STOLEN HORSES

STOLEN HORSES

BILL BROOKS

FIVE STAR

A part of Gale, Cengage Learning

GALE
CENGAGE Learning·

Farmington Hills, Mich • San Francisco • New York • Waterville, Maine
Meriden, Conn • Mason, Ohio • Chicago

GALE
CENGAGE Learning·

LIBRARY OF CONGRESS CATALOGING-IN-PUBLICATION DATA

Names: Brooks, Bill, 1943– author.
Title: Stolen horses / Bill Brooks.
Description: First edition. | Waterville : Five Star Publishing, [2016]
Identifiers: LCCN 2015046099| ISBN 9781432832001 (hardcover) | ISBN 143283200X (hardcover)
Subjects: LCSH: Horse stealing—Fiction. | Frontier and pioneer Life—Fiction. | BISAC: FICTION / Action & Adventure. | FICTION / Westerns. | GSAFD: Western stories.
Classification: LCC PS3552.R65863 S755 2016 | DDC 813/.54—dc23
LC record available at http://lccn.loc.gov/2015046099

First Edition. First Printing: April 2016
Find us on Facebook– https://www.facebook.com/FiveStarCengage
Visit our website– http://www.gale.cengage.com/fivestar/
Contact Five Star™ Publishing at FiveStar@cengage.com

Printed in the United States of America
1 2 3 4 5 6 7 20 19 18 17 16

STOLEN HORSES

CHAPTER 1

Ballard stood with his hands thrust down in the back pockets of his faded dungarees as he stared at the charred and still smoldering remains of what had once been the house of Foley and Uda Promise.

"What you think, Mr. Ballard?" Charley Redleg said.

"Think what was ain't no more," Ballard said.

It was a surprisingly chilly and raw day in the Texas Panhandle for September. Overhead clouds like masted sailing ships drifted by unimpeded over an ocean of blue sky. Tumbleweeds rolled and rolled until they snagged on something or other, strands of barbed wire, some old fence post, even the crashed-in timbers of the house.

"They look like what surely used to be folks," Charley said, his gaze fixated on two forms within the ruins, unmistakably human but black and tarry and curled as if the heat had shrunken them first with fear and then with the fire itself.

"They were once, that is a fact," Ballard said. "But I can't say who exactly those two are, for there used to be three that lived on this place. Foley had that boy working and living here as well. So one of them is missing. We've looked all over this place and I've not seen another, have you?"

"No," the Indian said. "And a mare is also missing. Less it run away on account of the fire, got loose somehow or other."

"It could well be. But the real question is, where's the other one that lived here?" Ballard mused as much to himself as to

7

Charley Redleg.

Charley shrugged, hunkering down inside his sheep-hide coat, the wind whipping his silver-streaked braids about his face. He was descendent from a line of proud peoples, Comanche. But these days all the Comanche left were tamed Indians, pumpkin growers who dressed like white men in calico shirts and denim jeans and low-heeled boots.

"Let's bring the wagon around and get these two loaded and see if Doc can tell us which these two are."

"What do you reckon's happened here for it to be a fire and them two not gotten away from it?" Charley asked.

"Damned if I know," Ballard said. "I guess it's what this county pays me for, to find out."

By the time they got the two charred remains enfolded into a tarp they'd found in the work shed along with lengths of ropes, dried and cracked harnesses, a whetstone, and hoes and such, the sun lay slanted to the west, its light stabbing down through a distant copse of trees. The wind was colder and more brisk now that the sun had gone down some.

"That wind is coming on us like we're trespassing," Charley Redleg said, climbing up into the wagon seat alongside Ballard. They'd harnessed their two saddle horses to the wagon and set their saddles in back alongside the bodies.

"Let's get on before it blows our hats and us to the piney woods," Ballard said and snapped the reins over the team's haunches.

"You won't get no argument out of me," Charley Redleg said, his fists balled in the pockets of his coat.

They went on.

Einer slept to the music of night sounds.

In the outer dark, coyotes howled their hunger as they loped on padded paws through sage and buffalo grass, their movement stalking, silent, ghostlike, nostrils scenting the presence of jackrabbits, mice, ground squirrels. Cave bats on the wing darkening an already dark sky. Wind shuffling through the brush as if searching for something lost.

Einer dreamt of a woman of his long-ago past, someone he knew that from the first moment he'd set eyes on her he would forever yearn for no matter the time or distance between them. He was always pleased to dream of her, though such dreams came infrequently the older he got.

The dream was always the same. She was there in the room with him, naked, standing at the window, the shape of her outlined against moonlight. She had not changed, still young and beautiful.

"Magdalena," he said in his sleep without knowing he said it. Just her name alone filled him with remorse at having lost her.

A barn owl throated his name and immediately he woke.

He swung his legs off the side of the bed and his bare feet touched the cold floorboards. The night chill was upon the land—early warning of coming winter not yet fully arrived, but soon. He knew it and dreaded it.

He sat with face in hands, hungover still from last night's drinking over in Lost River. It was a long ride but worth it. And so he'd gone after dressing in his best shirt and combing his sparse hair, patting it in place with scented hair oil.

By the time he got to town, the dance was already in motion, the music fine and lively, the dancers stomping around the dance floor.

For a long time he stood along the wall drinking punch he spiked with whiskey and watched the dancers, aching to get in among them but hardly a gal not already taken. And then he spotted one across the way sitting by her lonesome. She was young, but then they all were compared to him. And she was a tad on the homely side and a bit heavy too. But Einer felt as sorry for her as he did for himself seeing her just sitting there and went on over on the chance she might dance with him.

She looked up at his approach and he gave her his best friendly smile and asked her if she'd care to dance.

"I know I'm probably about your daddy's age," he said. Then laughed and added: "Maybe even your granddaddy."

She smiled back and stood up and Einer guided her out onto the dance floor amid the other couples and was amazed at her grace for being the size she was. In his mind he compared her to a good cutting horse, one that knew in advance every move the cow was going to make, though Einer refrained from saying any of what he was thinking. He was just pleased she was such a good dancer.

He didn't know how many dances they danced and was disappointed when a fellow cut in on them; Einer went back along the wall a little winded and thirsty too. He found his cup and took it up and wondered if he shouldn't just go on back home now that he'd had his dance.

He waited a bit, then set his cup aside and gave one last glance to the floor and saw across the way her chair was still empty and so went on outside to where he'd tied his horse, a long-legged black stallion with a blaze face and four white stockings. He stood a moment drinking from the pint bottle he carried in his saddlebags, the same one he'd spiked his punch with and used to ward off the night chill, then plugged it and slipped it back into place before untying his sheep-hide coat from behind the cantle. He was buttoning it up when she said, "Are you leaving, Einer?" It near startled him.

She stood a good head shorter than him and wore a shawl over her shoulders.

"Why I was about to," he said.

"I was hoping we might get in another dance," she said. "I don't suppose you've enough left in that bottle for me a swallow of it? It's durn chilly."

"Why I reckon so," he said and took it and handed it to her and watched as she took a pull from it without making a face as she drank.

"That's one way to get warm," she said.

"I don't suppose you'd care to go off aways with me," he said. It just popped out of his mouth before he could stop himself from saying it.

"Why, Einer!" she said in mock surprise.

"You'll have to excuse me, Cillia," he said. "It's the liquor doing the talking. I . . ."

She giggled like a schoolgirl.

"Well, it sure is saying all the right things, Einer."

He could see she was a bit drunk herself but was stunned into silence for a moment until she said, "Don't you think it might be too cold to . . . you know?"

"I reckon maybe one of these carriages around here would have a blanket or two we could borry."

She nodded and Einer searched two or three of the hacks to find a couple of lap blankets and they walked off aways and found a quiet spot; Einer spread the blankets on the ground and the two of them shed just enough clothes to accomplish what they'd come to do.

Afterward Einer said, "You don't know how much I appreciate this, Cillia."

She smiled and kissed him on the mouth.

"We all get lonely sometimes, Einer. I know what it's like too. And seems to me we did each other a kindly favor. But now I best get on back before my sister and her husband come looking for me."

He wanted to ask if she came to the dances often, but she'd gone before he had a chance.

Boy, you ain't as young as you once was, Einer, he told

11

himself. But I reckon you ain't quite as old as you thought you were, and grinned foolishly, then rode that long ride home alone, not sure if he felt better or worse for the experience, but knowing he felt something.

His sleep was short and fitful and now he sat half awake, half asleep, head throbbing like it was a drum somebody was beating inside his skull.

"You don't know whether to git up or shoot yourself, do you?" he said to the empty room. It was that darkest hour before dawn, the deepest kind of darkness. There was nothing to recommend it. He'd been living in the shack for almost a year, the longest he'd lived anywhere in recent memory.

He'd come upon it abandoned and dragged his belongings inside and patched the old cottonwood corral good enough to keep his horse in.

The single room was full of dust and scorpions and one large rattler that he killed and cut off its rattles and tied to his hatband as a warning to other snakes.

The outer construction was weathered boards gray as the flesh of the dead; some of the sideboards were curled and pulled away from the nails. The roof needed patching but he slept out from under the leaks.

The walls were lined with yellowed and curled newspapers and pages torn from catalogues. The crudely knocked together cot was without a mattress and he used his soogins to sleep upon. A potbelly cast-iron stove in the middle of the room stood with its black tin chimney lying on the floor and these he set back into place. Two ladder-back chairs were still usable, and a table missing one leg was easy enough to repair. By the time he finished the repairs and after nearly a year of living there, it felt akin to some sort of home.

The night music had stopped as soon as he sat up, as if the

outer creatures knew of his stirrings and waited to see what he'd do.

We all just waiting for the light, he thought. Even night's creatures don't care for the dark. The only reason they carry on so is because they're afraid, like kids whistling past a graveyard 'cause they're afraid.

He stood with slow deliberation, letting his bones realign, and pressed both hands into his lower back. It was like sleep rearranged him and at each rising he had to put everything back in its proper place.

His mouth was sour and his tongue rough as sandpaper and felt too big for his mouth. He cussed himself for drinking so hard. Any damn fool would know better, he thought. Any damn fool but you.

He thought first of the woman in his dream and then of the woman he danced with just hours before, Cillia, who was plump as a hen but sweet as candy. Something shivered through his blood thinking about it.

He stood and padded to the window and looked out but there was only the darkness still. Even the stars had left the world and just a sliver of a crescent moon resting on one end getting ready to hide from the dawn.

"You ain't nearly what you think you are sometimes," he said aloud simply to hear a human voice. "You can't just go off whenever you want and do what you want. If'n you could, you'd already done it."

He stepped outside and relieved himself and noted again how weak his stream. "One more damn thing to remind me how age weakens and breaks you down, slow but sure. As if I needed any more reminders." Muttering all the while to himself, to whatever creatures might be listening.

He went back in and lay down again but could not sleep. He wanted to dream some more of her, the love of his youth whom he'd given his heart to, and have her there in the room with him again, even just for a few minutes. He wanted to hold her just once more and smell her fresh washed hair and have the smoothness of her naked flesh under his fingertips as his hand mapped the landscape of her body. He wanted to taste her mouth and all the rest so that the long ago would become the now. Just once more is all. The woman last night had not sated him in the way he needed; she had simply stirred the dying embers of memory for Magdalena, his truest love.

Tears leaked from the corners of his eyes and down his weathered cheeks and were trapped by his ears.

"Just once more, goddamn it, just once more. Is that too fucken much to ask?" The bitterness of his words tasted metallic in his mouth.

He didn't know who he was talking to but himself, for he'd come to determine a long time ago that there was no God. He'd seen and done too many wrongful things to have gone unpunished, and there were a hell of a lot worse than him still riding around out there. No just God would have allowed the things he'd seen and done to happen, would allow others to do these things.

"When you was a young man . . ." he muttered. "Lord, how easy it was. You should have taken more care to hold onto her and you didn't. You damn fool."

He grimaced at the thought of how it had been but was no longer, the reality of what and who he was. Close as he could hope for was what had happened earlier that night, with the homely gal, and even that was a rarity. But it meant less than nothing to him and left him feeling poorly about himself for having done it now that he had time to think about it. How many others had she let take her off and lay on a blanket?

Jesus, he thought. Jesus.

14

★ ★ ★ ★ ★

There was something moving out there, but Einer did not hear its sound for thinking of the woman in his dream.

A single figure outlined against the night sky moved, hunched over toward the small cabin.

The figure stopped, stayed still, then moved again, then stopped, listening.

It was the horse he was after and he aimed to grab it.

What the shadow was most listening for was a dog's bark. He hated barking dogs. If a light came on in the shack he'd get down and wait till it went off again. He had decreed if it came to it, he'd strangle a dog to quiet it. He needed that horse bad.

He stopped and squatted down again and examined by feel the poverty of his boot soles. There were holes worn through the thin leather, allowing stones to press up through and bruise his feet. He was hobbling like some old broke-down cowboy after having walked so very far through rough country afoot.

You're a poorly son of a bitch, ain't you?

He looked at the sky off to the east and saw the palest light washing through. It would be full on light within an hour and he'd need to get down there to that shack and get that horse before it did.

He removed a lump of cloth from inside his shirt—an old ragged bandanna with something tied inside—untied it and took out the hard biscuit and chewed on it with deliberation, savoring each crumb licked from his dirty palm. He'd tried his best to make it stretch and had imaged it into a proper meal: a plate of potatoes with cooked beef and carrots and a glass of buttermilk and a slice of huckleberry pie.

He could not remember when he'd last had a proper meal; it had been so long. Even when he was back working for Foley and Foley's sister, he'd rarely gotten a full meal. They were miserly folks to be sure, and asked overly much of him. Too much, as it turned out.

He thought of her as he nibbled the biscuit—a crone of a woman, dried up as a peach left too long in the sun. Scrawny as a chicken and no beauty to her. Foley was just as bad, like old whang leather with that bullet head of his no hair would sprout on. Poor seed indeed them two. But even such he could have stood if not for her, the sinister demands she placed on him— the threat she held over him.

For every time Foley went off somewhere, she tried to get at him, tried to get him to do ungodly things with her, promising to feed him better, whatever he wanted if he would do what she wanted, get him a pair of new boots and a fine hat if he would. She was old enough to be his ma and that's all he could think of when she came at him.

He'd hear the two of them in their room nights carrying on like man and wife. Goddam. He'd bury his head under the pillow so as to muffle their sounds.

He'd held out for the longest time, but there came a point where his poverty and the hard labor left him in such a sorry state and her threats more ominous that he finally did her bidding one hot afternoon while Foley was off somewhere for the day.

Thing was, once he gave into her she told him if he ever spoke a word of it, she'd claim he raped her. He said he had no need to say anything.

"I tell my brother you set upon me, he'll kill you and if he don't, he'll get the laws on you and you'll go to prison, maybe get hanged."

He never got the things he'd been promised, either. The meals were just as poorly and the living conditions no better and the work just as mean. Seemed like Foley worked him even harder, even as her depraved demands increased. He finally had enough and told her he wouldn't do it no more unless he got what she'd promised. And again she threatened to lie on him, and clawed his back and he realized it was to confirm her lies if she laid claim to such madness as she threatened. Too late he felt more trapped than ever.

When he finally slipped away that night, he took all the food he could carry in a poke sack, Foley's mare, and Foley's pistol heavy as a brick, and rode away against a storm of flames rearing into the night, splintering lumber and shattering glass.

He foolishly rode the mare hard for two days and the second night it stepped in a prairie dog hole and snapped its foreleg. He'd had no recourse but to shoot it. He looked about and felt lost in the sea of nothingness but prickly pear, sand, rock, earth and sky. He started on foot west by southwest and by the fourth day he was just about used up.

His original plan to cross the Llano Estacado—the Staked Plains—seemed to have gone awry. He'd figured if he could make it across, he'd be safe from Foley's pursuers, if there were any. He didn't know if there were. Two more days of sleeping during the heat and walking at night had brought him thus—on the lip of the small canyon in watchfulness of the cabin.

He squatted down eating the last of biscuit and hoping to steal himself the horse in that corral like it was just waiting to be stole, he told himself. Had he seen a light wink on and off in the late dark or was it early morning? He no longer knew what time it was.

He'd squatted a long time, watchful, wrapped up in the horse blanket he'd taken off Foley's horse once he'd shot it. But a horse blanket wasn't any good against cold nights. It was just something to put over you and now a cold wind rattled through the chaparral and prickled his flesh like icy fingers. He wondered as he squatted in the cold, half starved like some old dog, if he would have been better off staying at Foley's and putting up with it till he'd thought things through better.

He could still smell the hotness of the room she'd taken him to, the water-stained peeling wallpaper of tiny red roses, the smell of her fetid breath from under him. The whisper of the cornhusks of the mattress as he ground away doing her bidding. How she liked to claw his back, clawed him and bit his shoulder like some feral cat and warning him to "Keep going damn you!"

And all he could think the whole while was about murder, relief brought only by her ordering him to get the hell out of her room when she'd gotten her pleasure.

His stomach lurched as much from the memory as his hunger.

His teeth chattered gnawing on the biscuit, catching the crumbs in his off hand so he could lick them up. He felt so tired and footsore all he wanted to do was lay down and never get up again. Sleep at best, since leaving that small scrub of a ranch, had been intermittent, restless, fraught with dreams of fire and screams, blood and crackling timber, and each day left him more exhausted.

Just go on and sleep, he told himself. You gone die any damn way. Nothin's gone save your sorry ass now.

He let his eyelids close and in a moment he was drifting skyward, or it felt like it. Then a coyote called not far away—off in the brush—and he alerted to its sound thinking it might have been a gray wolf. He'd heard stories about wolves running a man down and tearing him to pieces. Those old wolfers who hung around the saloons back in Tascosa told stories about wolves.

"They get the taste of human flesh, they won't eat nothin' but a pilgrim," they said.

He took hold of the thick stick he'd been carrying—a length of cottonwood limb he'd found a few days back in a dry wash—to help him walk. The previous sun had heated the rocks all day long and for a time their warmth was soothing. He'd caught a number of scorpions and roasted and ate them as well after tearing off their stingers. They had made him sick for a day and a half.

"You best not come no closer," he said to the direction of the movement in the brush. "I'll bash your damn brains in."

His hand trembled, whether from fear or weakness, or both, he didn't know.

Whatever it was, called no more, nor was there the sound of the passage of it going on through the chaparral. Just a wind stirred silence.

He wished now he hadn't done what he'd done but there was nothing he could do for it. He wondered if it was the law out there somewhere looking for him. You know the law ain't gone leave you alone he told himself. They'll come after you for killing them folks.

After a time of squatting, he slowly rose to his feet and started down toward the shape of the cabin, carrying the club in his right hand ready to swing it if he had to. He'd bust anything that came at him.

CHAPTER 2

After depositing the bodies with the town's medico, Ballard aimed for home knowing it might be a time before Doc could determine who they were.

Mayra was there in the kitchen when he came in. Her smile was warm and welcoming and her body compliant when he held her.

"I'm glad you're home," she said. "I'm always glad when you are."

He knew that some of what she meant was that she was glad that he was not dead, killed by some miscreant or other, and he was glad too.

Ballard was a man of middle years, nearly forty and hard-lived till the day he met Mayra. He'd been to war as a young man and seen and tasted its horrors and thence tried to wash away such taste with whiskey. And after the war he used the only skill he'd learned to find work with. The choices were two: lawman or outlaw. He still wasn't sure why he'd chose the one over the other, but since having met his wife, he was glad he'd chosen right.

He had given up the bottle for Mayra. He gave up the whoring and gambling too, and thus his tumble toward early destruction stopped short of actuality, and she was pleasing to him in ways he could not define.

The baby child was a surprise and a miracle all at once. He wallowed in the happiness it brought. And now, in a way, it seemed like a home to him he never wanted to leave, and in a way, the severity of the land had taken on a kind of beauty that forged itself in the mind and soul of a man otherwise happy just as it seemed to him now, and she too had grown accustomed to their life in the harshness of the Texas landscape.

He tried not to think of the charred bodies in the wagon's bed, what they must have gone through before the flames consumed them. It was a bad way to die. But then there was no good way to die, was there. If they were lucky, somebody had killed them first. He hoped that they were lucky.

He knew Foley and his sister, Uda, as bitter hard people, ugly as a pair of mudhens, the both of them. He only got out their way once every several months in his circuit to check on folks in the county. They seemed to him suspicious of everyone who came round and especially of the laws. John Paul seemed subdued, cowed, and he hardly ever spoke a word and was standoffish. The first time Ballard met the threesome, he thought John Paul was their son, but then come to find out from town rumors, he was just a boy who lived out there. And who knew the circumstance of how John Paul came to be there in the first place or what his role was, for he wasn't just a mere boy, but somewhere between a boy and a man, sixteen or seventeen he imagined, but it was hard to tell. And he sure hadn't looked like either Foley or his sister. Ballard rightly deduced that John Paul was of no relation to the pair.

Ballard had no good or bad opinion of any of them, but even if they were hard and bitter they deserved a natural life, no matter how they chose to live it.

"You look tired," she said.

"Yes," he acknowledged. "I could stand to eat something."

"Sit down and I'll fix you a plate."

Soon he was eating and Mayra sat across from him watching him, the baby at her breast nursing and he watched the infant sucking, its tiny hands reaching for the soft flesh as it sought the warm milk.

"What did you find?" she asked him.

"A fire," he said. "Bad one. Found two bodies burned up. Got 'em over to Doc's now hoping he can tell me if one of 'em is the woman or John Paul."

She looked at him quizzically.

"Woman or boy?" she said.

He nodded as he chewed the piece of fried ham she'd given him.

"You probably don't know them, but it was these people named Promise. There was a brother, Foley, his sister, Uda, and a boy lived out there. Some boy they hired on, no relation. Well, of the two we found, I figured one to be Foley, but the other one could either be John Paul or the sister. Hard to tell the way they were burned like that."

"What caused the fire?" she said. "Do you know?"

He shook his head. "Still trying to figure it out, but might not ever learn the cause."

"You said you found two bodies. What happened to the other one?"

Again, he shook his head, sipping some of his coffee.

"I don't suppose you have any sort of a cake?"

She stood and went to the cupboard and took down a pan with sheet cake in it she'd baked that morning and cut him a piece and put it on a plate and set it before him.

"That'll hit the spot," he said as she sat back down, curious as to what happened to the missing person.

"Well, anyways," he said cutting a piece of the cake with his fork. "That's what I'm also hoping to find out. If I can find the one that's missing I can find out what started the fire. This is good, Mayra. Real good."

"I'm glad you like it."

"I do," he said.

CHAPTER 3

John Paul did his best not to stumble down the caliche slope that led to the shack. Jesus but he was tired and sore-footed, so hungry his head swam.

He slipped near the bottom and tore his knee. He felt the warm wetness of blood oozing down his shin and forced himself not to cry out in pain.

He just had to have the horse and get away clean. The pistol fell out of his waistband when he stumbled and cracked his knee and it clattered and slid on down and he had to search around in the dark to find it. He shoved it back inside his waistband, and felt the cold steel along his hipbone. It wouldn't do him no good anyhow. He had no bullets for it, had used them on the mare and taking potshots at rabbits for meat but missed every one. Still it gave him comfort to have it, and besides nobody but him knew the hulls in its chambers were spent.

You'll wake the damn dead, he berated himself. Overhead the sky was beginning to lighten more, making shapes of things before unseen.

Finally he was down to the bottom and duck-walked toward the cabin. He saw the small cottonwood corral between the cabin and outhouse and the shadow of the horse as it came to the top rail and looked at him. His hope rose he wouldn't have to walk no more.

The horse held its head high, its ears twitching, alerted to his coming. Horses could see in the dark real well, he'd heard seasoned hands say. It must have seen him too, then.

He whispered to it.

"Easy boy," he said, holding forth his hand trying to make it think he had an apple or something to offer it. "Easy now."

The horse snuffled as it stood there watching him.

"I ain't gone hurt you," he said glancing toward the cabin to see if anyone inside was alerted. Its windows were dark still.

"Come'n now, let me get in there with you and we'll just ride on off of here."

He eased himself between the rails but the horse moved to the other side, then stood watching him.

"Look here. Look it what I brung you. A nice fat apple," he said, holding out his hand with the nonexistent fruit.

The animal took a step forward, then halted.

"I guess your eyes ain't so good you can't see this apple," he whispered. "But I got it, right here."

He reached back and took a coiled rope hung on the gatepost and let it out into a loop. Shit, he didn't know if he could rope the horse or not, but it was plain to see it wasn't buying into the apple scheme.

"I'm just going to put this rope over you," he said judging the loop he let out. He swung it three or four times round and round, then let heave. The rope slapped the horse's nose and it spooked and snorted and stamped its hooves and ran along the back rails first one way and then the other.

"Damn it all to hell," he cussed himself as he gathered the rope back toward him.

He started to make another loop when he heard a voice behind.

"You know how death comes?" the voice said. It sounded old, phlegmy, and like the crackle of fire eating at pinewood.

He froze, the rope dangling from his hand.

"What?" he said without turning around. He hated to think that he was caught and probably about to be shot dead.

"You know how death comes?" the voice repeated.

He turned around slowly, raising his hands, and looked to see who was speaking such nonsense to him.

"What in the hell are you talking about?" he said soon as he saw the bandy-legged man in his long drawers with a wild thatch of snow-white hair sticking up like rooster feathers. He saw the other thing too—the shotgun in the man's hands aimed directly at him.

"I'm askin' if you know how death comes, by what means does it come?"

"No, I don't know," he said.

"It comes like a thief in the night is how it comes," Einer said. "Like boys who steal other men's horses. You are a thief and this here I'm holding is death."

"I wasn't trying to steal nothing," John Paul said, his voice quavering not just from fear but hunger and weariness too.

"Well then, was you trying to mate it?" Einer said. " 'Cause if you was, Lucifer yonder will kick your brains out, he ain't no mare, he ain't even gelded. I don't know what else you'd be doing in there but trying to steal him."

John Paul looked back over his shoulder at the animal, who stood stiff-legged and head held high with ears alert.

"Hell no, I wasn't trying to mate it," he said. "You crazy old bastard."

"Maybe I am so, but I ain't crazy enough to come up on another man's property and try and steal his horse in the night. And another goddamn thing, long as we're at it. Was I wantin' to, I'd be in my rights to hang you from the nearest tree. Round in this country they hang horse thieves. It'd save me a shell to hang you and the rope wouldn't be no worse the wear of it."

"Well, shit," John Paul said. "You might just as well go on

and do what you're going to do, 'cause I'm done wore to a nub-
bin and I'd just as soon be dead as to go on in this godforsaken
country as to spend another day trying to cross it."

And just like that he sat down still holding the rope.

"Toss away that pistol," Einer said.

John Paul took loose the pistol and tossed it aside.

"Now come on out of there."

"I can't."

"Why can't you?"

"I told you, I'm used up. I'm about starved to death and too
weak to carry on one more step. So just go ahead and shoot
me, or hang me, or whatever the hell you've a mind to do. You'd
be doing me a favor."

The man stood holding the shotgun. Something with heavy
beating wings flew overhead and was gone as if a ghost, or
winged angel lost and looking for home.

"Where you hail from?" Einer said.

"Somewhere back yonder aways," John Paul said, jerking a
thumb back over his shoulder. "Hell, I don't know rightly."

"And you're out trying to cross this Llano afoot?"

The hoary old head shook with disbelief at such nonsense.
The canyon was slowly filling with light, like bright water in a
black bowl.

"I was trying to cross somewhere," John Paul mumbled. "Had
me a horse but it broke its leg stepping into a damn hole way
back yonder. Been walking since."

"You on the run from the laws, maybe?"

"No, damn it. I was just leaving one place for another and hit
a patch of bad luck."

"I'd say so. Only a feller running from the laws, seems to me,
would try and cross this ground at night or any other time
without a good horse under him and a poke of supplies to tide
him over. A feller not too damn bright would try it as you've

done. I reckon you know that now, don't you?"

"I reckon so, mister."

"How old are ye, boy?"

"I'm sixteen or maybe seventeen, if I reckon right. But just now I feel like I'm a hundred."

"Come on to the cabin, I got some grub. Don't want you dying on me, it'd mean I'd have to dig a grave and I ain't up to it."

"Thought you aimed to shoot me, or hang me—if'n you could even find a tree tall enough to hang me from in this barren country," he said. "I ain't seen nary a tree in three whole days."

"Like I said, I ain't up to digging graves."

John Paul slowly unscrewed himself from the ground and came on out of the corral and Einer waved him on toward the cabin with the twin barrels. John Paul could see now that there was a small light glowing from within. He'd been too fixated with trying to rope catch the horse to have noticed it had been lit.

The door hung open and he entered and saw the lamp with a tiny guttering flame inside the blackened glass chimney there on a table.

"Go on, sit down, I'll fetch ye some victuals," Einer said, leaning the shotgun against the wall.

First light had fallen against the canyon's west walls draining away the darkness and shadows and illuminating the rock and declivities to a glowing red like virgin's blood, and if John Paul had looked out just then he would have seen juniper, salt cedar, willow, soapberry, cottonwood, and mesquite—trees aplenty from which to be hanged.

There was an old black iron stove with a pipe elbowed up and through the roof. Next to it was a shelf with some bone china cups, a tin of Arbuckle coffee, some canned goods, beans, and potted meats.

He watched as Einer got down two cups, then went to the plated stove and struck a match to its innards to light the kindling already inside for that coming morning's breakfast.

He took a butcher knife and chunk of cured ham wrapped in cheesecloth and cut off some slices and put them in an iron skillet and then poured out some coffee still warm from where he'd heated it in the night as was often his habit, night or day, to soothe his nerves and maybe his soul. He set one of the cups down before John Paul.

From a warmer shelf above the stove's plates he took a pan of day-old biscuits and set them before John Paul too.

"I got lard you can smear on 'em," Einer said. "Bacon won't take long. Go on, dig in."

"Ain't you scared I'll grab that old gun and blast you to rags?" he said. He didn't know why he said it except he was feeling poorly and raged with anger at his condition. Hadn't been for Foley's mad sister he believed he'd be in a better place than he was. Yet another goddamn mad person there in the room with him now, feeding him for what purpose, he did not know, but was suspicious.

"I don't reckon you'd be such a damn fool as to try it," Einer said, tugging a revolver from his waistband and laying it on a shelf next to some cans of beans and potted meat by the stove. "Less you think I'm too old and slow to snatch this here up and send you straight to your maker, if you even got a maker, poorly as you appear to be. It's probably where you belong anyway."

John Paul looked at it when Einer put it there. It was a damn fine-looking gun with horn grips.

"I'd fill you so full of lead you couldn't swim a creek without drowning for the extry weight," Einer said, forking out the bacon onto a plate and setting it next to the pan of biscuits before taking up a chair himself.

"Mister, I couldn't swim a creek without drowning even

without the lead. I never learned to swim a lick."

He studied Einer's weathered face, the gray nearly colorless eyes, the thin shoulders as if he'd filled his union suit with a bunch of old bones, the liver-spotted hands, the horned yellowish nails and knobbed wrists. Why the old son of a bitch could have got himself a job as a scarecrow in some peckerwood's field of corn, he thought.

"You're kinda behind the eightball, ain't you?" Einer said.

"You ain't gone eat?" John Paul said as Einer took his makings from the table, already laid out from the night before. With his Bull Durham pouch and cigarette papers, Einer built himself a shuck, then looked about, stood, and went over to the wall shelf and got down a box of Blue Diamond matches, striking one to flame off the table top and lighting his smoke.

"Naw, I ain't hungry just yet," he said, and blew twin streams of smoke through his nostrils. "I'll eat when I'm ready, but you go on."

You're awful damn scrawny, old man, John Paul thought and dug right in. He ate all the bacon and wiped three biscuits against the grease sheen left on the plate and drank all his coffee and Einer refilled both their cups.

He sat studying John Paul for the longest time until John Paul said, "What you looking at anyways? I hope to hell you ain't getting no funny ideas."

"How'd you come by that mark?"

John Paul reflexively fingered the large irregular birthmark that covered the right side of his forehead touching the outer edge of his eyebrow. It was the color and shape of spilled wine.

"I just come by it is all. Born that way."

Einer nodded acceptance of the explanation.

"T'ain't none of my business," Einer said. "But what were your plans once you stole my horse?"

John Paul shrugged, said, "To git somewhere."

"Hell, you're already somewheres."

"I know it."

"You mean to git somewheres else?"

John Paul nodded. Einer waited, the burn of his cigarette paper and scent of tobacco smoke almost soothing to John Paul. He looked at the makings.

"You want to make yourself a shuck?"

"I don't know how."

"Damn boy, you don't know how to swim and you don't know how to make a smoke," he said. "And you sure as hell don't know how to steal a horse. I'd say you ain't good for much."

John Paul's face felt hot but for the birthmark, and the anger in him rose up like a fanned fire and when he closed his eyes, even briefly, he could see those raging flames licking at the night as he rode away from Foley and all that mess.

"I reckon you don't know nothing about me," he said.

"I reckon I surely don't, but for the fact you were trying to steal my horse, which would leave me afoot. You steal a man's horse and leave him afoot way out here, you might as well put a bullet in his head, 'cause either way he's dead. You get that part why they hang horse thieves?"

"Yeah," John Paul said. "I git it."

He could hardly keep his eyes open and it felt like his nerves were just a bunch of taut barbed wire in a howling wind.

"Go on over and lay down and git you some rest," Einer said.

John Paul stood silent and walked over to the bed and set down and pulled off his boots and lay down and was immediately asleep. Einer could see the poor condition of his boots, the soles all worn through, same with his socks, those frayed clothes.

Jesus Christ. How is a young feller get in such a condition? Never in my worst days was I so bad off.

31

Einer was wise enough, experienced enough, to know that John Paul was in trouble more than just his physical condition. He was running from something or somebody and willing to risk his life to get away from whatever it was. Boys just didn't wander around in this desperate country at night, alone and horseless in the middle of nowhere.

He'd et like a starved dog, and look at him, dead asleep afore his head hardly hit the pillow.

Einer went out into the just-now dawn of an oyster sky with enough light to make sense of things, to show details that night had hidden, the snorting mustang, the outhouse off to the side, its boards as weather-beaten as the shack's lent no color to anything. Yonder stood a pile of rusted cans grown from years of man's hunger, Einer's and the ones who were there before him.

Jeez Christ, he thought, if only there was a market for rust.

He eased himself between the rails of the corral and walked over and picked up John Paul's pistol and examined it. Broke it open and extracted the empty hulls, not an unspent one in the bunch. What the hell did he think he was going to do with an empty gun? It was otherwise in working order and he admired it.

It was one of those Russian model Schofields he'd heard about—a .44–40 and had gutta-percha grips. It was a hunk of gun for sure; only if it had live rounds in it, he might could have done me some damage. Be my piss-poor luck some kid come along and steal my horse and shoot me dead in the process.

He sort of smiled at the notion. It's what the smart people call irony, he thought: all the bad things he'd done and never got shot doing 'em and then some kid who can't so much as swim or build a shuck comes along and kills me. Shit.

He stuck the gun into his waistband and thought amusedly, I'm a goddamn two-gun sumbitch. Then fetched a feedbag and filled it with oats and hooked it on the horse's nose and watched as it crunched until the bag was empty, then took it off and stroked the muscled neck.

"You'd have stomped that child to death, wouldn't you of?" he said. The horse snorted and tossed its head like it knew what Einer was talking about.

He saw the water tank was low so he went out and pumped up a bucket of water and emptied it into the tank; then he pumped three more buckets worth and poured them in, then set the bucket down and went off to the outhouse to relieve himself.

When he came out the sun was up over the Caprock Escarpment, turning it tawny. When the sun sank to the West, it turned the rock a fine reddish pink before it blackened and disappeared in the full-on darkness.

He went back inside the shack. John Paul still slept in the same position and Einer took out the two pistols and set them on the table and got himself another cup of coffee and set down.

He didn't know what was wrong with him. Here lately, he'd had no appetite. He knew he should eat something besides sugared coffee, but he hardly found it in him to do so.

He looked over at John Paul.

Sure wish I was your age again knowing what I know now, he thought.

He got out his gun-cleaning kit and cleaned that big Russian and saw that the barrel was somewhat pitted and could have been better cared for, like John Paul, he reckoned, but it was serviceable. He swabbed the barrel and down in the workings and rubbed it all over with a cloth, then set it aside and put away his cleaning equipment, wrapped up in a piece of soft hide.

He took his coffee and one of the chairs and went outside and sat looking off toward the Caprock; he made himself another smoke in the gentle warm wind of late autumn that searched out the canyon as if looking for something and he thought autumn was the best time of year. He'd met her in the month of September lo those many years ago and remembered how she reveled in the leaves of color and how the aspen twinkled like gold coins up in the high country.

It was that way now, there in the canyon. It was a pretty place to be early mornings like this. But with each glorified thought came the realization he wouldn't be around forever to enjoy it. What about when your time comes? he mused. Hell if I know. Just go in and lay down and let it come, I reckon.

A slight smile touched the corners of his mouth, beneath the heavy white moustaches.

"Boy, you've seen the elephant, ain't you? I surely have, two or three times. More'n most men ever will." It was often his habit to have conversations with himself just for the company of a human voice, even his own was better than none at all.

He often wished he had learned to play the fiddle or the guitar just to keep him company now days. But when he'd had the chance as a younger man, he never lacked for company.

"You never did learn much did you, old man," he said stubbing out the cigarette on the heel of his boot, then making himself another one, his blunted fingers surprisingly agile, delicate with the thin paper and tobacco, caressing it into a round nicely made cigarette, running the edge of the paper along the tip of his tongue, then sealing it before striking a match to the end.

He sort of wished he had a bottle of something. Good liquor always calmed his stomach discomfort. It felt like something was in there that didn't belong in there, something alive that was trying to eat its way out.

He exhaled smoke into the clear bright air, the sun's wash now touching the toes of his boots. The wind died and lay still and patches of shade sprouted under the trees.

All getting old was, was discovering some new ache or ailment most nearly every day. A pain that wasn't there yesterday seemed to spring up overnight and you found it like a scorpion in your bedroll the next morning. Stiff elbow, pained knuckles, aching jaw tooth, kink in your back. Never a morning free of something or other.

"Goddamn," he said at the wonder of it. "If'n it ain't someone or something else trying to kill you, it's your own damn self trying to do you in."

Then he laughed, hocked, and spit and looked over at the horse that'd come to the edge of the corral and stood watching him.

"You rotten sumbitch," he said. "You'd like to stomp my brains out, wouldn't you?"

And laughed again.

"We all the same thing, ain't we, horses or men, all the same, all wanting to be free and unfettered by other men." He wondered if horses understood human talk at all. It seemed sometimes they did.

He sat and smoked and wondered about things—the woman in his dreams. She'd been coming more often lately. For years she hadn't, even though he thought of her about every day. How many times had he tried to summon her and still she wouldn't come. Then lately she'd be there in his dreams, real as anything. He wondered if maybe she was calling to him across time and distance from somewhere wanting him to come to her, if there was something bad wrong going on with her and that is why she was showing up.

"Aw hell," he said. "You're tetched in the goddamn head you believe any of that folderol."

"Who are you talking to?"

He turned and saw John Paul standing there still looking tired.

"Nobody, I just talk is all, to hear myself 'cause there ain't nobody else way out here to talk to."

John Paul sat down cross-legged in the dirt.

"How long'd I sleep?"

"Not too very," Einer said.

"What's your name, anyways?"

"What's your'n?"

"You say first."

"Damn it boy, I ain't up to playing games."

"John Paul," he said.

"John Paul what?"

"That's it, just John Paul."

"So Paul is your last name?"

"I don't know if it is or ain't. It's all I ever been called, John Paul."

Einer took another drag from his cigarette and said, "Mine's Einer Fish."

"Well, that's a damn funny name, Einer," John Paul said.

"I'll advise you not to go slandering my name," Einer said.

"It sounds like something made up, Einer Fish."

"Why would I make it up?"

"Maybe you're a damn outlaw hiding out way out here in the middle of nowhere."

"Outlaw? That what you believe I am?"

John Paul shrugged.

"Why'd I make up such a name if it wasn't it?"

"Shit if I know."

"My outlaw name is Einer and you best fear me 'cause I am a doubly bad man."

John Paul wasn't sure what to believe of this old fool.

"How come I ain't never heard of you? I heard of most bad

men. I never heard of no one named Einer nor Einer Fish, either one."

"Shit, boy. I imagine there's a lot you ain't heard of."

Then he ground out his shuck beneath his boot heel and went on in the house.

CHAPTER 4

The ghoulish man with his beak of a nose and watery eyes bent low over the charred bodies that lay on the tarpaulin. The room smelled of alcohol and garlic from the arsenic he used to embalm the dead when needed. He would have no need for the arsenic this day, however. The room was in the back of the medico's two-story brick house with white gingerbread gables and tall windows that sat on a slight rise that overlooked the town, as if a sentinel over all.

"What do you think, Oral?" Ballard said, trying not to breathe in too much of the fetid air.

"I think there is no way I'm going to be able to do much with them," the doctor said. "Shit, they look like over-roasted hogs at a fourth of July picnic."

"No, I mean do you think that smaller one is Foley's sister, Uda, or could that be John Paul who lived out there and worked for them?"

"Look here," Oral said, and prized open the jaw of the smaller one. The jawbone cracked and fell away and charred bits of flesh crumbled under his fingers, thus exposing upper incisors the color of piano keys.

"You see that—those two front teeth?"

Ballard saw it then, the bucked teeth he knew Uda had. First time he saw her she reminded him of a skinny squirrel and of that old joke about being able to eat ear corn through a picket fence. It was the woman all right.

"You think that other'n's Foley?"

The medico shrugged, probed at the body and head with a metal stick, and shook his head.

"Couldn't say for sure, but my guess is it would be him if you found them together in the fire. Ballard?"

"I'd tend to believe it is Foley, too, but I can't be a hundred percent certain either. You see any other reason they could have died?"

"I'd say the fire was plenty enough."

"No, I mean gunshot or something, maybe?"

"It's possible, but their skulls are intact so if they were shot, it wasn't in the head. Otherwise there'd be no telling for sure the way that fire got at 'em. What do you suppose caught them unawares?"

Ballard shrugged, fished out his makings from his jacket pocket, and built a cigarette, even though he'd promised Mayra he'd give up all his bad habits. He hated going behind her back, but a man's got to have some sort of vice in his line of work, something to relax him with. He just made sure she didn't catch him at it.

"Don't smoke in here," Doc Oral said. "There's lot that could catch afire and I sure as hell don't want to end up like these two."

They went out and into the parlor at the front of the house, where fine oak floorboards were covered with a huge Belgium rug, and where two wingback chairs covered in blue damask stood before an unused hearth and a padded footstool; a horsehair sofa completed the furnishings but for a side cart of liquor. Upon the carved marble mantel, two framed daguerreotypes—a man and a woman young and unsmiling in wedding clothes—looked down upon the room.

A few paintings of country scenes hung on the walls—a river winding down from mammoth mountains with some deer grazing by a stand of birch trees. The other was of a laughing couple riding on a horse-drawn sleigh over a snowy field; Doctor Oral was proud to point out that it was a Currier & Ives.

Another above the mantel was of a somewhat beautiful woman staring down at them formally in a low-cut silk dress that showed the fleshy swell of a creamy bosom. Ballard privately thought she was just a couple of roast beef sandwiches shy of being fat. Her imperious face was framed in dangling black curls and a slight smile played at her lips as if she was keeping a secret she desperately wanted to tell someone. Ballard guessed that the oil painting was of the mortician's wife—the one who'd moved back east according to rumor, that, or a paramour.

Ballard was anxious to get home to his own wife and child and later to bed. The smell of arsenic and alcohol still lingered in his nostrils until he got the cigarette made and lighted and inhaled deeply, then exhaled through his nostrils.

Doc Oral sat down across from him and crossed his legs at the knees. He was gangly, which only added to his ghoulish appearance. A long boney face with hollow cheeks and deep-set eyes under a furrowed brow to go with that beak was a face that would have frightened children and most women.

"I was always a ugly kid," he blurted out once in the Rising Sun Saloon as he shared a drink with Ballard, who wondered at the time why he would.

"It could have been a lightning strike that set the house afire," Ballard mused, unable to keep his mind on other things, for such was the workings of his mind. "Could have been somebody kicked over a lamp, but I don't see how if that's so they wouldn't have known it and gotten out."

"Could be somebody aimed to kill them," Doc's gravel voice said.

"Yeah, I thought of that too. The likely suspect would be John Paul if that was the case."

"It would most likely be John Paul," Doc agreed, "elsewise he would have reported it his ownself. I mean that place is so far off the road you'd quicker get to China. 'Sides, they didn't have nothing worth taking if it was a robbery or some such."

Ballard nodded.

"Thing is, if it was a robbery or some such, whoever did it might not know what all they had. There was rumor about that Foley kept his money in glass jars buried all over the place."

"Yes, I've heard such as well," Doc said. "I reckon you'll figure it out."

"Maybe so," he said, taking a draw off his smoke and studying the stamped tin ceiling done in coppery fleur-de-lis, wondering what it cost to have a ceiling put in like that.

"I got to get on," Ballard said and stood. His size seemed to fill the room and the lamps' light threw his shadow up against the wall behind him, a dark enormous thing.

"You'll see to their care, then?"

Doc nodded.

"Like always." He shook his hoary head, his hair like a tattered cloud.

"Submit a chit and I'll see you get paid," Ballard said, then resettled his hat on his head to just about the way it was, and went on out into the long night.

As always she was there in the kitchen baking a pie, cooking a stew while sewing when he came in. He never got tired of seeing her no matter if he was gone for a week or an hour. Small and pretty with her red hair tied up in a bun, its color like autumn maple leaves. The infant in a cradle she rocked with her foot as she sat stitching some patches on the elbows of his favored denim jacket.

"How'd things go with Doc?" she asked, looking up at him.

He paused to pour himself a cup of coffee from the pot on

the stove, sniffed at the simmering pot of stew, and then sat across from her.

"Well, we pretty much figured out that one of them was Uda, the sister," he said, blowing steam off his coffee.

"Oh, my," she said. "How terrible. And the other was her brother?"

"Could be. Ain't for sure." He bent and looked down in the cradle at his child, their child, the miracle of it all, and was filled anew with love.

"Say, maybe we should call it a night," he said and she saw that hungering look in his eyes and put aside her sewing.

"Soon's the pie's done, is that all right?"

"Of course it is," he said.

After she'd removed the pie and set it aside and set aside also the pot of stew, she said, "I'll put the child to bed." And after a few minutes she came to him and he took her in his arms and rested his face atop her head, the fine threads of her hair like silk against his cheek.

"You always smell so nice," he said.

"I washed my hair in the rainwater," she said. She felt the movement of him down below, pressing into her.

"You really did miss me, didn't you?"

He kissed her mouth and her tongue toyed with his.

"Terribly," he said.

"Come, we'll go and lay down," she said, taking him by the hand and leading him back to their bedroom. They quickly undressed each other and he stood in deep admiration for her beauty.

"Sometimes I think of you as a girl," he said. "A young and pretty girl and it shames me to think of you that way and how my desire burns through me."

She became coy, knowing that he was so much older than her and understood what he was alluding too.

"You can think of me however you wish," she said. "I'll be whatever you'd like me to be, but I'll always be myself. Would you like me as a young girl, now?"

He nodded.

"I believe I would, against all my principles, but I know the truth and so that knowledge saves me from an otherwise shame."

"Above all, I'm your wife, Ballard," she whispered.

"Yes, I'll never forget that you are."

She tugged him to the bed where they lay for a time caressing and kissing, exploring with their hands, their eyes shut, as if two blind souls on a journey together upon which they had to rely one on the other.

He loved the soft weight of her small breasts, their smoothness like polished stone, yet warm in his hands, delicate to his tongue.

She squirmed under him, her strength surprising as she rolled him onto his back and mounted him, straddling him.

He looked up into her oval face, her mouth open, her eyes closed. She reached down and guided him into her and the sensation always took his breath no matter how many times it happened.

She arched her back and seemed supreme atop him, a woman warrior ready to ride into battle, unafraid. He nearly wept.

Time was a thing lost and it was only later when she awakened him saying that supper was ready that he glided back to earth. She kissed him once, on the mouth, for a long full moment.

"I love you. I love my man."

"And I love my woman."

Later they sat together wrapped in a blanket, the room dark with night complete and surrounding them and everyone and it felt to him peaceful, innocent, the dark, whenever it found them together like this. He held the child to him and knew that everything important in this world was important because of love.

"I'll have to be gone for a few days," he said. "Maybe longer."

She rested her head against his chest and remained silent.

"Maybe you could get your aunt Josie to come and stay here with you and the baby."

Still she said nothing.

He thought perhaps she was disappointed with him. Silent women were the biggest mystery of all.

Finally, she said, "When will you go?"

"Tomorrow, first light."

"Where are you going?"

"To find John Paul, if I can, Foley's boy."

"Why do you need to find him?"

"He might have killed those people."

"He might not have."

"No, he might not have. But I'd like to know the truth and bring him to justice if he's responsible."

"But he could be anywhere, isn't that so?"

"Yes."

She fell silent again and for a long time they set in the room staring into the darkness, pressed against each other, knowing that the light of another day would too soon come again.

The child stirred and began to cry from hunger and she took it from him and lifted one breast to its mouth and it took hold and suckled and became still but for its tiny fists waving as if eager to get all the milk it could, its gurgling sounds like water over stones.

He knew, too, that even though the darkness seemed peaceful that darkness was the devil's hour, a time that took hold of men's souls and caused them to do terrible things to one another.

"Let's go to bed," he whispered. "The three of us."

She raised her head like a fawn awakening in the forest.

"Yes," she said sleepily, and he led her to the bedroom still holding the infant who'd fallen asleep again, a drop of milk at the corner of its mouth and another drop at her nipple like two pearls. He placed the child in the cradle and removed her robe and once more, even though he was exhausted, he became aroused at the sight of her.

He lay down next to her pulling the coverlet over them and she was warm against him, warm and sleepy and vulnerable. He lowered his head to her milk-swollen breasts and suckled the milk, thinking it would content her. Her milk was warm and sweet and she sighed half asleep as he was at her breasts. There was something about her vulnerability that aroused him even more, and as she turned her back to him he slowly pressed against her backside as she sank into sleep, until he reached a moment of sexual release.

It was tantalizing and the first time that he had taken her like that and he was filled with wonder at the power this woman's beauty held over him.

He put his arm around her and held her then and slept.

CHAPTER 5

The autumn sun was weak behind a glaze of sky that couldn't seem to make up its mind whether it wanted to shine or devolve into rain.

Einer was up and was making them breakfast by the time John Paul awoke. It was the smells that woke him.

"Damn, boy, you're a late bloomer," Einer said. He had a smoldering cigarette dangling from the corner of his mouth as he fried the last of the bacon. There was a pot of coffee boiling on the stove as well and a pan of biscuits fresh pulled from the oven and setting on the warmer. Einer was dressed only in hat and boots and long handles and John Paul looked at him and shook his head.

"What time is it?" he asked.

"It's way past time for doing whatever needs to get done is what," Einer said cryptically and knocked the ashes off his shuck with a fingernail. "Come on, get a shake on, there's something I want to find out."

John Paul stood and stretched the kinks out, then gathered his blanket off the floor and set it aside. He felt like he'd just crawled out of a grave.

"Go on and warsh your face and hands before you sit down at my table," Einer said. "You can warsh out in the horse trough, take you a rag to dry off with."

John Paul took a rag from a pile of them and went out and straight for the privy and relieved himself, then came out and washed his hands and face and neck in the horse trough, the horse watching him.

"What you lookin' at?" he said.

Then he went into the shack again and set down at the table where the pan of biscuits and two plates of bacon already set. Einer poured them coffee and set down and started in eating.

"I see you're hungry your ownself this morning," John Paul said.

"You don't worry none about what I am," Einer said, pointing with his fork. "Wish I had me some apple butter for these biscuits, they'd taste a sight better."

"I wished I had some too."

"You ever have a ma?"

" 'Course I did," John Paul said. "What'd you think I was, hatched?"

Einer offered a grizzled grin.

"Hell, boy, far as I know you could have done crawled out from under a rock."

"Well I didn't."

"She a good cook, your ma?"

"Don't reckon I remember if she was or wasn't," John Paul said.

"How could you forget something like if she was a good cook or not? My old lady couldn't boil water if my daddy built the fire," he said.

"I just don't remember her all that much. She died when I was real little. My daddy shipped me off after a time, hired me out to some folks."

"Hired you out?"

John Paul filled his mouth with biscuit and bacon as to avoid the question about Foley and his sister, Uda, who he'd either been hired out to, or sold to. He didn't rightly know.

"I bet them folks is probably missing you," Einer said.

"They ain't."

"Why ain't they?"

"Jesus Christ, mister, you writing for a newspaper or something?"

"I get it," Einer said, washing down his food with a slug of the coffee, making a face at it as he did so, tasting coffee grit in his teeth. "You run off, thinking you'd cross that ol' Llano out there and start you a new life and you don't want them folks to know where you run off to because you probably robbed 'em blind a'fore you took off. Ain't that about the way of it?"

"What if I did? What's it to you?"

"It ain't nothin' to me."

"All right then."

They finished their meager meal and then Einer went over to his bed and pulled on a pair of canvas trousers but not his shirt. John Paul watched as he tucked the stag-handled revolver down into his waistband and took the other one—that of John Paul's he'd cleaned and oiled—and carried it over to him.

"I cleaned it and put in fresh loads. Come on outside, I want to see something."

John Paul stood from the table, uncertain whether to put the dishes in the dry sink, like Foley's wife always had him do when she wasn't in a hurry to get him off somewhere alone.

Einer was already out the door before John Paul decided just to let the dishes set and followed him out.

He watched Einer gather some rusted cans from the can pile and go over to an old stump of a post somebody had once driven into the ground, for what purpose could only be guessed—a gatepost, maybe—and set a can on it; then Einer walked back about twenty five paces and said, "See can you hit that."

"Shit," John Paul said as if the request were an insult to him.

He raised the Schofield, thumbed back the hammer, took

aim, and fired. He was surprised when the can didn't move, even though he shouldn't have been. The only thing he'd ever shot with it was Foley's racer after it'd broke its leg.

"Shit," he said again and fired a second time, and still a miss. "The damn sights are off," he said.

Einer took the piece from him and shot the can and before it landed from twisting into the air, he shot it a second time and then danced it on across the ground until his hammer fell on an empty. He broke it open and knocked the hulls out with due deliberation, reloaded it from shells in his pocket, and handed it back.

"You think you could shoot a man from here to that tin can?" Einer said.

"If I wanted to," John Paul said and took aim at the can again lying out there and his round spit up dirt just in front of it.

"Well you sure can hit the earth, that's a natural fact. Maybe you ought to practice a bit while I have my second cup of coffee and another shuck."

"Why you want me to do this any goddamn way, just so you can make fun of my shooting?"

"No, it ain't nothing to do with making fun of you, boy."

"Then what is it?"

"You finish off these shells—" he said, taking the rest of the cartridges from his trouser pockets and setting them in John Paul's hand—"and I'll tell you why. But only if you can hit that can three times in a row from right here," and he drew a line in the sand with his boot toe.

John Paul fired and fired and then reloaded his revolver and took careful aim as Einer went into the house and shortly came back out with his cup of coffee and squatted in the dust and built himself a smoke watching John Paul shoot and miss and shoot again.

He ain't got no kinda eye for shootin', you crazy old bastard, what give you the idea anyway?

He'd dreamed of the woman again that night and at the most critical point came away blinking away the darkness in trying to discern her presence in the room, and when he realized it was just him dreaming, his body felt like a clenched fist of disappointment and anger. The dreams of her always left him wanting and filled with abiding sorrow so deep it seemed infused in his bones—love like that gone missing was the most terrible kind of love.

Damn it to hell, he'd told himself lying there, you're crazier than a bedbug to think she's still out there somewhere. And even if she was, what'd she want with you now, after all this time? She'd run you off is what she'd do.

He'd lain there the night long regretting, feeling the anguish of a man who was old and lonely and knowing his time was running down faster than a two-dollar pocket watch and that his one and only true love had become lost to time and wouldn't it be real damn nice to find her again if for nothing more than to explain himself and seek her forgiveness. That would be the least of it. He didn't even want to think about what the best of it might come to.

It came to him then, near dawn, that he could either live out what little time he had just hanging on way out here in no man's land with naught but snakes and hawks, spiders and scorpions and such, nothing but the sameness of each day come and gone, or he could go in search of her and state his case and hope it wasn't too late.

And the more he thought of it, of her, the more the idea buoyed him, put his mind right. And if he could find her, if she wasn't already dead, if she didn't run him off or was married, well, at least he'd know one way or the other and he could close the book on that chapter of his life and die in peace. In his mind there wasn't a greater sin than to let love go unspoken to the beloved, for love was everything. A lesson he'd learned too late for the learning. Maybe.

And maybe this kid was the answer, some sort of sign that if he was going to go, now was the time. In spite of his kid's paltry condition, he had at least showed the gumption and belief in himself that he could steal a horse and cross that damned Llano on his own. The kid had sand even if he was something of a fool.

Shit, you don't even know if you could cross the Llano your ownself without some help getting across it, he thought. But maybe the two of you could.

Now he squatted there in the dust with his makings, and just as he finished rolling the smoke and lighted it, *Bang!* He heard the ricochet of the bullet.

"See there, you old bastard."

"Hit it again," Einer called.

And he did.

"One more time and I might take you with me."

John Paul stopped and looked back at him.

"Take me with you, where?" he said.

"Somewhere. Hit it again and I might tell you."

"Shit," John Paul grinned. "I don't know where it is you'd be taking me. What makes you think I'd go anywhere with you?"

"You said you wanted to cross that Llano, didn't you?"

John Paul weighed what that meant—crossing over into New Mexico, leaving his problems behind because he didn't see how some Texas Ranger could have any sway on the law in New Mexico if one was after him on account of what happened.

"You saying you'll take me across?"

"I might consider it—if you can hit that can one more time without missing."

John Paul swung back around, faced the deadly enemy that

51

lay with its sharpened jaw laid open, and fired, and the bullet nicked it enough to spin it around.

He stood for a moment holding the hot-barreled gun. Might just be the right time to hold Einer up and steal his horse, seeing as how he was just squatted there smoking a shuck.

He aimed the gun straight out.

"Nothing's stopping me from finding out can I shoot a man or not," he said, a sickly grin on his face.

Einer stood up slow, his own gun still tucked into the waistband of his trousers. His gaze narrowed.

"No, boy, nothing is, but me."

"Shit, I don't believe you could draw that piece a'fore I put one in you," John Paul said.

"Well then, I guess there is just one way to find out," Einer said. "Ain't they?"

"Hell," John Paul said, lowering his weapon. "I was just seeing what you was made of, is all. Case you and me become pards, I want to know you'll stick."

Einer stood a moment longer without moving and John Paul wasn't so cocksure he might not draw his piece and shoot him dead and it left him with a queasy stomach. You shouldn't have drawed down on that crazy old bastard.

"Pards?" Einer said.

John Paul swallowed hard.

"Well, ain't that what you're talking about, me and you?"

"Here's the thing," Einer said. "You ever again point a gun at me, it will be your eternal undoing. Just remember that."

John Paul nodded.

"So when are you taking me?" he said.

There was a long silence with naught but the sound of the cigarette burning down and not a breath of air to indicate one way or the other what the weather might turn to. The cigarette smoke just hung there.

"You were willing to risk your life to steal a horse," Einer said. "Would you do it to steal a bunch of horses?"

"Why would I want to steal a bunch of horses," John Paul said, "when one is all I need?"

"They is only one reason a man does anything," Einer said. "For money. Walking around money."

"Walking around money?"

"There's something I got to do requires money," Einer said. "You know what walking around money is, boy?"

"I reckon its money you walk around with," John Paul said.

Einer snorted.

"It's a lot more than that. It's what gives a man the means to have what he wants when he wants it and not have to wait till the end of the month for payday. It's what will put a new shirt on your back when you see one on a store shelf you admire. It affords you a proper bath with a fat whore in a pricey bordello. It stakes you to a poker game and even if you lose you still have plenty for a bottle of top whiskey. It's pissing away money on whatever a man wants to piss it away on and not have to worry about it. It's go to hell money, boy. That's what kind of money I'm talkin' about."

John Paul saw that faraway dreamful look in Einer's gaze. Einer, standing there wistful with that cigarette in the corner of his mouth.

"Thought you said stealing horses was a hanging offense?"

"You ever had a woman, boy? No, I reckon you are too young to have had you a woman. But let me tell you, you have a beautiful woman just once—especially one you don't feel you deserve—it's something that you'll never forget in two lifetimes, and it sure as hell *is* worth the risk of being hanged."

"I still don't understand all this about stealing horses. Where you gonna steal 'em from and who you gonna sell 'em to, to get all this going to hell money?"

" 'Cause you got no ears to listen with. You can't get you no woman like the kind I'm talking about being poor-assed and rundown with empty pockets. You can't buy you a dream sitting on your duff just dreaming about whatever it is. You got to get you a plan and then set to it if you want something out of this old world."

"You just now figured all that out?" John Paul said. "A man of your years?"

"I just now did," Einer said. "Thanks to you."

"Lord God almighty," John Paul said. "I just want to keep on going is all . . ."

"See, I've been thinking," Einer admitted. "And I about decided to go and get me some walking around money because of what I need to do. And it sure as shit beats the hell out of staying around here and waiting for the Lord to call me on home. Why even He'd be ashamed to have me in His house as I now am, and I would be ashamed to enter it as I am."

"I do believe I will just go on now," John Paul said. "Leave you to your dreams and such. I ain't about to get myself hanged over some old man's screwy ideas."

"You do and you'll die out there. You'll become buzzard bait and nobody will ever know nor care who or what you were. You'll just be some old bones somebody come across one day."

Again the boy swallowed, for he halfway believed the old man was portending the truth of the matter. That part about being dead and nobody knowing or even caring.

"Sure," he said. "Sure, I can understand that." Even though he didn't, but maybe the old coot could lead him on across the Llano and then he could make it to wherever he was going on his own.

"All right, then," Einer said, casting aside his burned-down shuck. "No time like the present to get on going."

"So I'd be doing you a favor by going along with you?"

"Just like I done you by not blasting you for trying to steal my horse."

"So just like that, we're going to go and steal a bunch of horses and sell them, so we can have walking around money so we can find us women?"

"Why you're slower than maple syrup in winter," Einer said. "We ain't gone steal a bunch of horses—not just yet. We just got to steal one—so you have something to ride. Then we're gone steal a bunch of goddamn horses."

"Just like that? Go out and steal one horse, when the only horse I've seen in days and days is that one of yours in the corral?"

Einer shook his head.

"Yeah, that's the plan if you will shut up with your damn ignorance."

"How come you want me in on this deal? Why don't you just go on and do it on your own?"

"Ever thing is easier when there is two," Einer said. "One to do the planning and one to do the doing. See if you'd had yourself a partner when you come to steal my horse, I might not have been able to stop you. But you didn't and I did."

John Paul considered the logic of this.

"It's why I needed to see could you shoot and hit the broadside of a barn," he said. "Now that you showed me you possibly can, I'm feeling much better about our prospects."

They left within the hour, riding double on the stud with nothing more than the clothes on their backs and everything Einer owned rolled up in his bedroll tied on behind the cantle of his Mexican saddle.

They rode away toward the west, toward Einer's dream and who knew what else.

A man can only wait just so long for something he's craved his whole life, and Einer was through waiting.

CHAPTER 6

Ballard left out when the first of the sun sifted through the distant mountains and sought out the rest of the world, everything west of east. Its light snaked along the dusty landscape and down into the arroyos and over rocks and canyons and crawled up the sides of red sediment hoodoos sculpted by wind and rain over eons of time, since the earth was first formed and it was void of life until life formed too from a muddy soup and crawled onto land and became wholly man walking on hind feet, or by the use of Adam's rib, depending which story a man believed.

The wind and rain and heat and winter cold had scarred the land like an old man's face in a losing knife fight. It was a landscape both sere and umber, of white gypsum and mudflats that spoke of misery and desperation of all those who would dare live in it and dare travel it. Even the few trees that grew were twisted and gnarled as arthritic limbs of sickly men. And the mudflats were imprinted with large footprints of long-ago creatures, some with thighbones as tall as a man, but now held the rainwater until the sun drew it up into the sky again.

He hated the idea of chasing a man or a boy across such land, hated everything about the prospects of not finding the kid sooner rather than later. Ballard was of middle years and no longer immune to hardship as he was in his youth. He was by turn too old to be young and too young to be old and felt half the time as being lost in between the two and regretful that he was.

Every passing year he'd grown more and more to the idea of settling down, maybe opening up a livery stable with a blacksmith forge, work he could do with his hands, at his own pace, and go home every night muscle worn, knowing he'd put in a good day's labor, that he was respected for his work, paid decent for it. And if a man wanted to bring his animal by for a new set of shoes and he further wanted to hang around and talk about the weather or what it had been like when the fellow had gone to the Philadelphia Exhibition, why that was an idea whose attraction settled with him nicely now that he had everything else he wanted.

He reached Charley Redleg's place just after high noon, saw him standing out in a planting of corn, him and his woman called Little Moon, the pair of them with bushel baskets picking the ears, and he reined to a halt, then dismounted.

Kids ran around like a brood of spooked chickens playing tag, too little to be of much use in the real work. Charley and his woman doted on those kids and he wondered if they'd say so much as boo to any of them even if they were to start eating the dog—an ugly old half-crippled black thing that lay belly down in the hot dusty yard raising only its eyebrows when he'd ridden up and dismounted.

Charley came out of the cornfield with his bushel full and set it down and mopped his forehead with the back of his sleeve.

"I'm going after that boy," he said.

Charley looked back at his wife still out in the field filling another basket.

"Can't go," he said. "Wish I could, but I got too much work. I've not even gone hunting yet either and she'll have me sleeping in the shed if I don't bring her a fat antelope or deer."

"I figured," Ballard said, "but thought I'd ask anyway. Looks like your corn came in good."

"Pretty fair considering how little rain we got."

"You ever see a good year for rain in this country?" Ballard said.

Charley shook his head.

"Not hardly in my lifetime I ain't. But we had a couple of pretty good storms last month and that saved us."

The woman had stopped picking and stood now watching. Ballard waved a hand but she didn't wave back, figuring rightly so that he'd come to take Charley away from her again.

"Tell you what," Charley said. "My cousin could use the work."

"Who is your cousin?" Ballard asked.

"His name is Elkhart Truth and he lives about ten, twelve miles up the road in Skull Flats. He's not a flesh and blood cousin, he's more like shirttail cousin."

"He any good a tracker?"

"Better than me, even."

Ballard looked off. Another ten miles of riding just to find a tracker, he thought.

"You think if I took him back out to Foley's he could cut that boy's sign?"

"It was John Paul then? That's what Doc said?"

Ballard nodded.

"Least I believe so. One of 'em was definitely the woman."

"Hell, if he can't cut sign for you, there ain't no sign to *be* cut."

"He's reliable too?"

"He might drink a little, but long as you keep him off the bug juice too heavy he'll be worth it."

"All right then, I'll take your word for it. How will I locate him when I get to Skull Flats?"

"Just ask around, everybody knows him, a name like his, how

could someone not know him?"

They shook hands and Ballard mounted up and rode off toward the nothing community known as Skull Flats. There was no skull to have named the place after, just a crossroads of a place with a trading post such as it was. A few shacks scattered about in all directions for half a mile, but Ballard could not have said why there was anything there at all. The outpost sold about everything necessary but only one or two of each. Sold more liquor than anything and it was a lot shorter ride there than into either Mobeetie or Tascosa, the nearest other settlements.

It took him under an hour to arrive there and he went straight to the trading post.

He knew the owner to be Mexican and who lived within. During business hours, which were irregular at best, he manned the counter and a belted Walker Colt as advertisement that required no sign or other warning about trouble making or mayhem if that's what you'd come for.

The owner was the grandson of a Mexican officer who had fought at the Alamo and had told him how he and the others had rounded up the remaining survivor defenders—including the now legendary Crockett—bayonetted them, and burned their bodies on one great pyre, though the grandson did not advertise the fact to the populace, knowing that any Texan worth his salt would promptly drag him to his death from the back of a horse for such blasphemy.

"Oh, it was a very terrible thing Santa Anna had us do," the grandfather had told him when he was just a boy and with eyes full of tears. "Those were some brave Americanos. I wish the commander had spared them."

The Mexican nodded when Ballard came in. Lawman or not, the storekeeper did not trust anybody.

"I'm looking for a fellow named Elkhart Truth," Ballard said.

"His cousin, Charley Redleg, said I'd find him around here."

"He know you're looking for him?"

A man of suspicion no doubt, one who aimed to keep whatever regular customers he had.

"He will, soon as you can tell me where to find him."

Theirs was and always had been an uneasy truce. In the shopkeeper's mind lawmen and thieves were of the same rank and not to be fully trusted, but their money was always good in his place.

"Back there," the owner finally pointed with his chin.

In the back of the place was a small sitting area with a table and some chairs occupied by several men sitting, cups in their hands, silent but for the clack of ivory dominoes they played, one against the other.

They all looked up at Ballard's arrival.

"Which one of you is Elkhart Truth?" he said.

A fellow in a checkered shirt sitting under a rounded crown hat with a feather of some sort sticking out of the band made eye contact.

Ballard thought it looked like a turkey vulture feather.

"Whatever it was I didn't do it," Elkhart Truth said. "Whatever it is the law's looking for me for. These here others can attest."

"Nobody said you did anything," Ballard said. "Wondered if I might buy you a drink of that bug juice, have a little palaver with you?"

"Why, hell, yes, you most certainly can."

He stood and carried his cup up-front. Ballard followed.

"Gonzalo, you ol' thievin' bastard, pour me another, Ballard here's buying."

"How'd you know I was a lawman?" Ballard said.

" 'Cause you look like one," Elkhart Truth said.

He had that thin half-starved look of a lounger, of a man

who'd never known a hard day's labor in his life. He also seemed to have that lounger's carefree happy-go-lucky outlook. Take life as it comes, and surely it will come if you are patient enough.

He wasn't very tall, with chopped black hair and stuck-out ears. Denims to go with his checkered shirt, no obvious weapons about his person, but several rings on his fingers and a dangling silver ring hanging from his left ear. A wood crucifix hung from a leather thong around his neck.

"Let's talk outside," Ballard said when he'd paid for the refill.

They stepped out into the bright Texas light, the ground as white flour dust.

"Your cousin Charley said you might be needing some work," Ballard said.

"Long as it don't have nothing to do with lifting heavy objects or digging holes or patching roofs," he said, taking a long swallow of his pulque—a whitish liquid commonly known as Mexican beer. "Also I don't herd pigs or sheep. They are stinking creatures—they go against my religion."

"What religion might that be?"

"Any that calls for handling filthy creatures. Cloven hooves and all that."

"Look, I don't care nothing about any of that," Ballard said. "I just need a good tracker. Charley recommends you highly."

"I can track a fish through water," Elkhart said with a wide grin that showed just how bad he was in need of dental care.

"I don't need to track a fish, I just need to track a boy."

"Don't sound too hard. What you pay?"

"Dollar a day, ten dollars bonus if we catch him."

"Grub included?"

"Yes."

"When do we start?"

Simple as that.

"Right now."

"Haven't finished my drink yet."

"Finish it, then."

"Getting so a man can't hardly take a day off," Elkhart Truth said.

"I imagine life for you must be a burden," Ballard said with no small degree of sarcasm. "You do have a horse, don't you?"

"Not one I own outright, but I can borrow one from my cousin Beaver."

"By borrow you don't mean steal, do you? Round these parts they hang horse thieves and you'll do me no good swinging from the end of a rope."

"You're pretty funny for a lawman," Elkhart Truth said and drained his cup, then set it aside.

"Don't mean to be."

"No, I didn't figure you did."

"Go find that horse and meet me back here," Ballard said. "I'll wait in the shade."

When the tracker left and came back in ten minutes riding a dish-faced Appaloosa, Ballard was impressed.

"Your cousin must be well set to loan you such a good-looking horse," Ballard said. "And well trusting."

"A man bet him this horse that he couldn't stand without flinching while the man shot an apple off his head from forty paces. Beaver took him up and won the horse. But I'll tell you this: where that bullet creased his scalp hair won't grow no more. Looks like a long pink worm and his ears won't stop ringing. Other'n that and the constant headaches he suffers, he came out okay on that deal."

"Let's go," Ballard said. He wanted to show no interest in Elkhart Truth's stories about winning horses and getting apples shot off somebody's head.

CHAPTER 7

John Paul and Einer rode double, taking their time so that the horse beneath would not break down. About every hour they would dismount and walk afoot over rough loose earth that ground beneath their boots like broken glass.

"Goddamn, they ain't hardly a damn thing in this country worth a damn thing," John Paul grumbled.

"It's good for one thing," Einer said.

"What the hell would that be?"

"Hiding from the laws."

"Shit, I ain't hiding from no damn laws."

"I know that's what you said and I tend to take a man at his word," Einer said. "But that is what this land is good for."

"I don't see where we're going to find any damn horse to steal," John Paul said. "Shit we ain't seen so much as a homestead in the last four hours."

Einer's original thought was to ride into German Town and steal them a horse there, but the place was so poorly and in the wrong direction from what he had in mind he didn't see the point of going there. So he chose another direction, one that would get them closer to where he wanted to get them.

Buzzards wheeled in the sky off to their left.

"Something's dead over there," John Paul said.

Einer barely bothered looking.

"It's a rare day in this country something's not dead, or dying, or wishing they were."

They went on under the blistering sun. To the north they saw dark clouds brooding over a scribble of ridgeline and Einer knew that a storm was headed their way. His bones told him as much. His feet and left shoulder ached.

"We best get on before that storm hits," he said.

John Paul looked, visoring his eyes with the edge of his hand.

"You read weather too," he said, a doubtful look on his face. He judged those mountains and clouds to be miles and miles away still.

"I know enough to come in out of the rain, unlike certain humans who are like a damn turkey what will drown 'cause they ain't got enough sense to come in where it's dry. Creatures with no sense often die before their time from strange and wondrous events."

"Shit, is that a fact?" John Paul said feeling every step of the animal's haunch bones knocking against his own.

"That's right," Einer said and fetched his makings to build himself a shuck, lighting it with a match struck off his saddle horn, then heeling the horse into a canter.

"You got a place in mind where we're headed?" John Paul asked. "Or are we just wandering around the earth hoping we run into a place, maybe something where a nice lady is cooking supper?"

The wind suddenly blew mightily and stung their faces and hands with blow grit that felt like thousands of needles.

Einer did not answer John Paul's question because he deemed it not worth answering. In his estimation most questions that John Paul asked were not worth answering. He was a young fool who might or might not learn a thing or two before this was all over. He admitted to himself at having been a young fool once and knew that by their very nature, fools, young and otherwise, had no sense whatsoever and would do foolish things until someday they came up against some hard reality. And sometimes then it was too late.

They rode on parallel with the darkening approach of the sky.

"Why don't we just ride in the opposite direction, away from it?" John Paul said. It was closing in on them now and John Paul could see it was.

"What for, we can't outrun it," Einer said. "And besides, there ain't nothing that a'way for a hundred miles."

He touched spurs to the stud and put it into a gallop anyway knowing they couldn't outrun the storm but maybe they could get somewhere up ahead that might afford them shelter. John Paul nearly tumbled off at the sudden change in speed.

"Whoa, goddamn you got to warn me when you're going to take off like a bat out of hell."

"Shut up and hold on."

They went on and the black sky continued to crowd them. First raindrops splattered down. It was hard to tell the time of day but on ahead they saw the makings of some sort of settlement just as the rain hammered down harder, soaking skin down to bone. Bolts of lightning like mangled silver wire raced through the blackness and thunder boomed all around them so loud it reminded Einer of the cannonade at Gettysburg and a dozen other places he'd fought at during the war, and him but sixteen years of age. It had hardened him real fast, that war did.

By the time they dismounted in the nameless town and entered a nameless saloon to get in out of the rain they were as wet as drowned cats and rain sluiced off their hat brims down their necks.

Einer took off his hat and slapped the water out, then settled it back on his head; John Paul followed suit, then trailed Einer to the bar and he ordered a whiskey. The barkeep poured and looked at John Paul.

"Him too?" he said, fixated on the wine stain birthmark on

John Paul's face.

Einer looked at John Paul.

"You want whiskey, or would you prefer root beer?"

John Paul gave him a hard look.

"Whiskey," he said.

"Pour him one too, then," Einer said to the barkeep.

"Two bits," the barkeep said.

"Two bits it is, then," Einer said and dug a gold coin out of a leather purse he took from his jacket pocket and set it on the wood.

The barkeep's eyes grew large when he saw it to be a gold twenty-dollar double eagle.

"You want, I can run a tab."

"No," Einer said. "These here will do us for now. Just something to warm up the blood is all."

The barkeep's hopeful face dissolved into one of disappointment. It had been ages since anybody had come in and put a gold double eagle on the wood. He made change and returned what was due Einer.

The whiskey hit John Paul like he'd swallowed a lit match; he screwed up his face and made a sound like a sputtering steam engine trying to start or stop.

"What the hell you put in that stuff?" he crowed.

"Put whiskey in it, sonny," the barkeep groused. "What'd you expect would be put into a whiskey bottle but whiskey?"

John Paul glared at him.

"Pour me another," he demanded.

The barkeep looked at Einer for approval. Einer nodded and circled their glasses with a forefinger.

"I reckon one more won't kill nobody—him maybe, but not me."

The barkeep was happy to oblige and poured them out and Einer separated out from his change two more bits and pushed them forward.

The barkeep put the coins in a wood cigar box he kept under the counter next to an unseen shotgun.

"Drink up," Einer said to John Paul as he held his own refill between finger and thumb.

John Paul tossed it back and fought off making any sort of face, but instead one that seemed a forced approval of the quality of the liquor.

"Shit," he said.

"That about the only word you know?" Einer asked.

"Grub's another one, how about you?"

Einer tossed back his drink and said to the barkeep, "They got a place in town that slops rootin'-tootin' gunslicks like us?"

"Up the street, Fannie's," he said.

Einer liked the sound of that—Fannie's.

"Hotel, too?"

Barkeep shook his head.

"Had one, but it burned down a month back."

"Let's go," Einer said and turned and walked out, John Paul trailing him, but less steadily so. The liquor had already found its way to John Paul's legs. The barkeep watched them go, thinking of where that twenty-dollar gold piece had come from and wondering if there were more of the same in that purse, and where'd the hell would an old broke dick like him have gotten such money in the first place. Then he thought, never mind where he got it, he's just got it.

They found the café easily enough and went in and grabbed seats next to a plate-glass window with streaks of rain running down like God's own tears. It overlooked the muddy street and across the way the sodden clapboard buildings. To Einer, the whole shebang looked as sorry as a three-legged dog's future. It was raining even harder now and the rain boiled out in the street in puddles newly formed. The lightning put on a hell of a show, too, like the Fourth of July, only wet.

A limping man in stained apron and greasy hair came over to take their order, and Einer was disappointed.

"Where's Fannie?" he said.

"Fannie?"

"This is her place, ain't it?"

The waiter was grizzled with a wattle of bristling unshaved hairs silvery as cholla needles. One eye didn't quite open fully, the lid pulled down like a busted shade.

"Why ol' Fannie left out a year after she opened the place," he said. "Married a prospector and gone off to live out in the desert with him whilst they search for gold last anybody knows. I bought the place two years back. Never bothered to change the name. Better Fannie's than Pecker's. That's my name, Leo Pecker. You imagine anybody coming in here to eat with the name of Pecker on the sign out front?"

He offered up a phlegmy laugh.

"No, I don't imagine nobody would," said Einer. "I wouldn't, would you?" he asked John Paul. The whiskey in him caused him to feel expansive.

"Shit, hungry as I am I'd eat a cow's pecker if you fried it right," John Paul said and returned Einer's mood with a grin.

"Then you boys's come to the right place. Just happen to have cow peckers on special tonight."

"You're shitting me, right?" John Paul said.

"Yeah, he is," Einer said. "Order you some eggs and bacon if he's got 'em. That's what I'll have," he said to the waiter.

"I can order for my own damn self," John Paul protested.

"Then go ahead and order, unless you plan on sitting here all damn night."

"I'll have some eggs and bacon," John Paul said.

"Bring us coffee too," Einer said and looked across at John

Paul. "That okay with you, we have coffee with our eggs and bacon?"

John Paul sat silent while the waiter went off to get their order.

"Cow peckers," Einer said with a crooked grin as he built himself a smoke. "I wouldn't eat one to get to watch you eat one."

"I bet you was hoping to court her, wasn't you?" John Paul said with a grin.

"Court who?"

"Fannie who used to own this place."

He didn't want to admit John Paul to be right in a manner of speaking. He was not completely unfamiliar with this town, having passed through here years back when it was still rowdy and expanding. But whatever false designs he might have had of meeting Fannie, they were only that, simple fantasies from living alone so damn long, hid out for years, of studying the renderings of women in corsets on those old catalogue pages back at the shack, and of course, the dreams of the woman he aimed to see again, who came to him in the nights but was never really there.

They ate and watched the rain and the waiter refilled their coffee cups several times and Einer made himself another shuck, his legs stretched out and crossed at the ankles.

"So, what now?" John Paul said.

"We'll rest the night and be gone in the morning, hopefully with you your own horse to ride."

John Paul leaned forward.

"Steal one from here?"

"That'd be the plan."

John Paul glanced out the window, up and down the street, saw no saddle horses tied up but Einer's.

"It don't hardly seem like it's an overabundance of horses

round here," he said.

"They's horses," Einer said. "You just need to know where to find 'em on such a poorly night as this."

"Well, shit," John Paul said. "And here I thought all this time we was just lost and hoping for some miracle, for the Lord Jesus to deliver us a horse down from horse heaven—like he gave them wandering Jews manna that time in the Bible."

Einer shook his head as he lighted the end of his smoke and snapped out the match and laid it on his plate.

"Jews in the Bible?"

"That's right. I bet you didn't even think I could read, did you? Probably figured me for an ignoramus."

"Ignoramus? Damn, boy, you're just plum full of surprises."

"And I ain't no damn boy so you can stop calling me that!"

"You need to temper that mouth of yours," Einer said, his gray gaze leveled at John Paul's mud-brown ones. "It's gone someday write a check your ass can't cash and you are damn close to doing just that with me."

John Paul shrank back, sat sullen for a moment, drank his coffee, and looked out at the rain-filled night, the rain looking like silver threads in the greasy light of the diner, falling outwards.

"I guess I just been too long disappointed in the quality of others to know how to act," John Paul said softly, "to believe in anybody but my ownself."

"Well, might do you some good to have a little faith in something other than yourself," Einer said, exhaling twin streams of smoke through his nostrils. "I don't say or do a damn thing I don't mean. And you can take that right on across the street to the bank, if'n there was a bank right on across the street to take it to. You see any bank when we rode in?"

John Paul shook his head.

"Me either. A disappointment to be sure."

"Why so?"

"I figured if'n it still had a bank, we might take it in our heads to rob it. It'd save a damn heap of work over stealing a bunch of horses."

"It'd probably get us slaughtered too—like the James Younger gang in Minnesota when the whole town opened up on them."

"Well we ain't the James Younger gang, and this sure as hell ain't Northfield."

"How you reckon it ain't?"

Einer leaned in close, lowered his voice, and said, "That building yonder," pointing with his hand that held the cigarette, "used to be a bank."

"You know this how?"

" 'Cause I robbed it."

John Paul sat back, still staring out into the rain-soaked night at the lifeless building, not entirely sure whether to believe the old man or not.

"Used to be a lively ol' place, lots of pretty demimondes, too."

"Demimondes?"

"Whores, boy. Whores."

"You're as hard to decipher as third-grade arithmetic," John Paul said.

"Ain't I, though."

They sat while Einer finished his cigarette and coffee and put a dollar on the table and told the waiter to keep the change.

"Change?" the waiter said. "Hell mister, your bill come to ninety-five cents all told."

"Well go on and keep the change anyway," Einer said, uncrossing his legs and standing up. "I guess you earned it. Maybe next time we'll order them cow peckers if you got any. By the by, they still a livery in town?"

"Still is, where it's always been, up the street a couple of blocks."

They walked out, the waiter watching after them.

"Where to now?" John Paul said as they stood under the overhang, the rain about let up to nothing but a drizzle, the storm moved on eastward.

"After we get you a horse we're on to El Paso, then on to Mexico."

"They got horses aplenty down there, huh?"

"They got enough for us," Einer said.

"Why we stopping in El Paso?"

"Never you mind why. It's enough to concentrate on one thing at a time."

"All right then."

They stood under the cover of the boardwalk for a moment, Einer looking up and down the street. It had been a long time since he'd been here. He didn't know the name of the town just that the bank was THE FIRST TRUST OF TEXAS, and he trusted there was plenty of money in it, him an' ol' Joe Grace, his sidekick at the time. Gracie, as Einer often referred to him, got himself shot-gunned by a farmer who caught Gracie bending his wife over his kitchen table one day when he came home early from town. Least he went out having himself a good time.

As they led the saddle horse down the street Einer recalled a Kate, or was it a Callie, who worked out of a crib joint somewhere along in here, a pretty filly but for bad teeth, who giggled the whole time he was fornicating with her like she was being tickled. He wondered if she might still be around, but then realized if she was she'd be damn near old as him. No sir, his was a higher aim he reminded himself. There was only one woman he was interested in finding. He was nearly afraid to think of her name for fear it would break his heart all over again.

Magdalena. He thought of it anyway, unbidden.

"We sure as hell can't sleep out in this rain," John Paul said. "You got any ideas?"

"Yonder, in the livery. You, me, and my horse."

"Livery?"

"Oh, you ain't opposed to sleeping on a man's floor whose horse you were bound to steal, or out in the bresh on the cold ground, but now all of a sudden you have a taste of finer things? A livery is too good for the likes of you?"

"Naw, I just thought a hotel with a real bed might be nice."

"I ain't one to disagree, but a livery floor is the best we can hope for in this burg."

They led the horse over to the livery and were glad to be getting out of the rain. The double doors had an unlocked hinge hanging from the hasp and Einer swung the doors open and led the stud inside and put him up in a stall before finding a grain bin and graining the animal. There were two or three other horses put up in there and they snuffled and moved around a little in their stalls before settling down again.

"Looks like maybe we found you a horse," he said. "But first we'll get a little shut-eye. I'm about wore to a nub."

Einer and John Paul found two empty stalls for themselves and Einer split his soogins from the blanket wrapped inside and gave John Paul the blanket.

"Go on and get you some rest. We'll leave before it gets light and take one of these horses with us when we go."

They lay in the dark listening to the rain scattershot the roof as the storm seemed to have returned, undecided in where it wanted to go. They lay in the dark listening, Einer in one stall, John Paul in another across from him.

John Paul was already snoring.

Einer, in spite of his weariness, could naught but think of her and of seeing her again. He was on his way now. That's what mattered.

He lay clothed with the old coach gun he always carried in lieu of a rifle because his aim at distance wasn't so good no more. The gun had been a trophy from a stage he and Gracie had robbed this one time and got the strongbox, which took them hours and hours to bust into, and when they finally did all was in there was a bunch of papers and two hundred dollars. But Einer got that coach gun from the messenger and it was just about right for the work Einer had in mind. He lay with it up close to him like a woman of bored steel and comforting, his pistol in his belt. Like in the old, old days.

CHAPTER 8

Ballard and the tracker, Elkhart Truth, rode in ever widening circles around the charred remains of the burnt structure until Truth cut the sign—sand-blown, pocked hooves barely visible leading away to the west.

"There he rides," said the tracker pointing with a gloved finger.

Ballard sat his horse but bent at the waist to get a better look at the vague declivities, then straightened again and looked off in the direction the tracker pointed to, a never-ending emptiness.

"Well, if he's headed out there he's going straight into a death trap unless he knows that country," he said.

The tracker stood and brushed dirt off his one knee, removed his hat, and mopped his forehead with the sleeve of his shirt.

"He'll cross the Llano, or try too," the tracker said, "unless he turns south and even then . . ."

"I know it," Ballard said.

"Unless he's got plenty of water, supplies, a real good horse, and the directions scribbled across his brains, all we're likely to find is just one more dead man who's tried crossing it."

Ballard nodded.

"I reckon," he muttered, then heeled his horse forward.

The tracker mounted and fell in alongside Ballard.

"You know your way across it—the Llano?" the tracker said.

"I do," Ballard said. "But that don't mean I'm anxious to cross it."

"We'll need to get some supplies if you do aim to cross it. A packhorse maybe."

"There's a place I know not far," Ballard said.

"It's no place to even think about getting lost in, the Staked Plains ain't."

Ballard rode on in silence, trailing the tracker, who then rode out front, eyes scanning the ground, reaching back every once in a while into his saddle pockets for the bug juice, taking a nip and putting it away again. He sang loudly off-key fragments of songs he'd either made up or memorized. It was caterwauling, like two whores in a hair-pulling fistfight, like tomcats set afire. It was just plain god-awful to Ballard's ears and so he held back to let the space between him and the tracker increase.

Don't be a fool, he could hear her say, hear himself saying it too. Why do you want to risk what we've got for a cause uncertain, for a crime that might not even have been committed, to find a boy who might be completely innocent? She never said it, but he imagined she was thinking it.

He had no real answer for her or himself, except it was his duty, an oath he had taken, sworn to uphold the law and arrest miscreants, to investigate crimes.

What was an oath anyway?

Just this: when a life had been lived and looked back on, a man's word was all he ever had that was truly his own, and either it stood for something, or it didn't.

They made night camp in a slash of earth not quite an arroyo and not even close to a canyon. It was as though the land had simply been cut open by a large dull knife enough for a body to crawl into, something out of the wind.

The good thing was there was a ledge of rock they could get

under and out of the weather in case it rained during the night. Earlier they'd heard distant thunder. The season was iffy when it came to rain: might be pretty and pleasant one minute and raising hell the next.

Ballard built a small fire and set upon it a can of beans. When the beans got to bubbling, he took it off, lifting it by the pried open lid with his kerchief, and stuck in a spoon he took from his shirt pocket.

"You want to go first?" he said to the tracker.

"First?" Elkhart Truth said, looking at the meager meal, if a meal it was to be considered at all.

"Okay then," Ballard said and began eating. The tracker watched with the eyes of a starved dog.

He watched until Ballard finished his portion, then set back; the can with the spoon in it rested on the ground between them. Ballard lowered his hat down over his eyes and placed his head on his saddle seat, his boots stretched toward the fire. The night had drawn down the cold and you'd have never thought it was as warm as the day had grown earlier.

There under his hat Ballard heard the tracker scramble to take up what was left of the beans, heard him smacking his lips and scraping the bottom of the can with the spoon, licking the spoon itself, then tossing the empty can away.

"That it? That all we gone eat?" he said.

"Get some rest, tracker," Ballard said. "We'll leave early and get us some supplies tomorrow."

"Well holy damn. I thought you promised grub included?"

"You ate what I ate," Ballard said.

"Half a can of damn beans?"

"Stop talking, I'm trying to sleep."

Night came on full dark but for a sky overhead salted with stars and the thumbnail of a moon. The tracker lay on his side staring into the dying fire

"What was I thinking," he muttered and cradled his bug juice, knowing he'd need it to warm him from the inside when the fire extinguished from lack of care. It was just some dead sticks of greasewood and not overly much tinder.

"You think there might be snakes in around here?" he said. He was deathly afraid of snakes ever since one killed his older brother when they were kids. Damn red rattler six feet long coiled under some Manzanita waiting for something to come by, a rabbit or something, only it was his brother Darenot who came by. The thing struck with the power of a club to the calf of the brother's leg. Together they ran all the way to the house, more than a mile—a fatal mistake. That much venom injected into one scrawny little leg was just a death warrant his daddy had said. Brother Darenot fell dead in the yard.

"Do you?" he said when Ballard did not answer.

"Do I what?" Ballard said, his voice full of irritation.

"Do you believe there would be snakes crawling around a night as cool as this?"

"Who knows for certain what a snake will do," Ballard said. "Now leave me to my sleep."

The tracker rose and took his rope from his saddle and spread out a loop all the way around him.

"Ever body knows a snake won't cross a rope," he said the next morning when Ballard arose and looked at the tracker encircled by his rope on the ground.

"I knew a fellow once who thought the same thing," Ballard said. "Turned out he was wrong about snakes not crossing ropes. He woke with one in his soogins lying up against him like a lonely wife. Damn thing bit him in the face when he yipped. Died before they could get him to a doctor's."

The tracker looked at the rope, sorely disappointed if the story Ballard told him was the truth.

"Let's get moving," Ballard said, already in the process of

saddling his horse.

"No breakfast neither?" the tracker said, his voice rising to near panic. "Damn I can't ride all day with no grub and go to bed hungry."

"You won't have to, there's an old Mexican woman not far from here makes the best tamales I ever ate."

"Well, shit. What we waitin' for?"

"I'm not," Ballard said and forked his horse and turned it out. The tracker stood there scratching his head.

"You just a real damn hound dog, ain't ya?" he muttered, watching the ass end of Ballard's horse.

"What if he ain't even gone that way? You ever stop and think about that?" he shouted.

He finished strapping on his saddle and went after Ballard.

"So damn hungry my belly thinks my throat's been gone on vacation," he grumbled. "Git along there, cayuse!" and quirted the horse into a gallop to catch up.

CHAPTER 9

Einer heard it: the slight creak of a door being opened, light footfalls stirring loose straw. He cocked back the rabbit ear hammers of the coach gun, holding it across his belly, and waited to see if the steps halted; then he turned around and went back out again, wondering if they had heard him prepare the shotgun for killing. Could be just the owner come along and found the clasp flung back and looking to see what it was caused it. Could be worse than that too. His instincts, however, told him it was worse than that. He lay there cradling the shotgun, unwilling to stir more for fear of giving away his position.

He heard a match struck, saw the brief glow of flame, then heard a voice whispering low.

"You sure they in here, Pecker?"

"I follered them over."

"Hesh."

There was a pause, a silence, for even John Paul had stopped snoring. Einer didn't know if he'd awakened to the entry of others too, or he'd just stopped snoring. If the kid was awake, this would be a show of his mettle, Einer thought—unless they killed him. Killed them both. He knew he shouldn't have flashed that double eagle. But shit, if a man had to worry about every damn thing he did, well, what was the fucken point of even living?

He thought he heard John Paul stir, tried to communicate silently: *Git ready, boy, they're coming.*

"I can't see shit," the harsh whisper of one of them said.

Another match struck, another brief flame that almost as quickly glowed down to almost nothing.

Einer scrambled up and pulled both triggers and the boom of both barrels firing was deafening.

He heard them cry out, one and then the other.

"Git up, boy, kill them bastards!" Einer yelled, jerking free his revolver, cocking the hammer back as he did.

The darkness was complete again until John Paul fired off two, three, four quick shots that flamed from the end of his gun barrel, blinding him in the process and Einer too.

Whoever they were, they weren't dead for they returned fire just as quick, bullets splintering wood, and one at least ricocheted off something metal.

"I'm empty," the kid yelled.

"Well I goddamn ain't. Reload that sumbitch." Einer fired in the direction he thought they were and then the kid fumbling to reload got two or three chambers filled and excitedly fired off those.

Then everything ceased as Einer reloaded his own revolver.

Horses were kicking the slats of their stalls and shrieking like scared women. At least one of the shot men was moaning.

"Oh, sweet Mary," he cried. "I'm shot clean through. Don't shoot me no more, goddamn it."

Einer breathed heavily as he waited, his chest hurting, tight like there was a steel band around it.

"Boy," he said.

"Yuh?"

"You hit?"

"Maybe. Something's hit my head. I've blood leaking into my eyes."

"In the head?"

"Something hit me in the head a splinter maybe, 'cause I ain't killed."

"Can you get to your feet?"

"I am on my feet."

"I'm going to strike a match, don't shoot me."

"Shoot you?"

"Thinking I'm one of them."

"One of who?"

"Oh, shit, just shut the hell up and let me light a match."

"Go on and light it."

He found a match in his shirt pocket where he kept some and his makings and struck it. Its flame jumped up in his hand, then settled as he came out of the stall and went to the men lying on the hard packed floor, his hand holding the cocked revolver. He heard John Paul come in behind him.

"Just don't let that iron go off and shoot me in the back, goddamn it," he said.

He caught a glimpse of a pair of boot soles, toes pointed toward the rafters. Horses continued to be skittish and stomping around. The match burned down and he flicked it out before it burned his fingertips.

"You see anything?" John Paul said.

"Yeah. I'm gone light another match."

"I'll shoot anything that moves."

"Just don't shoot me, goddamn it."

"You already told me that about three times already."

"I'll tell you three more times I have to," Einer growled.

He struck another match and arced it around and found a bull's-eye lantern hanging on a nail driven into a stall post; he took it down and raised its chimney glass and set fire to the wick, then lowered the glass. The light inside the soot-grimed chimney swelled to fill a circle ten feet wide around them.

Einer knelt by the man with the heavenward-pointed boots and saw that the top of his head was blasted away with nothing left but skull fragments and brain matter the consistency and color of strawberry jam, but the man's eyes were staring upwards like he was surprised and Einer thought, I imagine you was. Then realized it was that barkeep.

He held the lamp higher and saw that the side of a stall was wet and a red sludge was running down its boarded side and there at the base of it lay a chunk of skull bone big as a peach can. He stood and went to the other, who was making miserable noises.

He held the light close to the pained features.

It was that waiter, Pecker.

"Help me, mister, go and get me a medico, I'm bleeding out. Oh glory, you done shot me all to hell."

His eyes darted in the light like moths trying to get inside a house through a screen door.

"You know how death comes?" Einer said.

The man's mouth opened, his lips trembling as he held his shirtfront, which was heavy enough with blood he could have wrung it out and had him a pail full.

"Wha . . . ?"

"I asked, do you know how death comes?"

The shot man rocked his head side to side.

"No . . . no . . . Please, mister, go and get the doctor. I got a wife and kids. Don't let me die lying in horseshit."

"It comes like a thief in the night is how it comes, which you have now learned, but it's too late for the learning in your case. I surely am sorry for your wife and kids. She should have married a better sumbitch than you."

"You want me to go see can I find a doctor?" John Paul asked, standing over them.

"Ain't a doctor in the world can do a thing for him," Einer said standing, gazing downward.

"We just gone stand here and do nothing?" John Paul said, so much blood on both men he thought he would puke, especially

83

that fellow whose head was nearly blown off.

"See if either one of these'ns boots might fit you," he said. "They ain't got no more need for 'em and yours is worn to nubbins."

John Paul hesitated. Einer reloaded his weapon, discharging the empty hulls beside the body of the dying man.

"Well, suit yourself. Them look like good boots to me," he said.

John Paul squatted and pulled off their boots and found that the dead man's was a decent enough fit when he pulled them on and was glad that the still dying man's was too small.

"They fit good enough," he told Einer after walking around a bit testing them.

"Now take their guns and find you one of these horses, get it saddled, and let's get the hell gone from here before word gets spread and the rest of these vultures come and hang us for *their* own crimes."

John Paul glanced at the dying man. Pecker was just about gone. His mouth was moving but no words were coming out and that alive look a creature has was all but gone out. He gasped two or three times like a drowning man and then stopped altogether. John Paul was relieved that the fellow's suffering was finished.

In moments they were riding off into the black night, the wind in their faces and Einer in the lead, the hooves of their horses throwing up muddy clods ten feet into the air.

John Paul told himself that the men had asked for what they got and if they hadn't wanted to end up killed they shouldn't have tried to rob him and Einer. But they had and now they were dead and it troubled him more that he wasn't at all troubled by their deaths. Told himself it could have as easily been him when he tried stealing Einer's horse.

They rode until near daylight, then slowed, and Einer

watched for a place to get off the road and lay up until they'd rested enough to go on more.

He found a small brush arbor of leaning willows sprung from the banks of a live creek and they eased in there and dismounted and unsaddled their horses and stretched out on the ground.

Einer felt the weight of his years pressing down on him, the deep ache in his hips and nether regions and down along his lower back from the pounding ride. He would have liked a cigarette but was too tired to build one.

"What is it, boy?" he said after a long silence and sleep still not having arrived yet.

"I was thinking, is all."

"What was you thinking, about them two killed?"

"Yeah."

"You worried you might have killed them instead of me?"

"Maybe," John Paul said. "I guess it don't matter much who killed them."

"You are damn right about that."

"I know it."

"You never shot nobody before have you?"

John Paul remained silent.

"Hell, here all the time I figured you to be a young killer— like that Billy Bonney over in New Mexico."

"Who?"

"Some boy who shot a lot of men, they say. But then he himself got killed by the laws."

"What made you think of it?"

"I just figured . . ."

Then John Paul heard Einer snoring.

He lay there awake for a long time, and before he knew it the morning light was spread like golden water over the land, chasing away shadows and turning them into rocks and greasewood and crumbling red earth and sparkling in the stream water like broken pieces of glass.

He got up and went and knelt by the stream and cupped up the cool wetness into his hands and lavered it over his face and neck. He cupped more and drank of it and it tasted good and clean and clear as a dream of water.

He squatted there looking about and saw nothing that identified where they were or where they might be going. Just knew by the position of the sun in the east they were still headed west. He looked over at the horse he'd stolen—a not very tall bay with a blaze face. Then he glanced down at the handle of his revolver sticking from his waistband, and the dead man's boots on his feet. They felt good and tight and were nearly new.

He pulled the pocket watch from his pocket—the one he'd taken surreptitiously from the dead man whose boots he wore. He'd spotted the watch in the pale yellow light, it having slipped out of the man's waistcoat pocket, and he'd picked it up and put it in his own pocket. Einer had said nothing. Maybe he hadn't seen him do it. Maybe he had.

He couldn't quite figure Einer, and it troubled him that he couldn't. He didn't seem nothing like ol' Foley at all. He was older than Foley but he acted a lot younger. He'd probably done things in his life that ol' Foley would never have even considered doing.

He looked back over his shoulder at Einer lying now on his side, his legs pulled up, his hand between his knees.

If he wanted he could just take the horses and ride off with them. But when he gave it more thought he remembered about what Einer had said about horse thieves and leaving a man afoot in the wild and somehow it seemed more cruel than letting a gut-shot man pass on in his natural time.

Thinking it over more, if not for Einer, they might both be dead, be the ones lying on the stable floor, their brains running down a wall instead of the other two. Einer had braced them.

And maybe he had braced them too. In the end, he felt like the two of them needed to stick together if either was going to make it through.

He lifted another handful of water to his mouth, then stood and went over and lay down.

It was time to sleep.

CHAPTER 10

Elkhart Truth had scouted on ahead, having lost the faint tracks to wind and shifting sand and dirt and wetness from a scattering rain, and when Ballard caught up with him he saw what the scout had found.

"Here's a saddle horse," he said. "Was you looking for it or one like it?"

It was Foley's mare all right, what was left of it anyway, with most of its meat ripped away from the rib bones. The saddle was uncinched and the horse blanket gone. A nest of flies lifted away, then resettled as the men stood there.

"That's a darling saddle," the scout said.

"It and the horse belonged to the man who was killed, maybe by the boy we're after. One thing's sure. He stole this horse and it makes me more than ever of a mind he had a hand in those people's death."

"Real bad sort, huh, this boy?"

"Couldn't say for certain. But I don't know why else he'd have fled if he didn't have anything to do with the couple's death."

"Foreleg's snapped. Probably stepped in that old gopher hole. It'll sure do a trick on a horse."

The sun was hot and unkind to the men who stood beneath it and their shirts were darkened in patches with sweat.

"There's an old woman runs a place not far from here, the one I was telling you about makes such good tamales. We'll eat there and maybe she's seen our quarry come past. We'll be able to buy a few supplies off her if she's got any," Ballard said.

"I hope she's got some bug juice to sell," the tracker said.

They rode on.

They sat their horses and Ballard called the dugout and soon enough the blanket that stood for a door was pulled back and a stout built woman dressed in shirt and trousers and a rope of hair near to her broad bottom came out and looked them over. She had a brace of pistols strapped to her waist and carried a long-barreled shotgun.

When she saw Ballard she eased the gun down.

"Ain't seen you in awhile," she said.

"Mary," he said. "You still selling those good tamales?"

"Same as always," she said. "Git on down and come in and get you some."

They dismounted and tied off at a wood hitch rail and entered the cool darkness of the earthen hovel. The roof was braced with cottonwood timbers from which hung several lighted lanterns that offered a cozy sensation. There stood a small handmade table and a pair of chairs formed of thick vine soaked for days and shaped, then left to harden.

Along one wall, there was a pantry and an old iron stove with a length of black stovepipe that was going straight up through the earthen overhead and was poking out through the grassed roof.

"Sit y'selves down," she said and they sat each one side across from the other. The chairs were low with woven bottoms of river reed and she reached into a covered Dutch oven and filled two plates with tamales wrapped in corn leaves and set the plates before them.

"Drink too, I suppose?"

They nodded and she dipped into a clay jar and filled two

cups and set these down next to their plates, then pulled up an old crate and sat on it between them while they ate.

"What is this here?" the tracker said tasting the drink in his cup.

She eyed him appraisingly.

"Potato beer," she said. "Good, huh?"

He made a face but his system had long ago adapted to all manner of brew and he knocked it back and held it forth for a refill. It had a kick but not much of one.

She watched them eat with pleasure for it was too long between times of serving visitors. Hardly nobody ever came out onto the Llano unless lost or foolhardy. She truly did like to watch a man eat and enjoy himself among other delights.

They could smell her muskiness, which was somewhere between dark earth and unwashed flesh. The way the light fell from overhead she looked very much a man of middle years; she even had several chin whiskers.

"Have you seen a boy with a stained face recently pass this way?"

"Stained face?" the woman said wiping her red hands on her trouser legs.

"Birthmark," Ballard said and swiped the area of his own face to describe it. "Like somebody spilled wine on him and it just dried into his skin."

"Lord no," she said. "Last humans I seen was a couple of buckos coming up from the south looking for work. Had no money, but I fed them anyway."

She sighed with the remembering of those two and how it was she worked out payment for the food. They didn't hardly want to do it, but they did it anyway and she was sorry afterward to see them ride off.

"What you all looking for him for?" she asked.

"Just looking for him is all," Ballard said.

"I was to see something like that, I'd keep him," the woman snorted. "I could use me something young and unusual."

She looked directly at Elkhart Truth.

"Why you ain't such a bad lookin' feller y'self," she said patting him on the knee. He flinched like he'd been burned.

She poured them more of the potato liquor.

Even as hard a drinker as he was, the tracker was feeling a bit loose in the limbs from the drink, its potency having slipped up on him after about four cupsful. Ballard had stopped after one cup.

"Did he do something bad, this stain-faced boy?" she asked, trying to go at it from another tack.

"Maybe something, maybe nothing," Ballard said. "I'll know when I catch up to him."

"You'll be lucky as hell to catch anybody yet alive and walking around on the Llano," she said, her voice like the sound of sandpaper rubbing against brick.

"I can track anything that moves, and if he's still alive, as you say, we'll find him," Elkhart Truth said in a boastful manner, but not sure why he said it except the potato brew was causing him to fill giddy and loose-tongued.

They ate half a dozen of the tamales each and scraped the black beans she'd served with them off their plates.

"These are about the best tamales I ever put mouth to," the tracker complimented as she watched him closely.

The day's light had drained out of the sky and the sun already had begun melting into the western horizon.

"Ye boys feel free to settle your hash for the night," she said. "I'll whip up some breakfast in the morning."

"We might just as well," Ballard said.

She went to a pile of old wool blankets, some with designs woven into them and handed them each a blanket.

"One of ye can sleep in the wagon bed and the other under

it," she said. "Pay me afore you leave in the mornin'."

"Obliged," Ballard said, taking one of the blankets. The tracker followed him out to where the wagon stood off to the dugout's side next to a small cottonwood corral with a water tank that collected the rain.

They unsaddled and watered their horses and turned them out into the corral with a pair of matched mules she had in there and then Ballard climbed into the bed of the wagon and lay down.

"I reckon you'd already decided who was to get the wagon and who the ground," the tracker said. The potato brew had caused his head to feel afloat like a pumpkin in warm wet sea so that it didn't matter much to him where he slept. He just needed to lie down.

"Me chief, you Injun," Ballard said mockingly.

The last light bled out and full dark came on over them like a tarnished metal shade pulled down. Wind shuttled through the grass and underbrush, then died, then regained itself and shuttled again like a thing struggling to stay alive.

Ballard was fast asleep when the woman came out of the dugout and crept to the wagon and crawled down under.

"Tracker," she whispered, shaking his shoulder. "Tracker."

He was half asleep, dizzy, and loose feeling from those cups of potato brew he wished now he hadn't drank so many of.

"Wha . . . ?" he started to say before she clamped a strong hand over his mouth.

"Ye want some more potato beer?"

He blinked into the darkness, started to sit up, and bumped his head.

She kept her hand over his mouth.

"Come on to the house and git ye some and ye can sleep in a nice bed too," she said. And led him like a tamed dog out from under the wagon, two night shadows skulking toward the dugout. She'd had a single lamp lit and the jug there on the table with two cups. He sat down rubbing his head where he'd bumped it on the wagon and she poured his cup full of the bug juice and some into her own.

"Drink up, Tracker," she said and he did and she refilled his cup. "I got plenty. Drink all ye want."

It didn't take much more.

Sometime in the night he thought he heard her harsh voice singing, but that's about all he remembered until he awakened on the lone cot there in the dugout, the blanket for a door pulled back and away—the doorway full of hot white light and him naked as a fresh born babe.

"Jesus Christ!" he yelped and jumped up covering himself, then quickly finding his clothes in a heap and shucked into them before running outside.

She was out there shoeing one of the mules and Ballard stood leaning against the wagon, his horse saddled and waiting.

"You have a good time with Mary last night," he said stifling a grin.

"I'm a sumbitch," the tracker declared. "That woman drugged me!"

"And who knows what all," Ballard said, trying hard not to laugh.

"She took advantage of me, goddamn it."

"She didn't do nothing to you that you didn't want done," Ballard said. "Mary like most of her ilk can easily spot the weaknesses of others and uses it to her advantage. I thought about warning you, but knowing how much you like the bug juice, figured it wouldn't do any good. A man best learns from his mistakes."

The tracker stood there cussing and hopping about like a rooster on a hot stove lid.

"Get saddled," Ballard said. "We're burning daylight."

The tracker vowed to himself he would forever more remain a teetotaler and begged Ballard never to mention the incident to anyone.

"Who the hell would I tell that would give a damn?" Ballard replied.

He had a point, the tracker figured.

Still.

CHAPTER 11

John Paul craned his neck around, jerking it like a chicken as they rode along, him and Einer.

"Seems to me we ain't headed west no more," he observed.

"That's because El Paso ain't west, it's south of here," Einer said as he rode casual, the almost constant cigarette dangling from the corner of his mouth, its blue smoke curling in the air above his head. "You got a rather sharp eye," Einer sarcastically accused.

"Well, I never went to too much school," John Paul said, "but I do know that the sun rises in the east and sets in the west and we been riding another direction than east or west for a day or two now."

"Sonny," Einer said, hocking up a gob and spitting off to the side before replacing his shuck in his mouth, "you're quick on the draw, sure enough. We headed south by west, or west by south, take your druthers, otherwise we'd end up in New Mexico instead of *old.*"

"Well, hell, I was sort of looking forward to crossing that ol' Llano."

"Whatever in the hell for?"

" 'Cause that was my aim and just so I can say I did."

"You think anybody would care if you crossed it but for the buzzards?"

John Paul scratched the back of his neck. The new boots were breaking in real well.

"I reckon somebody might," he said.

"Like who would it be who cared if you crossed the Llano or the Red River, or the Brazos or anything else?" Einer liked a good verbal tussle now that he had a chance at one.

"There's some who might," John Paul said.

Talking to this old booger was like trying to get out of quicksand. The more you fought with it the deeper you got caught up in it. But John Paul wasn't the kind to give up an argument easily. In that regard, he was a lot like Einer in his temperament.

John Paul suddenly hauled back on the reins. Einer stopped too.

"Now what is it?" he said, his voice like broken glass somebody was walking across with hard sole boots.

"Seeing's how we're supposed to be pards seems to me you'd give me a little more respect and not treat me like an idjit," John Paul sulked.

Einer took the cigarette from his mouth, holding it with thumb and forefinger like it was something dangerous and looked at it, then flipped it away.

"Pards?" he cackled. "Even pards don't make us the equal of one another. You'd have to live about another thirty, forty years before that came to pass."

"Well, damn you then," John Paul said. "I'll head my own way."

"Hell, you don't even know where the shit you are. Head your own way?" Einer said shaking his head. "You'll die out there without me to show you the way. Road agents will kill you for them boots and that gun and that horse too. You'd as sooner march through hell as go your own way out here."

"Well, where are we then?" John Paul said. "I reckon I can find my own way it comes to that. And I reckon I can steal my own damn horses too."

"Here," Einer said swinging his arm about in an arc. "This is where we are at, right here, in the middle of no goddamn place and be glad of it. Those backshooters had their way t'other night, we'd be worm food and it wouldn't matter where you were at. You'd just be graveyard dead—like them two we left in that barn."

"Well, shit," John Paul said. "I held my own, didn't I?"

"I reckon you damn well did," Einer said. "But if you don't quit being so tetchy you'll die for trying to do things dangerous you got no experience at."

"We'll see about that," John Paul said.

Einer watched John Paul turn his mount's head around and heel him forward.

"All right, damn it, hold on," he called.

John Paul turned back around.

"Pards it is then, equal as two sides of the same coin. That satisfy you?"

John Paul felt proud, Einer's equal.

"Shake on it," he said, holding out his hand and spitting in the palm.

"Jesus, boy, your mind just won't let nothing rest, will it? Wipe off that damn spit and I might shake with you. Where'n the shit you ever think of doing that—spitting in your hand?"

"Read it in a book once," John Paul said, wiping his hand down along his pant leg before sticking it back out again.

"Well maybe you ought to read a different kind of book," Einer said.

Then he reached over and shook John Paul's hand.

"All right, then," John Paul said. "I reckon we ought to go on to El Paso."

"I reckon we oughter instead of sitting around here swearing blood oaths to one another. Next thing I know you'll want to be taking out a marriage license."

John Paul grinned.

"You sure are a crusty ol' sumbitch."

"Ain't I, though."

They rode on, the sun a fiery watchful eye upon them, the land full of unseen things—a desert tortoise crawling its way toward shade, a jackrabbit stock still but for a twitching nose, a red coyote trotting along with another jackrabbit caught in its jaws. Life abounded even though you couldn't see it unless you really watched for it. But neither Einer nor John Paul were looking for such things, they just saw them is all.

"How many you figure we can steal at one time?" John Paul said.

"Maybe a couple hundred is what my aim would be. Split three ways would give us fair sight of walking around money."

"Three ways?"

"That's right. We need to take on a partner, a man I know down in El Paso."

"Why we need a third man?"

" 'Cause this one knows where the horses is to be stolen, and how to steal 'em without getting our damn fool heads blown off."

"Well shit, you might've mentioned something about this beforehand."

"Why?"

" 'Cause we're partners, is why."

"Oh, I forgot," Einer said. "I must be getting old."

John Paul didn't think Einer meant it, but he let it pass.

"What's you gone do with your share?" John Paul asked.

"Like I told you, go see a woman I used to know. What you gone do with yours?"

John Paul shrugged.

"Get me some new duds, I reckon. Maybe buy myself a right smart horse and one of them Stetson hats."

"What about a gal?"

"Gal?"

"Sure, that's what most young sprouts would do they come into a pocketful of fresh money."

"No thanks."

"Well," Einer said, "you are of a different stripe then."

"I don't know what you mean by that."

"I don't mean nothing by it."

John Paul notched his flop hat back so that the stain on his face showed like a large rose petal; a shock of brown hair fell down across his forehead.

"Where we gone sell 'em after we steal 'em?" John Paul said

"My friend'll know where we can sell 'em," Einer said, the pain of sitting a saddle for so long a time rising up through his nether parts and into his back. He used to could ride a horse all day and all night, sleep in the saddle and eat in it too. It was another thing he missed about his youth, the strength he used to have for enduring hardship. Such got him thinking about other things he missed as well.

I used to could make love to a woman morning till night, he thought. But for the other night, I wasn't even sure I could do it at all no more. I reckon I got a few miles in me, but not all that many. He shuddered at the thought.

He wondered what would happen if Magdalena—Maggie as he used to call her—would want to take him to bed, renew old times. Lord what an embarrassment it would be if she did and he'd spent it all on that little chubby gal. He reckoned no matter what, a man was born with just so many of each thing: so many heartbeats, so many miles he could walk, so many meals he could eat, and so many times he could make love to a woman. Now he wondered if maybe he'd spent his last turn and there wasn't any more left in him.

You can't let yourself think on them things anyhow, he told

himself. She's probably married and forgotten you a long time back, that is if she'd not passed on.

All of a sudden John Paul let out a whoop and swept his hat in the air and set spurs to his mount, running him full out.

"Now what the hell?" Einer wondered. He watched as the kid rode hell bent for leather for about a mile, then spun his horse around and come running back still whooping and slapping the air.

He reined his mount to a sliding stop.

"Now what the hell has gotten into you, Geronimo?" he said.

"I'm just real happy is all," John Paul said.

" 'Bout what?"

"Everything."

"Well that's good, I reckon. Now stop all that damn catar-wallering and wearing out that horse."

CHAPTER 12

They saw the line shack down in the declivity, not quite a canyon.

"Don't look like nobody's down in there," the tracker said.

"Well, let's ride down and see," Ballard said. "The tracks we lost a day back seem to lead to this place and we've not seen another so far."

They heeled their mounts forward, slowly working their way down to it, keeping a cautious eye open just in case somebody *was* there or about.

Nobody came to their call and so they dismounted and went forth and pounded on the door calling out. And when again nobody answered Ballard lifted the latch and swung the door outward and stepped inside, followed by the tracker.

"Looks like whoever it was just up and left it," the tracker observed. "They's still matches and candles and wood in the stove and dirty plates on the table."

"Could be whoever lives here is out there somewhere and will return later."

"Maybe so."

"I can't feature nobody living down here in the middle of nothing," the tracker stated.

"There's plenty who live like this and worse," Ballard said.

"He made sure he had enough reading material," the tracker said, looking at the newspaper- and catalogue-page-covered walls.

Ballard did not answer. He'd seen other hovels like this one. Seen hovels with entire families living in them, all crammed into a space no larger than this shack. He went out to the corral and knelt and picked up a horse apple, tested it, stood, and looked about.

"There's lots of dung and not all of it completely dried out," he said. "I don't know why whoever lived here would go on with that boy but it looks as if he might have done it."

The tracker studied the signs, and said, "Shod horse, deep tracks, like maybe it was carrying a double load."

"Which way?" Ballard said.

The tracker walked about a bit, then pointed the direction they'd been traveling—west.

"Looks like maybe he's got a hostage?"

"No," Ballard said. "If it was that, we'd have found a body— one or the other one. He'd have no reason to take a hostage."

"Accomplice, maybe?"

"Could be."

Try as he might, Ballard couldn't feature John Paul having an accomplice, either, so far out from Foley's. But hell, he'd been a lawman for a long time and never was surprised by much.

"Let's go," he said, mounting up.

"We could take a rest, you know," the tracker said. "There's a good cot in there and it's nearly nightfall."

Ballard thought it a sound enough idea. They'd stayed on the march steady since leaving the old woman's place and the horses could use a rest as well.

"We'll stay the night, then go on," he agreed. "There's a town on ahead. If they're riding double we might catch up with them there."

"I'll flip you for the cot," the tracker said. "Call it."

He flipped a silver dollar in the air and slapped it down onto his wrist.

"Heads," Ballard said.

The tracker lifted his palm.

"I'm a son of a bitch!" he groaned.

They arrived the next night after riding through a thundering rainstorm. Some of the greasy light from a saloon's windows fell through the streaky rain and lay in a muddy square on the ground. Rain in that country was often quick and violent, then ended almost as quickly as it began. And when it rained at all, the rain fell with great passion, as if the dry hatched earth summoned the gods to quench its thirst and the gods would sometimes acquiesce and other times not.

They reined and noticed black bunting in the window and went in, Ballard's curiosity piqued by the bunting, wondering if someone important had died.

Ballard ordered coffee and the tracker whiskey.

A thin mustachioed fellow with sallow skin served them.

"You gents in for the funeral?"

"Funeral?" Ballard asked.

"Fellow what owned this place is who it is for. Funeral's tomorrow. Him and Leo Pecker's both."

"Never heard of either of them," Ballard said.

"Oh," the barkeep said. "It's been real big news round here. We ain't had no murders in nearly three years and then we get two in one night."

"What happened?" the tracker said, then tossed back his whiskey and tapped the glass on the oak and twirled his finger over it.

The barkeep refilled his glass.

"Some old man and a kid gunned them down night before last over in the livery. Everyone figures they was in there stealing a horse and Wally—fellow what owned this place, and Leo Pecker, what owned the diner up the street, come in on them."

Ballard looked at the tracker, the tracker saying, "Sounds like them."

Ballard thought something wrong with the story, however.

"How'd they conclude that?" Ballard said.

"Conclude what?"

"That they'd gone there to steal a horse? What made this Wally and Leo fellow follow 'em in there? Were they deputies?"

"No. We ain't got no law in this town, just what is done by whoever is wearing a gun and willing to use it."

The tracker listened. The whiskey was good. He could feel its warmth spread through his tired limbs.

"This boy," Ballard said. "He have a mark on his face?"

The barkeep wiped the wood with a towel he wore over his shoulder.

"I wouldn't know. I was off the night it happened, but Slim yonder seen 'em when they was in earlier before all the blood-letting."

Ballard turned toward the direction the barkeep pointed with his chin to where the man sat in a darkened corner, alone and watchful, chin whiskers down to the middle button of his waistcoat.

The man sat under a ruined hat; the brim looked like it had been chewed on by dogs, and the crown torn open and hanging like a stove lid not quite shut.

Ballard crossed to where the bearded man sat and pulled out a chair and sat down opposite so he could look into the man's face. He smelled like a goat, his gaze baleful.

"That barkeep said you saw who it was shot these two local men," he said.

"I seen 'em, I sure as hell did. 'At boy looked like somebody had a big red mark burned on one side of his face. And that old crow with him looked like maybe he was in the game of murder, judging how he stood and how well armed he was. I seen men

104

like that before. Cold-blooded in every way. Say, I don't suppose you could afford me a drink, could you?"

Ballard turned toward the bar and signaled for the barkeep to bring over a drink and once he had, Ballard watched the bearded man smack his lips, which were loose and folded into his mouth because he had no teeth and slobbered his words when he spoke.

"I get the shakes I go too long without a drink," he said then, raised the glass trembling to his mouth and drank and set the empty glass down again and looked at it with the same longing some men might look at a woman they knew they could never have.

A shudder suddenly went through him.

"You have an opinion as to what happened the night of the killings?" Ballard said.

The man shrugged, still looking at the empty glass, and Ballard turned again and called for the barkeep to bring over the bottle. When he did, he said, "Just leave it and give that damn fool standing over there another drink as well."

The barkeep nodded and went away.

The bearded man looked like it was Christmas morning and himself a child who found everything he ever wanted under the tree as he stared at that bottle.

"I reckon what it was," the man said, reaching for the bottle and forgoing the glass altogether, "is Wally and Leo went to rob them two of the money that older feller was flashing about and probably believed it would be easy enough, him old and that boy just a strange-looking kid, only it wasn't and that's how it all began and how it all ended—believing something that wasn't true. Lots die thinking that—believing something that ain't true."

Ballard nodded. Now the story made sense to him.

"You wouldn't have happened to have been outside and seen

105

which way they rode off?" he said.

The bearded man swallowed from the bottle direct, a good long pull, and then rested it again on the table, his grizzled lips wet with whiskey dew.

"Matter of fact," he began. "I sleep over in that barn most nights and had heard them two come in and didn't think nothing of it. Tramps will sometimes go in there and bed down for the night and leave first thing, present company excluded of course.

"It was only when the shooting started that I ducked on out of there. They rode off on the El Paso road, and I thought when they did, God speed, for you have killed two of our town's worst and they won't be robbing unsuspecting strangers no more."

"You don't sound like you'll be going to the funeral," Ballard said.

"Hell, no. Wally always treated me like a damn bummer, would make fun of me in front of others. He had no respect for anyone, old men especially. Fuck him! And thank ye kindly for this," he concluded, his hand still wrapped around the bottle like it was the most precious thing in the world.

Ballard reckoned it was.

He stood and went back to the bar and paid the tab for the drinks.

"Let's go," he said to the tracker. "I think I know where we can find 'em."

The tracker looked longingly at the shelf of liquor bottles.

As they mounted their horses Ballard told the tracker what Slim had told him about the shooting.

"Could be he's just telling you some story," the tracker said. "Old drunks like that will tell you anything for the price of a drink."

"That include you?" Ballard said.

"I got you this far, ain't I?"

"I reckon so," Ballard said.

"Goes to show you, some can hold their liquor and some can't."

"Just keep on holding it for a time longer," Ballard said.

They rode on through the night, the rain having quit, and found an arbor of live oaks grown out of a dry creek bed, then made camp for the night, that crazy tracker serenading himself to sleep as Ballard tried to ignore what to him sounded like pigs mating.

Overhead clouds passed before a half moon, ghostlike, and it left Ballard feeling lonely for his wife and child. After his first wife passed he thought he'd be alone forever, and then he'd met Mayra and fallen in love so sudden he felt lightning struck. She proved to be all he could have hoped for and it still seemed unreal to him that she'd loved him back so hard and faithfully.

"Could you kindly shut the hell up with that racket?" he called. His mood was bad for the missing of her and he hated that it was.

If things go sideways and I don't ever get back to her, he ruminated, it's only 'cause you can't stop getting caught up in what you think is your sworn duty. But this is the last of it. Once this is over, that's it. I aim to stay with her the rest of my days and hers too. I promise. I damn well do. Enough is enough.

Then he closed his eyes and slept, for the tracker had passed out drunk finally.

CHAPTER 13

Camped that night by a blaze of fire constructed of an old blackjack stump, the upper part lightning struck but its roots still anchored in the soil, for nothing could destroy a blackjack tree but lightning and God, Einer and the boy sat around eating from a can of beans and some strips of jerky, the pair of them silent, like strangers in a strange night.

"You think maybe I shot one of them men in the barn the other night?" John Paul said.

"I thought we already went through all that," Einer grumped.

John Paul seemed to ignore him.

"At first it didn't bother me, right after, but most recent I can't get it off my mind. Maybe, I'm just a plain damn killer and not pretend I'm anything but."

"I reckon you might could have shot one of 'em," Einer said ruefully patting his pockets for his makings. Seemed like if he wasn't smoking he was getting ready to smoke out of habit.

"I can attest that it was me that probably got 'em both with the scattergun. Hard to miss with a gun like that. Sure didn't kill 'em on first blush, for they returned fire pretty fair for a time. But even shot men will do that lessen they're dead outright. Desperation keeps some men alive longer than they ought to be. You could have shot that one what lingered, that Pecker fellow."

Einer didn't know why he said it, he just said it. Maybe if the boy got over his vacillating on the subject he'd forever shut up about it.

"I know it," John Paul said. "When you cut loose with that scattergun I couldn't hear nothing for a while. I just come up shooting is all. Didn't even know what I was shooting at, couldn't see nothing. Figured it had to be something bad for you to let loose."

"You hear 'em come in?" Einer said, finding his pouch of tobacco in one pocket and his papers in another.

"No, I didn't hear nothing until you pulled the triggers, damned near pissed my pants."

"I heard 'em."

"How'd you hear 'em?"

"It's from my old ways. You learn not to sleep so hard you can't hear what's coming up on you."

"When you was a outlaw, you mean?" John Paul said.

"Yes, back before I become civilized and quit all that."

"Well, looks like you started it up again."

"Shit, if anything they should give us a medal for ridding that burg of them two."

"No, I mean getting ready to go steal horses."

"Looks like maybe I have, then."

"What all you done—back in them old days before you become civilized?"

"About ever bad thing a body can do."

"You ever kill a woman, a child?"

"Hell no. I wouldn't do nothing like it. And I never raped a woman either like some of them did."

"Some of who?"

"Some of them I rode with. And if they was to, I'd leave them in my dust. It wasn't right some of the things some of 'em done. I wan't no angel, that was for sure, but some things I wouldn't do then and wouldn't now."

109

Einer ruminated, trying to remember past times that were equally fuzzy and clear to memory. It was a funny thing, he thought, how you'd not think of something for years and then it'd come to your mind, clear as a bell unexpectedly, and other things you'd try and remember you couldn't recall, just pieces of it maybe, like your old life was more like a dream than actual.

Magdalena was like that for him. There'd be times she seemed more like a dream than real to him. But he knew she was real. As real as anything and it ate at him to want to see her again.

He couldn't recall their first conversation or exactly how they met. It was just one day they had and it grew from there.

He could recall her eyes sometimes, the sound of her voice other times, but an entire picture of her all at once was incomplete, fragmented by passage of time. He could remember she was on the small side, real dark hair and brown sugar skin. He could recall the first time she'd let him kiss her and that her feet were small and fit in the palm of his hands, that her breasts were small too, small and perfectly shaped.

Every time he thought about her he wanted more than anything to see her again—just for even an hour if that's all it come to. Hell, even five more minutes. He wouldn't let himself think that she might be dead after all these years, though he knew it was a real possibility. She had to still be alive and he aimed to find her and show himself to her and make his case.

He didn't allow himself to wonder if she'd married. But surely she must have, a woman pretty as she was. Hell, she might have run through two or three husbands by now, had a bunch of kids. Kids hell, grandkids'd probably be more like it. Still he could only imagine her the way he remembered her and not any other—a seventeen-year-old beauty.

"How can you be sure?" John Paul said.

"Sure of what?"

"That you never shot a woman?"

110

"It ain't something I'd forget," Einer said, irritated by John Paul's questions. "Why the hell would you even ask me that?"

John Paul wanted to tell him why. He wanted to get things confessed, sins he'd been carrying around like a tote sack of bricks.

"But you shot plenty of men," John Paul said. "I reckon whether it's a man or woman, a life is a life taken, ain't it?"

"No, it ain't."

John Paul's face was seen through the flames, all shadow and light, big square jaw on him, that dark stain that grew darker in the night. He had queer eyes of a sudden, Einer thought. Something was troubling his damn fool head, all these questions about murder.

"I did what I had to do," is all the more Einer would tell him.

"You robbed banks?"

"Yes, two or three, I did."

"Trains too?"

"Yeah, them too."

He snorted the answer.

"There ain't no promise in train robbing."

"Why ain't there?"

"Well, first off it takes too many men and then even when you can get one stopped, you don't know rightly if it's carrying any money or if it is if you can get at it. The safe is the express car and too damn big to haul off and generally too damn hard to crack open. No, robbing trains was never my style."

Einer set his makings aside for a moment and finished his beans, scraped out the last of them with his spoon from the bottom of the can and tossed it aside, then reached for his makings and with great care built a shuck.

"You want some of this?" he said.

John Paul stood and reached for the sack of Bull Durham and the papers.

"I ain't never made a cigarette before," he said.

"Squat down and let me show you how," Einer said, and John Paul squatted on his boot heels and watched Einer do it.

"Just like that," he said, handing John Paul the shuck. "Reach in there and grab you a ember and light her up."

Einer watched him cough the first lungful.

"Stay on with it, you'll get used to it. You'll get so used to it you won't want to not smoke."

"Hell," John Paul said after he got used to it. "Sort of makes you light-headed, don't it?"

"At first it does," Einer said, lighting his own shuck.

"What's your story, now that you know mine?"

John Paul took up his place across the fire again, sitting cross-legged.

"Like I told you before, nothing much," he said. "I was staying with them folks I told you about and got tired of it, the way they worked me. Wouldn't hardly feed me enough to keep a dog alive. I was like a damn slave to 'em."

"We all slaves to something or other," Einer opined. "Work never hurt nobody, especially no kid."

"It liked to have *killed* me," John Paul said with a grin. He had large teeth up front, large but straight and white as ivory.

"Shit," Einer said. "You young folks don't know a thing about hard work, what it is. Try being harnessed up like a mule so your daddy can plow a row of beans and another of corn, you want to know what work is."

"I reckon you done that?"

"I sure as hell did and a lot worse too. My mam and pap had seven kids and not a pot to piss in or a window to throw it out of. We all worked like dogs just to stay alive. I left out soon as I was able, figured they'd have one less mouth to feed that way. Joined the Army and fought in the war some, then quit all that for it was pointless—just men slaughtering each other and for what?"

John Paul stared at the old man with a new respect to hear he'd fought in the War.

"That how come you took up the outlaw life, you figure as long as you was shooting at people and getting shot at you might as well get something out of it?"

"I didn't take it up right away," Einer said, remembering. "I first set out to be a drover. Helped trail herds from Texas up to Kansas and later on New Mexico. But then those goddamn grangers fenced off their land and the Union Pacific run trains into Texas anyhow so the droving business all went to shit. I tried other pursuits but learned right quick they wasn't a plow or bobbed wire fence my hand would fit. A man has to make a living somehow, and this country already had one president, so that job was taken."

"Well, there you go," John Paul said, puffing on his cigarette, exhaling through his nose like he'd seen Einer do.

They listened to coyote songs for a time.

"Them people you was with, what made you to finally decide to quit 'em?"

"I don't know, exactly," John Paul lied.

"What'd all besides that man's horse did you steal off 'em when you left out?"

John Paul remembered then the things he didn't want to remember.

"I took the old bastard's horse and saddle, this here pistol, some grub, and that was it. I figured three years of working me like a dog, it was the least he owed me."

"You shoot him when you left so he wouldn't send the laws after you?"

John Paul didn't answer for a time. It wasn't something he wanted to remember—what happened—those hot flames licking

113

up into the blackness of night, the crackling of timber caving in on itself.

"Nah, I just left," he said at last.

"So could be they got the laws on your trail?"

John Paul shook his head.

"I doubt they'd send the laws after me."

"Shit, I bet the laws is out there right now looking for you."

"Maybe they are, but so what?" John Paul said angrily. "Let 'em come on if they can find me. How the hell they gone find me after all this ways?"

"Laws—some of 'em, don't give up," Einer said.

John Paul didn't say anything but saw a single shooting star so quick he almost thought he hadn't seen it and looked for another.

Einer wasn't such bad company, he considered. He'd rather have some company than to be out here alone, John Paul told himself. It wasn't he was scared of anything, but being alone out in the middle of nowhere wasn't something he favored.

He didn't know why he started talking about it, he just did.

"This fellow's sister," he started to say, then cut his words off thinking it would be a mistake to say more about what happened back there at Foley's.

"What about her?" Einer said, now leaned back on one elbow as he burned down his shuck to where it almost touched his fingers.

"She was something else but not in any good way."

"How do you mean?"

"Why shit, you wouldn't even believe it if I told you."

"Try me out. I've been known to believe a lot of things. 'Sides, I like hearing a good story even if it ain't true."

"Trust me," John Paul said. "It's so damn strange and ugly it'd have to be true even if it wasn't."

Einer fashioned himself another shuck and lighted it off his last one, which was near burned out.

"Did she have no tits, something like that?" he said.

"No, she had 'em. Just not much of ones. Like two fried eggs flung up against a wall."

Einer laughed a phlegmy laugh.

"Go on and tell it, boy."

"Well to start with she was ugly as hell, same as her brother. I never seen such two ugly people in my life. But here's the other thing, the two of them slept together like man and wife. The whole time I lived with 'em."

"I've heard of such, women being as scarce as they are out here in the wild. How'd you come to live with 'em to start with?" Einer wanted to know.

"When I was little my mom died and a little later my daddy pawned me off to them, then left out. He might've even sold me to 'em. They wasn't too bad at first. It was later when I grew some they got worse."

"Where was you born?"

"Back east somewhere is all I know."

Einer nodded in silence knowing something was troubling the boy, and so he waited to see if John Paul would come out with it.

"It wasn't all she did," John Paul said. He'd been wanting to tell somebody for the longest time, just to get it said and off his mind. And now that he was telling it, he couldn't seem to stop.

"What else was it?" Einer said. He lay with his head back on his saddle, his eyes closed, talking into the dark of his hat as his cigarette dangled from the corner of his mouth—its glowing dot a curious light in the dark.

"She made me do it with her."

"Made you do it with her?"

"I sure didn't want to, but she threatened if I didn't do it with her she'd tell her brother I'd raped her and have him shoot me, or otherwise have me arrested."

"Well, hell. I reckon I would have gone along with it then were it me. How many times she make you do it with her?"

"Ever chance she could find when he wasn't around. Like she couldn't get enough."

"Was it really all that bad?" Einer said.

"I mean goddamn you should have seen how ugly Uda was," John Paul said.

"That was her name, Uda?"

"Her name was as ugly as she was."

"I've met some homely gals," Einer said almost consolingly, "but I can't say I ever met someone like you're describing. She sounds half crazy."

"She was *all* crazy in my book," John Paul said, tossing the butt of his smoke into the fire.

"Did you end up hurting those people for what they did to you?" Einer asked, and the question startled John Paul for he hadn't been prepared for it. He remained silent for a long time.

"No," he said. "I just left is all."

Einer wasn't sure if it was a lie or it wasn't. But either way, that time had passed already and nothing either of them could do about it no more than they could do anything about the killings in the stable the other night. History is a thing you think about but not a thing you can change.

John Paul lay back watching for more falling stars, seeing those flames eating away at the darkness, how they threw the light even into the trees and up against the sky and all around. How the sound of timber sounded like the breaking of bones. And of course the human cries, Uda's cries, and he just kept going, lashing the quirt against the horse, for he could not seem to get it to run fast enough.

CHAPTER 14

They arose, and before the sun even got up over the horizon fully, they were in the saddle and riding onward. And as luck would have it they came across a solitary homestead and rode over to it and called the house.

A man in faded dungarees with one sleeve pinned up came to the door. He wore a sidearm hanging in a holstered gunbelt around his skinny waist

"What you all want?"

"Breakfast," said Ballard. "I can pay."

The man eyed them and Ballard took the badge out of his pocket to show him and the man allowed them in and had them set at the kitchen table. A woman in a faded gingham dress was at an iron stove trimmed with nickel plating. The room was filled with warm smells—frying pork belly sizzling in a cast-iron pan and biscuits on a warmer and hot coffee.

"I'm Thane," the man said. "This is my Missus, Ellie."

She did not turn in greeting but kept right up with the preparation of the meal.

"Where you hail from?" Thane said, then saw the tracker staring at the pinned-up sleeve.

"Left it at Gettysburg," he said, "along with a bunch of other'ns. You was to look upon that place after three days of fighting, you'd have thought they was growing hands and legs and every form of human death. That ground was bought with

117

our blood. Bought and paid for." He shook his head remembering.

The woman silently poured them each cups of coffee and glanced at Ballard with a hardened gaze.

"You don't need to worry about us, Miss," Ballard said. "We'll eat and be on our way."

She wasn't bad looking but for a swollen middle and pale. She moved with efficiency. She reminded him of Mayra in some way he could not quite define: not in looks, but in something about her grace under hard conditions. Her quietness, maybe it was.

"Where you hail from, lawman?" Thane asked, reaching for the sugar bowl in the center of the table and spooning in some to his coffee and stirring it.

"Up north away," he said. "Up around the panhandle."

Thane looked at the tracker, saw that Elkhart Truth had his gaze cut to the back of the woman at the stove, and frowned.

"And you?" he said. It caught the tracker by surprise.

"Me? Hell up that way too. He hired me to help him. I'm no lawman. But I could track one of those yardbirds of yours if it was to go off in the night." He smiled.

"Who is it you all are looking for, you don't mind my asking?" the man said without taking his gaze from the tracker.

"A boy with a mark on his face," Ballard said. "He might be riding with an old man. Don't reckon you seen anybody like them come past in the last few days?"

"No," Thane said. "I was to, I'd remember. We don't get too many come by this way. Oh, once in a while might be some Mexicans or ragged Induns looking to steal horses, or a tin salesman ever once in a while."

"Indians?" the tracker said.

"You don't mind my saying you look like you're somewhat Indun."

"I do mind," Elkhart Truth said.

The woman served them plates with the fried sowbelly and biscuits with huckleberry jam but did not seat herself at the table, but instead went into the only other room.

"She's got to feed the baby," Thane said. "It's about ten days old, but sickly. Not sure if it will make it or not."

They had not heard an infant's cry.

"It's hard country, to be sure," the tracker said without looking up from his plate. He was sawing the sowbelly with a dull kitchen knife. The meat had a grayish cast to it, but the biscuits were warm and tasty, especially with the jam added.

"There a doctor hereabouts could see to the child?" Ballard said, thinking about his own child.

"Nothing close and even if there was, we couldn't afford to pay one. Ethan—that's his name—will either make it or he won't. Two others is buried out back. She don't seem to have much luck with carrying babies." He said this last in a low voice so as not to be heard beyond the curtain dividing the room.

"Maybe it's your seed," the tracker said.

Thane stared at him hard.

"I told her we can always have more. But you know how women is about them things. I feel bad too, but . . ." he shook his head and sipped his coffee.

They finished eating.

"How much do I owe you for the grub?" Ballard said.

He shrugged.

"Maybe a dollar if you can spare it. Normally I wouldn't charge y'all nothing, but like I said, times is hard. Real hard."

Ballard looked toward the curtain, envisioned what was taking place beyond it, and put five dollars on the table.

"Maybe if you can somehow get your child to a medico . . ." he said, then stood and said to the tracker, "We got to get on. Thank you kindly, Thane. And good luck to you both."

Outside he and the tracker watered their mounts before saddling up and riding out.

"That was a terrible thing you said to that man," Ballard said.

"I know it. It just come out. I sometimes do that—say the wrong thing."

They rode stirrup to stirrup for a time, Ballard keeping his own counsel.

"Some folks just have a tough go of it," the tracker said. "Generally a baby will squall when strangers come in and that one didn't."

"Leave it alone," Ballard said.

"Why I was just commenting on how some has got it bad. The man didn't even have but one arm neither."

"Leave it alone, goddamn it!"

The tracker watched Ballard spur his horse into a full-on gallop and ride away ahead of him and didn't bother to try and catch up because Ballard was in a damn poor mood and it caused Truth to want to keep his distance around men like that.

CHAPTER 15

Einer and John Paul reached El Paso, a hubbub of activity like John Paul had never seen before. It had changed since last Einer had been there, grown two or three times in size, and all the noise and movement caused him to blink his eyes with consternation. El Paso wasn't nothing like what he'd remembered when he was young and wild and woolly. Back then it was a sleepy little town just riding the banks of the Rio Grande. In the daylight it was just a town but at night there was plenty of liquor and women to be found both sides of the river. But nothing like what greeted his eyes now. It seemed all grown up, like somebody that had changed out of work clothes into a fine new suit. He tried hard to decide if he liked what he saw, and so too did John Paul who'd *never* seen anything like it.

"Man, this is something," John Paul said. "I bet a body could find anything he wanted in a place like this. Look at all these stores."

"I reckon they could and they have, them what's looking for whatever it is they're looking for," Einer said. "I hardly know which way to turn."

"I never seen so many people all in one place. Where'd they all come from?"

"I reckon from all over. And yonder lies ol' Mexico, across the Rio Grande—Ciudad Juárez."

"You ever been over there?"

"Several times. It's where you go if you want some low

entertainment, or more likely something you can't find this side."

"Dang," he said. "How're we gone find this fellow can help us steal them horses?"

"We'll find him if he's still around, and if'n he ain't, I reckon there's others we can hire on to do the job. Certain types of men are always looking for a little fast money."

They dodged the mule-powered streetcars with their clanging bells, and rode past two- and three-story brick buildings, business both sides of the crowded boulevard.

John Paul saw a sign that read St. Louis Street, and another that read El Paso Street and some of the streets were brick paved and he reckoned it would be easy to get lost in all those streets. He saw saloons aplenty and clothing shops, with rotating barber poles and signs cut like large teeth that read Dentist. There were men and women walking up and down, some Mexican and some white, all mixed in together, some dressed ordinarily and others dressed in finery. He saw a fat man smoking a large cigar and a yellow dog dodging traffic. Half the women carried parasols against the risen sun and the streets in some places were jammed with teamster wagons unloading their goods, burly men carrying cases and barrels and mopping sweated brows. Butcher shops displayed ropes of sausage links, cured ham, and plucked chickens hanging from hooks.

"Goddamn," he declared.

"What?" Einer said.

"I never seen nothing like it."

"You said that already."

"I know it."

"Well, you needn't say it again."

They reined in at a saloon with a large plate-glass window with lettering done in gold leaf like it was a bank's window that read EL DIABLO and dismounted and went in through one of two double doors that also had panes of frosted glass and brass knobs.

It was larger than John Paul expected inside and there were plenty of customers lined up at the oak and more playing cards and still more playing at games of chance: roulette, dice, faro. There were billiard tables toward the back and a stairway that led to an upper level with curtained rooms.

"What's up there?" John Paul asked.

Einer looked up.

"That's where a bucko can get his daisy plucked if he's got walking around money and ain't gambled or otherwise pissed it away."

"Daisy plucked?"

"Where he can fuck a woman if he's got the money," Einer said. "Let's get a drink."

John Paul whistled and grinned so hard his jaw ached.

They worked their way to the bar and Einer ordered them a whiskey each and when it was served, Einer said to the barkeep: "You know if Atticus Pinch is still around this town? Ever heard of him?"

"Atticus Pinch?"

"Am I speaking somethin' other than English?"

The barkeep shook his head.

"You the laws?"

"Do we look like the laws?"

The barkeep shook his head.

"I reckon if you are, you ain't like no laws I ever seen," he said, staring at John Paul's face. "Yeah, he's still around. Matter of fact, he's my father-in-law. I married his youngest girl, Callie. What you want with him?"

"That'd be between him and me," Einer said and tossed back his drink and waited.

"You didn't come to kill him, did you?" the barkeep said.

" 'Cause, me personally, I wouldn't mind if you did, but Callie might take it hard."

"No, I didn't come here to kill him. Is there a reason you'd believe someone would?"

"Reasons aplenty," the barkeep said. "You boys want another?"

Einer circled their glasses and John Paul quickly drank up so he could get a refill.

"You still ain't said where I can find him," Einer said.

"Try the city jail. That's where he spends most of his time."

"Don't tell me the old bastard's gone and turned legit?" Einer said, unable to imagine it.

"No, he sweeps it out in exchange for sleeping there and a couple of dollars a week."

"Now that sounds like Atticus alright," Einer said. "I remember where the old jail used to be, is it the same place?"

"No, they built a new one recent, could hold all the miscreants the old one couldn't."

The barkeep said it would be six bits for the drinks and this time Einer turned his back to the barkeep as he dug out the money. They didn't need to present no more temptation to would-be thieves.

"Out the door, turn left, two blocks up, and then hang another left. It's brick now. Fancier than some houses."

They drank their drinks, John Paul still watching the upper level where he'd seen some right smart looking gals taking men up to. Prettier than he would have believed whores could be.

"You want a piece of tail?" Einer said.

John Paul flushed red.

"Nah," he said. "I reckon it's best not to consort with whores."

"You do, do you? You think there is something improper about consorting with whores?"

"No," he said.

"First time is always harrowing, boy."

John Paul looked at him. Einer was grinning like a possum eating fish.

"Well, hell, let's get on and find this fellow if we're going to," John Paul said.

"All right then, if you're sure you don't want some of that upstairs there."

John Paul had flushed scarlet by such bodacious conversation in a public place, but he turned to the barkeep and said, "How much is it to go upstairs with one of the gals? I was just wondering?"

"Depends," the barkeep said.

"On what does it depend?"

"On what it is you want, how long you want it for, just a few minutes or all night."

"Dang," John Paul said.

They left, John Paul still wondering what it would be like to go upstairs. If anything, because of what Einer said about not being put off gals because of Uda, John Paul told himself maybe he ought to try it and see. Maybe it was different with a working gal, somebody *he* chose and not the other way around. He told himself he'd give it some thought but was in no hurry because it was sort of daunting too.

They found the jail and encountered two police, both large fellows in formal-looking blue coats and guns strapped to their hips. They looked like they could be twins: dark and mustachioed and barrel-chested.

"Heard we might find Atticus Pinch here," Einer said.

"Shit," one of them said. "What'd you be wanting that broke dick for?"

The other policeman looked on silent in his study of the two of them.

"Want to talk to him, is all."

"You pay his fine you can talk to him all you want," the first one said.

"I thought he worked here, swept out the place?"

"Yeah, he does that too when he's not drunk and disorderly and causing trouble," the talking policeman said.

"How much is his fine?"

"Five dollars."

"All right then, bring him out, I'll go his fine."

The silent one watched as Einer dug out his money and set the right amount down on the desk while the other policeman took out a sheet of paper and had him sign it to make things official.

The other one rose and went back through a door and came out again, prodding the miscreant Atticus Pinch ahead of him.

John Paul thought the fellow looked like a dump rat as poorly a picture he presented—ragged clothes, grizzled face, hard-set eyes that peered from under shaggy brows. What hair he possessed was wild and untamed as if someone had blown it up with a firecracker.

Atticus Pinch was a smallish man, his checkered trousers stuffed down into the top of mule-ear boots, his hands and feet as small as a girl's.

"Goddamn if it ain't ol' Ben Wilson!" he hooted.

Einer gave him a hard warning look for using the alias that Einer used back in their outlaw years.

"I knew some sumbitch sooner or later would take pity on poor ol' Atticus," he said, speaking of himself in the third person. "Ol' Atticus has all the bad luck in the world."

Then he looked at the two police.

"I'd just as soon be locked up for misdeeds than be known as a jail swamper," and he offered them a sour face.

"And I'd just as soon you clear out and don't come back till you've taken a bath. You stunk up this place so bad it'd make maggots puke."

"Come on, let's go," Einer said.

John Paul was confused by the name that Atticus Pinch called Einer by—Ben Wilson.

They went outside and Atticus Pinch paused, raised his face to the heavens, and drew in a deep breath.

"Boy, she sure feels good breathing free air again," he said. "I don't suppose you got a drink or a smoke on you," he said.

"Let's go up the street and I'll buy you a drink," Einer said. "Got something I want to discuss with you."

"Oh, hell yes. Let's do just that," Pinch said. "Who's this, your girlfriend?" he added, looking at John Paul.

"I just knew someday you'd go queer, living all alone all the time." Then he brayed like a mule and punched John Paul in the shoulder. "I'm just foolin' with you, boy. This here old fella was the damnedest I ever seen on the ladies. Tore 'em up. Attracted 'em like flies to a honey bucket, then tore 'em up." Again he brayed.

"His name's John Paul," Einer said. John Paul resented Einer speaking for him.

"Well, goddamn, nice to meet yer, John Paul. I'm Atticus Pinch, rowdiest son of a bitch this side of the Rio Grandee River!" Then added: "I'm nearly seventy year old and can still outfight, outdrink, and outfuck anybody in El Paso, and that includes all of Mexico, too."

More braying. Passersby turned to look at the trio.

"You're embarrassing yourself," Einer said. "Which is fine, but don't embarrass me too. Shut up, Pinch."

"Yes, sir, boss." He saluted like an ill-suited soldier.

They found a saloon and went in and Einer got them a bottle and three glasses and found a table off away from anybody and poured them each a stiff one and waited till they'd tossed them down, then poured another.

John Paul noticed that there was no upper floor to this saloon and felt disappointed because of it. He figured every saloon in town had an upper floor and he was hoping to spy a prostitute.

"How you been since last I seen you, Ben?" Atticus laughed.

"I've been all right, only my name ain't Ben no more."

Atticus Pinch nodded his head knowingly.

"What should I call you, then?"

Einer looked at John Paul as if seeking approval.

"Name's Einer," he said.

"Einer," Pinch repeated. "Now that's a hell of a name—hard to forget, too. Nice to meetcher, Einer."

They drank another.

"Me and this boy aims to steal us a passel of horses down across the border, run 'em back up, and sell 'em. Was hoping you'd throw in with us if you still know the game."

"Why, hell yes, I still know it. Just 'cause a man falls out of the saddle once in a while don't mean he's forgot how to climb back on, whether it's screwing or stealing horses."

"Well, ain't you just a font of wisdom," Einer said.

"A what of what?" Atticus said.

John Paul listened with interest.

"So once we steal us a herd," Einer said. "You know someone will buy 'em, no questions asked?"

"Let me check into it. I might know a feller would buy 'em."

"Just don't take all day doin' it," Einer said. "Me and him will be over at the hotel catching up on our rest."

"Okay, let me go send a wire to this feller and I'll get back hold of you. By the way, could I borry a dollar to send the wire?"

"Keep the bottle," Einer said and reached in his purse and handed over a silver dollar. "But one way or the other, me and John Paul here are crossing the Rio tomorrow, either with you or without you. I'm sure there are other waddies about who'd like to make some quick money if you ain't up to the task. You look a might sorry and worn out to me."

"I just might be sorry," Pinch said. "But you know me, I ain't one to let opportunity slip away."

They left out and let Atticus Pinch to the business at hand.

"You think he'll come through?" John Paul said.

"Can't say. He used to be a hell of a thief in his day if you could keep him on the tracks, but he used to derail a lot. And it looks to me like he maybe still does."

They walked to the nearest brick two-story hotel and got two rooms.

"They don't need to be nothing fancy," Einer said to the clerk.

"Don't worry," the pocked-face man said, "they ain't."

"How about getting a boy to take our mounts over to the livery and have them put up?"

"Sure thing."

The clerk gave them keys to rooms across from each other and they mounted the stairs carrying their belongings, what little they had; Einer, his coach gun carried in one hand by the forestock and his soogins draped over his shoulder, found the doors to their rooms.

"Go in and get you some rest," Einer said. "I'm about wore to a nub."

John Paul went in and set down on the bed and got up and looked out the window and set down again. Then after awhile he lay back and closed his eyes and before he knew it he was asleep.

When he opened his eyes it was dark out and the street below still looked alive and lively with horsemen and pedestrians being drunk and loud, and the commerce drew his desire to be down among it, just to walk around and see things if nothing else. But the real reason had to do with that saloon—the El

Diablo. He stood looking out for a long time, then went to Einer's room and knocked on the door. For a time nothing happened, then he knocked again and the door cracked open and Einer's face appeared, his white hair disheveled, his eyes reddened.

"What is it, boy?" he croaked. "Something wrong? Shit I thought you maybe was Pinch come with good news or bad."

"Wondered if I might borrow some money in advance?"

"Money, in advance? What for?"

"I sort of would like to go back to that saloon—the one with the whores upstairs."

Einer looked at him a long time, then closed the door and came back in a few moments and opened it a crack again and held out five silver dollars.

"Go on," he said. "Git you some. Just be careful is all. This town is full of con artists and bunko men and will knock you in the head over a dollar, they think you got one. The whores probably ain't that much better, so pick a good one." Then Einer closed the door, just like that.

John Paul had thought to ask Einer to come with him, but Einer never gave him the chance.

John Paul looked at the money in his hand and something bright and joyful as the silver itself filled his being, something hot as a fire blazing in a dark night burned in his blood. He felt joyful as a traveler who knew he was just about home again and there waiting for him was food, all he could eat, and the warm, warm love of a woman he'd never have to leave, ever again, this as he went down the hall whistling some old tune he'd made up, his feet feeling like they weren't even touching the floor. He went down the stairs and on out into the night, so loud and alive he wanted to shout, and hurried on to the saloon with the whores upstairs, hoping there'd be one for him and he hadn't forgotten how to get there.

CHAPTER 16

There was a rapping at the door like somebody was trying to break into hell. John Paul shot straight up out of bed, unsure of where he was or even who he was. Whatever that stuff was him and the girl drank last night left his head feeling like the inside of a bucket. His eyes and even his hair was sore.

"Whaaa! Whaaa!" he croaked.

"You dead in there?"

It was Einer pounding on his door.

"Jeez Christ, will you let off with that damn racket?"

"Git up, and let's git going. Our game's on."

John Paul cradled his sore head in his shaking hands.

"I'm coming," he cawed.

"Well, come on then."

He crossed the room and opened the door just to get the old fool to leave off with that racket, then recrossed the room and sat heavily on the bed, bending and reaching for his trousers that lay in a heap next to his boots and tugging them on one leg at a time.

Einer watched.

"Boy, you're about as pitiful as anything I ever seen."

"Yeah, well, you ain't no beauty yourself."

"How'd your luck run last night? You snag yourself one of them dancehall queens?"

John Paul groaned, getting on his socks before reaching for his boots. He started putting them on, then realized he was trying to get the left one on his right foot and switched it out again.

His memory of just hours or maybe even minutes—he didn't know how long he'd been asleep—before was yet fresh planted in the soil of his mind but too soon yet to bear growing into something greater than just a memory.

He finally got his boots on, then stood and found his shirt lying over in the corner of the room with no idea how it got there and little idea of how he even got back to the room after leaving the girl's company.

"Looks like she rode you hard and put you up wet," Einer said, taking his makings out of his pocket and rolling himself a smoke as he leaned against the door.

"Yeah, well, I reckon it was the other way around," John Paul grumped.

"Oh, I'm sure of that—you with all your worldly experiences with women and such."

"Whyn't you just leave off on me."

"Well, I can see whatever it was you was up to last night didn't put you in any better mood."

"That pal of yours ever find out if we can sell them horses we ain't stole yet? That Pinch, what's his face?"

"He's downstairs waiting for us. I explained how you like getting your beauty rest 'fore you get started."

"Shit."

Atticus Pinch was squatted on his heels out front of the hotel smoking a black cheroot and watching like some old dog the lady folk strolling up and down the sidewalks. He looked round at the approach of Einer and the boy.

"Well, hell, I was wondering if you two wanted to go get some goddamn horses, or what? Them Mesicans ain't gone wait all day to hand 'em over, they got shit to do too, you know."

He grinned around brown-stained teeth. John Paul thought

Atticus Pinch was about the worst specimen of human he ever saw.

"Let's get on," Einer said, and they went on down to the livery where they'd had their horses put up and saddled them and swung on out to the road headed for the Rio Grande.

John Paul lagged behind Atticus Pinch and Einer, who rode along jolly as a rapscallion boy headed for a picnic or a dance somewhere. He was half sorry he'd ever run into that old man. Seemed to him, with his head aching like it was, that being in the company of Einer, or whatever the hell his true name was, was just another form of enslavement, not any different than when he was dependent on Foley and Uda. But then on quick consideration, he knew that it was as bad.

Boy, I ever get my hands on some real money, I'm gone, he told himself. Gone and never coming back and that old coot can do whatever the hell he likes and good riddance.

By the time they reached the banks of the Rio Grande it wasn't anything like John Paul had featured it to be. It did not look grand at all. He'd imagined it would be this big, deep ol' river, bright blue as the morning sky, and had worried about crossing it because he didn't know how to swim. The fear of drowning had grabbed his gonads like icy fingers. But as he sat looking on, he wondered if so much as his horse's belly might get wet crossing over to the other side. It wasn't anything like what he'd imagined.

"You sure this is the Rio Grande River?" he said.

"Sonny, if it ain't then I'm lost as shit," Atticus Pinch said with a smirk on his homely face. "And I sure as hell ain't lost."

"Well, what are we waiting for, let's get on across and get them goddamn horses," John Paul said.

They went on across and came almost immediately into Ciudad Juárez, just a collection of shacks and squandered people. They didn't bother to stop but left it in their wake and followed the curve of the river northwest with low-slung hills off to their left that reminded John Paul of gigantic sombreros; eventually they came to a willow arbor late afternoon that grew along the grassy banks where the river was wider and riffled over rocks so that the water looked like white question marks.

"This is where we'll bring 'em across when we get 'em," Atticus said

"We'll camp till nightfall," Einer said. "Always best to steal a man's horses in the dark. Makes it harder for him to blow your brains out."

"Well, if'n that's the case, how come you had to roust me from my rest so damn early?"

"Sloth is a terrible habit to get into," Einer said, dismounting. "And you've already got enough bad habits as it stands. 'Sides, where we got to go is just a short ride from here and we'll be plenty rested when we snatch 'em and run off with 'em."

Atticus Pinch dismounted too and unsaddled his horse and stretched out lying on one side, his head propped up on the palm of his hand.

Einer followed suit, but for the lying down part. Instead he took a length of line and a fishhook from his saddle pockets, then dug around in the wet soil nearest the water till he came up with a grub, which he threaded onto his hook, and then hand-cast the line out into the current.

"Might see if I can catch us a fish or two for supper," he said.

John Paul unsaddled his mount and lay down on his back and closed his eyes under the shelter of his hat.

The memory of last night came back to him in bits and pieces, his mind still not of one thing, one solid piece of brain yet, it felt like, and the memory was like a puzzle he needed to assemble to get the whole picture.

She'd said her name was Mercy Blevins but she had changed

it—Blevins—to Love. Said she'd not want her family name used in such work as she found herself engaged in. She was smallish and pale-skinned and smiled coyly compared to the others he'd observed, who were brash and loud talking as he stood scouting them like some old cowhand trying to figure out which one to cut from the herd.

Their eyes had met and he nodded and she'd come over. She'd asked if he would buy her a drink and he explained how he only had five dollars and he was hoping to buy her company for the evening—some of the evening, anyway—and go upstairs with her to the rooms.

"You like me, then, eh?"

"Yes'm," he said. "I like you a whole lot compared to these others."

He wasn't sure soon as he said it if she'd take it as an insult—"compared to these others"—but she laughed and leaned against him and put her hand on his chest and instantly he grew aroused.

"It's okay about the drink," she said. "And yes, you can buy my company—for a little while at least."

He felt her hand slip down and touch his inner thigh.

"Damn," he said. "You sure enough know how to get to the point."

"You are man, I am woman. What more is there," she said, and took him by the hand and led him upstairs to one of the rooms.

He thought maybe everybody in the place was watching the two of them but when he looked down on the gathered below, nobody was paying a bit of attention and the air was just a cloud of smoke and noise.

She'd taken him into one of the rooms and closed the door behind them. It was a small room barely large enough for the narrow bed, a small wood stand with a chipped basin, and a mismatched ceramic water pitcher. There was a towel folded and waiting for whatever purpose it might be needed for. He didn't know its purpose.

She kissed him then, a long deep kiss and surprised him by darting her tongue into his mouth. That had never happened before, not even with Foley's sister, who was dry-mouthed and foul-breathed, and his knees buckled a little.

She stripped him out of his clothes quick as shucking an ear of corn and set them aside in a nice little pile by the bed. He watched there in the shallow light an oil lamp gave off as she undressed for him. He didn't think he'd be able to contain himself with all that had transpired already and when she was fully naked and came and climbed on the bed next to him and began to caress him as she kissed him, her hands everywhere at once it seemed and he tried to return the favor, but she was too good at what she did and before he knew it he seemed to bust loose. "Oh, Jesus, Jesus, I'm sorry, I'm sorry . . ."

"It's okay," she whispered, her mouth close to his ear and she held him like a mother might a child.

"I'm sorry," he repeated over and over again. "I didn't mean for my gun to go off so quick."

She kissed him full on the mouth and he thought his heart might just stop then and there, like a watch that'd suddenly been smashed by a hammer.

"Don't worry," she whispered. "We still have time to try it again if you like? Would you like to try it again?"

"Yes'm," he said. "I would."

"Please call me Mercy, not ma'am," she said.

Her touch and ways were soothing to him and he yielded to her direction as she guided his hands and mouth and aroused him again.

"Like this," she said.

He was surprised at how much he desired being with her and

was fearful their time would end too soon. He didn't know exactly how much time five dollars bought him. "There," she said. "Like that." And before he knew it they seemed natural together, nothing at all like what Foley's sister had him do.

"Say my name," she whispered.

"Mercy," he said.

"Say it again."

"Mercy."

He didn't know why she wanted him to say her name but it seemed to please her when he did.

"Say mine, too," he said.

"John Paul," she said.

"Mercy," he said.

Back and forth they said each other's name and whatever lay beyond the room for as far as the world extended, he knew not, nor cared to know. The only thing that mattered to him was right there in the room with her saying his name, touching and kissing him and he her.

And when he released inside of her she clung to him like they were both drowning in a forbidden sea and only he could save her even if he could not save himself.

When it was finished he lay there breathing hard, panting like a dog that'd just run across a hundred miles of hot desert.

She lay beside him, her head in the crook of his shoulder, her breath warm and soft upon his fevered skin.

"You know something," he said.

"Tell me," she said.

"I never been in love before, but I think what I'm feeling right now might be love."

She rose up on one elbow and looked at him but the shadow of her now kept him from seeing plainly her features in that low light. She was just a shape of a woman, but the shape of her seemed adequate.

He thought she was smiling.

Then she kissed him quickly.

"You are too young to know what love is or is not," she said. "But it is nice of you to say it."

His anger was quick to spark.

"I ain't that much younger than you," he complained. "I reckon I know what love is as much as you do."

"Ha," she said. "I don't pretend to know what love is. There is just this and the love of money and love of pretty clothes. That's what I know about it."

He felt sorely disappointed in her answer.

"I would like to stay with you longer," she said rising from the bed. "But I must go. Our time is finished. Do you understand? Unless you can pay for another hour?"

"No," he said. "I ain't got no more money. It was ever cent I had."

His disappointment was like a knife to the chest. He realized it was nothing to do with love—not for her it wasn't—no matter how much he'd like it to have been. He watched her pour water into the basin and set it on the floor, then squat over it and laver water to her nether region before patting herself with the towel, then slipping the dress on over her head.

She turned and looked at him, but again the light had grown so dim in the room from the guttering lamp's flame he could not discern her features finely enough to know what emotion her face showed.

"All right," he said and sat up and shucked into his clothes, then stood and came to the door where she waited.

"Can I ask you something?" he said.

"Yes, of course."

"Is Mercy your real name?"

She nodded.

"Yes," she said. "Mercy Belvins from Ohio," elongating the

O. "But don't bandy it about; in this place I'm Mercy Love."

"I'm going to come back for you, Mercy, whatever your last name is. And I'm going to take you out of this place and I'm going to marry you."

She touched the mark on his face tenderly then, as if they'd gone from being lovers to simply friends and heading right back to being strangers. A friend that she now felt sympathy for in his besotted condition, but also a welling of feelings she'd long ago forgotten how to feel.

"It is not possible," she said. "Many have promised me such things but they never happen. My life is my life just as your life is your life. We are simply what we are, no more. You're probably far from home and a sweetheart and I'm just a girl who works for a living. You'll leave here and forget all about me when you get back home again to your gal. It's okay," she said. "This is just something that brings us a little pleasure and for that we should both be grateful."

"Is it the way you feel with those other men?" he asked.

She stared at him a moment, silent, thoughtful, and he couldn't be sure if she was trying to conjure a lie for his benefit, or, maybe seeking the truth within herself.

"No," she said softly. "I don't always feel this way with other men. Lots of them are real bastards and not tender at all. You're a kind tender boy with a kind tender heart and it's nice."

"But sometimes you have had others like me—tender with you?"

She shrugged.

"Sometimes," she said.

"I'm coming back for you," he insisted. "Will you go with me away from here when I come back?"

She put a hand on his wrist.

"I want you to come and see me again," she said purposely keeping her answer vague. His pleadings had touched her in the most delicate way. He was still young and handsome even with his face marked by the stain, a stain she barely took notice of after first sighting it. And someday—if he lived long enough—he would be old and shed of such fanciful notions as love and trying to win the hearts of whores. She wasn't that much older than him, but she felt as if she was.

"John," she said. "I must go downstairs now."

And they went on out and down the stairs and she parted from him and he watched her immediately approach a man standing at the bar drinking a beer talking to another man. The man drinking turned and put his arm around her waist and said something in her ear and she laughed and he could tell she was asking the man to buy her a drink. And John Paul went on out into the night feeling hateful and mean-spirited and came across a drunkard staggering down the street singing wildly, a bottle of some sort of whiskey in one hand, waving it about, and John Paul went up to him.

"Say, mister," he said. "I got me a sister will screw you for two dollars."

"Oh yeah, where's she at?" the drunkard said, weaving about as if he stood on the deck of a rocking ship.

"Right back here," John Paul said.

The drunk followed him into an alley and John Paul hit him a blow across the temple and the man groaned and fell to his knees and John Paul snatched the bottle from him. He'd intended to rob him and get enough money to go back in the bar before she took up with that other man, but searching through the drunkard's pockets all he found were a few dimes, a nickel, and some Indian head pennies.

"You dumb old bastard," he cursed. "Spent ever damn cent on liquor, didn't you?"

The drunk lay on his back, his knees up, mouthing his complaints of pain and confusion.

"Shit," John Paul said and went on with the bottle back to the window of the saloon and watched through it as the girl led the man up the stairs; he soon enough had consumed all that was left in the bottle, watching her until he could stand it no more, and then turned away from the window and went on.

He wondered if she'd treated them like she had him, made them think they were special, made them want to say to her, I love you, only to watch her clean herself over the basin unless they had more money.

Between the liquor and sorrowing grief that filled his mind he got lost three times trying to get back to the hotel.

And now, resting in the brush arbor he could not but think of her the way any fool in love with a woman thinks of her in absentia.

CHAPTER 17

Night sky salted with stars ice cold and distant and a three-quarter moon casting just enough light to go by. They shook him awake.

"Damn boy, is it all you do is to sleep?" Atticus Pinch said, kicking the soles of John Paul's boots. "Git up. Them damn Mesicans will be up and cooking their beans in a few hours—soon as it's light again."

He staggered awake and numbly went and saddled his mount, head still heavy as a bucket of bricks. He had not dreamed of Mercy, but wished that he had. He longed for her in spite of everything, knowing her to take other men up to the room, knowing what she was doing with them, and each time a stab of pain sharp as a knife penetrated his heart.

He wished he could just rub her off his mind like that schoolteacher rubbed words off the blackboard back when he'd gone through to the fourth grade. But he couldn't.

He came over and squatted by the dying fire and poured himself a cup of coffee and spooned some beans from a near empty can.

"I sure do appreciate you fellers leaving me all this fine grub and good coffee," he said sarcastically. "Why I don't think I could eat another bite, and having them coffee grounds stuck in my teeth, well, I don't know how to thank you all."

Atticus Pinch laughed.

"Shit kid, you get any more sass to you you'll be wearing

flowers in your hair. Now clean up this mess and kick out that fire and let's hit it."

Einer was already getting into the saddle, much to his displeasure. He hadn't ridden so much in several years and his groin and inner legs were sore and blistered as well as his backside. He used to could ride all day and night. But then he used to could do a lot of things that he couldn't anymore. Everything was a young man's game. Gentlemen, the truest ones leastways, went about in carriages with padded horsehair seats where their asses wouldn't have to take a pounding. Well, soon enough, he told himself, he'd be riding around in his own damn carriage and pitching money out to the pilgrims and Magdalena would be right there with him, pretty as she ever was.

They rode on in the three-quarter moonlight on up through trees and across a wide stream, the hooves of their mounts splashing up white rags of moon-shined water that fell and settled back into the shape of what it was.

As they rode on, Einer waited for John Paul to catch up to him and then said around the glow of his cigarette, "Ol' Jesse Valdez has some real good stock and that's where we're headed according to Atticus," who rode out front of them.

"How many?" John Paul asked.

"Enough if we take a couple hundred he might not notice for a day or two."

John Paul whistled low.

"Atticus used to work for him, so he knows which pastures the old boy keeps 'em on and how many vaqueros he might have night hawkin' 'em and how we can get to 'em before . . ."

He didn't finish the thought.

"Before what?" John Paul said.

"Well, you know if they spot us they'll surely put up a fight and try and kill us for the horse thieves we are, gun us down or hang us if they can take us alive. But if they catch us, they might also take us to some Mexican jail somewhere. Trust me, boy, I'd as soon be shot dead or hanged either one as be locked up in a Mexican jail."

"Well, shit," John Paul said. "You make it all sound so romantic."

Einer took a long draw off his shuck and the tip glowed brighter still.

"You've any preference?" he said.

"Preference for what?"

"Shot or hanged or in a Mex jail?"

"I reckon neither one. But if I had to choose, I guess shot, something quick, straight to the heart."

"Well," Einer said, "it's something to hope for anyway."

They went on and it seemed the farther they went the more the dark deepened around them, the less the moon had its power to light the land or the horses ahead or them. Clouds also appeared and blocked out the moon's light now and again. John Paul wondered if they were lost and just riding around in the dark. He wondered if Atticus Pinch was just a damn liar.

"It's so dark I can't hardly see nothing," John Paul said. "Them clouds crowding the moon don't help a damn thing."

"Hesh," Einer said. "Voices carry of a night."

Up ahead they could hear the careful clatter of Atticus Pinch's own animal, as he guided it over loose shale trusting it to be surefooted and not slip and go down. It looked to John Paul they might be going up a draw but he couldn't be sure. John Paul's own horse followed in single file behind the other two.

At some point Atticus Pinch stopped and waited for them.

"Just up ahead," he whispered pointing. "He's got 'em ranged up in a grass pastured valley right yonder."

"How many you figure?" Einer whispered, having mashed out his smoke on the heel of his boot.

"A couple hunnert I figure. That's just one bunch. He keeps

'em all over about five thousand goddamn acres of his. This is the closest bunch to the border."

"Nighthawks?"

"I reckon—he usually has them out."

"How many of 'em you reckon?" Einer said.

"Four or five maybe, but only two awake this hour. 'At's how we used to do it anyway when I was working for him."

John Paul pulled the pocket watch he'd stolen off the shot man back at the livery and snapped open its face but he couldn't read the spider hands in the dark. Einer looked suspiciously at him but didn't say anything.

"Let's ease on down there, then," Einer said. "You two swing on around in behind them and drive them toward me. Anything starts a fuss, I'll knock 'em down with this here." He patted the coach gun. "Just drive 'em back to the river where we camped and on across. Don't wait for me, I'll catch up to you all the other side."

John Paul swallowed dryly. It was real. Real as anything: they were about to become real rustlers, real outlaws.

"We git 'em moving, keep 'em moving, full out. Don't stop for nothing," Einer warned.

They heeled their horses forward and in the faintest light of a momentarily cloud-free moon they saw the dark shapes of horses beyond, and beyond the horses a scribble of mountains pushed up against the blue-black night. The horses were bunched, some grazing still and others asleep standing up and some laid down. John Paul figured there were so many they wouldn't have been able to count in the daylight. Just a lot is all he knew—a big bunch his heart was eager to capture. He thought again of Mercy and getting enough money to go back and get her. It's all he wanted.

"You go with Atticus to get them horses," Einer said to John Paul. "You take the left side and he'll take the right. Get in behind them quietly and then you all drive 'em to me."

"I'll whistle you when we get in behind 'em," Atticus told John Paul. "When I do, pull that pistola and get 'em going toward Einer here, and keep 'em running till we cross that goddam river. Just don't shoot nobody. Shoot yer gun up in the air."

A Mexican wolf, they guessed it was, called into the outer dark and called again. When its call was not answered the night was silent again but for the falling of stars that could not be heard.

John Paul heeled his horse forward following the lead of Atticus Pinch, then they separated like water flowing around a rock, John Paul going one side and the outlaw the other. John Paul listened keenly for Atticus's whistle when they got far enough behind the herd. By leaning down over the neck of his horse he could still make out the shape of the horses.

They went silent against the silent night. Now and then one of the horses whickered, having scented their approach, but it didn't mean anything because they were just horses doing what horses do and they went on until they got in behind them.

Finally he heard the outlaw's whistle—like a nightbird, only it wasn't any nightbird he'd ever heard, and turned his horse around. Then he heard the crack of a whip and Atticus was going after the herd and John Paul followed suit, jerking free his revolver as he went and firing wildly into the air and shouting like a madman. And suddenly the herd was up and running before them as they drove them toward Einer, who now had the stock of his coach gun thrown up into the hollow of his shoulder at the ready, expecting the nighthawks to jump into the fray. He was knelt down in order to make out their shapes against the night sky—horses and riders, he just hoped that he didn't shoot the boy or Pinch when they came.

His heart racketed in his chest with excitement. It was like the old days again, doing wrongful things in the name of money, love, adventure, or just to be doing 'em.

"Goddamn," he muttered, his finger lightly on one of the triggers, the hammers cocked back, ready to strike, to deliver a fatal lesson if need be.

He heard the thud of a couple of hundred horses coming directly his way, the ground trembling as they came on. He'd positioned behind a twisted tree to keep from getting trampled over. He would let them pass, him keeping an eye out for the vaqueros that would surely follow and try and chase them down.

John Paul's heart pounded louder than the herd's hooves against the solid earth. He rode madly, shouting and calling, "Get on there. Hup, hup!" Across the way Atticus cracked the air with his whip, calling, "Get on you bastards. Get!"

It was like reading one of those dime novels, only better, John Paul thought.

Even their mounts seemed to catch the fever of the chase and stretched out their necks and bunched their muscles with each stride as if eager to catch the herd, to run 'em down just to be doing it.

The night exploded with their eagerness and rider and horse bared teeth as they rode toward the waiting river. They flew past Einer, leaned against the tree's trunk, shotgun at the ready, horses and men a rush of sweated flesh, four-legged devils heading straight to hell or glory. He reveled in the thunder and dust and they seemed more like a thousand than a couple of hundred.

"Keep going you hammerheads," he shouted after them, running riverward to that great Rio Grande and hopefully on across without losing too many.

In his excitement he once more felt young and vital and the feeling seemed to infuse his tired bones with new life, for he was doing something he'd long wanted to do ever since he'd vowed to quit the outlaw game, ever since that last stint in a

Montana prison of fifteen long and dreadful years that broke him of the fever, of being a hunted and haunted man. And when they released him through the gate and he tasted real freedom again, he vowed to never give it up—and had held to that vow. Until this very moment. What good's dying alone and safe in bed, he told himself as the last of the herd thundered past followed by Atticus and John Paul shouting like madmen.

He reasoned—rightly or wrongly—that John Paul's arrival was of a purpose; he knew not what or how. But surely the wandering boy had brought him a new vision of the life he had yet to live. It brought his dreams of her into a possibility again. But now John Paul was aware of it too and he was glad John Paul knew of the dream and the possibility and gave him a sense of kinship with the boy, one he'd have never thought he'd have.

As they thundered off into the darkness, he waited still. And sure enough he saw four riders coming, firing their pistols—the flashes of gunfire flaring against the blackness; he could tell by the wide sombrero brims who they were and that they sure enough wanted their herd back and he couldn't fault them for that. But the herd meant everything to him and he wasn't about to relinquish it easily.

He sighted down the short barrels, aiming low, and pulled one trigger; he stood the shock of the shotgun's buck against his shoulder and saw the first two horses crumble, pitching their riders. He heard them cry out in anguished Spanish. He didn't know what they said but figured it to be nothing kind.

The other two paused briefly but came on again and he cut loose with the other barrel when they got about forty yards away with the same results.

He sure hated to kill horses but it was better than killing men.

Satisfied he'd done his job, he mounted his horse and chased off in the direction Atticus and John Paul had driven those herd.

"Son of a bitch," he yelled to the night. "We did it!"

CHAPTER 18

They drove the herd northwest into New Mexico where Atticus said he knew a man who would buy every one he could get at a fair price, no questions asked. Atticus explained this man was a powerful and rich horse trader who could have fake bills of sales issued and alter any brands that needed it and no one would question him. He would then in turn double his money by selling the horses to the Army.

New Mexico seemed like a strange and alien land to John Paul with its lonesome black mesas and fields of lava like long jagged fingers that had flowed down from extinct volcanoes, rock that could cut through flesh and bone.

The sky was a dome of turquoise, of cooling breezes that came down off mountains with the slowness of melting ice and caressed the languorous grasses now growing brown from freezing nights.

"It sure is pretty country, ain't it?" Einer said as they camped of a late evening by a pebbled bottom creek under the flare of a sunset sky.

"It's a lot prettier than Texas," John Paul said.

Atticus nursed a bottle of liquor to his chest as carefully as a mother holding her infant.

"Had a good friend of mine killed by some laws 'round here," he said. "Shot him down like a damn ol' dog, they did. These New Mexican laws are hard as you'll ever find anywheres."

"What'd they shoot him for?" John Paul asked across from the fire.

The herd was settled and grazing contentedly.

"One thing or the other," Atticus said.

"One thing or the other?" John Paul replied, curious.

"He might a fucked this sheriff's wife. Maybe that was the cause of it."

Einer smoked silently, thinking about the thing most on his mind: seeing Magdalena again. He was as close now to seeing her as he'd been in more than thirty years. The very thought of it quickened his heart and stirred his blood the way he'd remembered it having been stirred those nights so long ago.

John Paul laughed over Atticus's story.

"Well, shit," he said. "I reckon I'd shoot him too if I caught him fucking my wife."

"You ain't married," Pinch said, dully.

"No, but I mean if I was."

"Oh. Well, that ain't all there was to it," Atticus said, languorous in his telling.

"What more was it?" John Paul said, reaching for the coffeepot to refill his cup.

"Well, this fellow—the sheriff, I mean—wasn't what you'd call on the up and up and supposedly he'd run with a gang of thieves, road agents and such, and my friend was one of 'em and that's how he met this sheriff's wife and afore you know it the two of them had taken up together and run off to somewhere down near the border. Well, anyway he tracked 'em down and caught 'em and he shot my friend about a dozen times right there in the bed where he was sleeping with the wife, aired him right out, then he took his knife and ruined her face so no other man would ever want to fool with her. I heard she begged him to kill her but he wouldn't. Told her she was lucky he didn't cut her nose off the way them Apaches'll do their women."

"What about him?" John Paul said.

"What about him what?"

"Well if he ruined her face like that, did he divorce her then?"

"No, you see, that's the other part of it. He kept her, said he loved her no matter how she looked."

"Loved her!"

"Love is the goddamnedest thing, ain't it?" Atticus said, taking another nip of the bottle.

John Paul thought about Mercy. Einer about Magdalena. Just sitting around together, the three of them, two hundred or so stolen horses, thinking about love of women.

"That don't make much sense," John Paul said at last. "I wouldn't cut up no woman I supposedly love."

Atticus grinned.

"I know it," he said. "Shit, was it me, I reckon I'd have killed her then and there. But that's just me, of course. I couldn't love no woman with a cut-up face."

"You couldn't love nobody, Atticus," Einer chimed in. "You just ain't that type to love a body. You'd fornicate with 'em, but you'd never love 'em."

"I reckon that's true enough," Pinch replied.

"You stand night watch, boy," Einer said to John Paul. "Atticus will spell you."

Einer lay back then, still smoking his cigarette and staring up at the darkening sky and thinking about her. Last he knew she lived in Santa Fe and hoped she still might. Maggie is what he called her back then, and he knew she was a settling-down kind of woman and figured if she was still alive she might likely still be in Santa Fe. He hoped she was.

I want to die in bed alongside her, he thought a thousand times before and thought it now as well.

★ ★ ★ ★ ★

They went on, and in three more days they came to the buyer's ranch and Atticus went into the big house and spoke to the buyer and together they came out. The buyer looked over the herd Einer and John Paul had kept bunched together and said for them to run them in the big corralled pasture up away from the house. And so they ran them in, Einer holding the gate open till the herd was all in, then he closed it and the counter, a man who was as old as Einer, counted out two hundred and fifteen horses and gave the tally sheet to the buyer.

The buyer was a thinly constructed man with a hawkish gaze and silver hair. He was neatly dressed in a finely made gray suit of clothes and black polished shoes and looked like a banker—which he was—but a rancher too.

He invited the three of them to come inside and offered them they stay overnight.

"Miranda will take your dusty duds and clean them for you while you bathe and shave," he said. "Then we'll eat supper and have something to drink and settle up if that suits you gentlemen."

They shook hands all around and followed the housekeeper up a long hallway with tiled floors and stucco walls and ceilings of heavy dark beams.

She showed them each to their rooms and where an inside bathroom was with a large cast-iron porcelain-coated tub that sat on clawed feet. There was even a sitting place for them to do their business with a flush water tank overhead and they marveled at the nicety of it all.

"It's like a San Francisco hotel," Einer said.

They flipped a coin as to who would bathe first and John Paul won the toss. He shucked out of his dusty duds and was almost ashamed to have anybody have to clean them, but the housekeeper had instructed him to set them in a pile outside the door and she would take them. There was a belted checkered wool robe in the bathroom and the tub was already full of hot soapy water. He climbed in and it felt warm and slick and he reveled at the sensation. He'd never taken a bath in anything more than a horse tank or creek. He sank down to his chin, his knees bobbing above the water's surface.

"Damn," he said in a luxuriant voice. "Damn."

After a time there was a knock on the door and he started, then said, "Yes."

"Might I come in?" He recognized the housekeeper's voice.

"I ain't decent," he said.

"It's okay," she said. "I've seen lots of men before. I've brought you some fresh towels."

"Okay," he said.

She entered and set some clean towels on a small stand next to the tub. She made no effort to look at him. "Is there anything else you need?"

"No ma'am," he said.

"Mr. Blaine likes his guests to be treated well," she said. "If there's anything you need, just ask."

He took note of her.

She was a large woman with dark hair though streaked through with silver. She had a round face and fat cheeks and a small mouth, wide hips and stout legs. Motherly. He figured her for a native of that country, but spoke good English.

"Thank you," he said as she left.

He leaned back again and looked about the cavernous room. Whoever this Mr. Blaine fellow was, he had a hell of a house and sure knew how to be cordial. He also had liked the looks of the country all around—the low hills shaggy with brown winter grass, he imagined, would be lush and green come the spring. And the water, the creeks they'd crossed not to mention the rivers, well, it was like a paradise in his way of thinking. He imagined Mercy would like this country too.

You ain't never had the likes of this before, he thought. This is what I'd like for Mercy and me, to live like this someday, in a country like this. He let his thoughts run wild with possibilities as he scrubbed his skin with a bar of good-smelling soap. Scrubbed his chest and arms and legs, one at a time and down in his crotch, thinking again as he did of the way Mercy had touched him. He scrubbed between his toes and his feet never felt nothing like it either. Then he dunked under and got his hair wet and scrubbed it till it squeaked and dunked again to rinse it.

By the time he finished the water was cool and gray and he stood and dried himself with the towel and went over to a dry sink with a large round mirror on the wall above it and looked at himself. He was whiskerless but fine whorls of brown hair graced his cheek and upper lip. His hair had grown longish and shaggy. He squinted looking at himself to try and see what Mercy had saw that night. There was a tin of baking soda and a fresh toothbrush laid out and he brushed his teeth until they felt slippery and clean, then took up the comb that laid waiting also and combed his hair back, then donned the robe and went out and back to his room, passing the housekeeper on the way, her arms holding more towels.

"I'm finished," he said. She nodded and continued on up the hall and he went to his room and lay down on the bed. It would be a few hours he reckoned before supper was due and he was saddle sore and weary and the warm bath had made him sleepier still.

He closed his eyes, wondering what his take would be and would it be enough to go and get Mercy and convince her to come with him.

When the housekeeper knocked at the door and he came

awake he thought it was Mercy calling to him from the other side.

"Come in," he said eagerly.

But it was simply the housekeeper with his clothes cleaned and his boots polished and she set them down and said, "Supper will be ready in twenty minutes. Just go straight down the hall to the other end of the house and you'll come to the dining room."

He thanked her and she left and he dressed in the clean clothes and though his jeans were badly faded and in places the threads showed, and his shirt was frayed at the cuffs and around the collar, they felt luxuriant fresh washed against his clean skin, and his washed socks felt new on his feet. He tugged on his boots and sat admiring how good they looked and smiled at the thought that they were still the boots of a dead man.

"Well, you couldn't use them no more," he said aloud as if the dead man were sitting there demanding an explanation. Then he stood. His gunbelt and revolver he left lying on the stand next to the bed.

"I reckon they'll not ask you to shoot your supper," he said to the empty room. Then he went out and found the dining room without trouble.

Atticus and Einer were already seated along one side of an elongated table with burl wood top and massive stout-carved legs. They each looked different, bathed and shaved.

"Well, don't we all look like proper gents," Atticus said.

The chairs had ornate carved backs and red damask padded seats. There were five place settings of china plates and elegant ivory-handled silverware.

In the center of the table was a large bowl of fruit, apples and peaches and grapes. There were leaded crystal glasses of water and a similar pitcher of water as well. There were also two carafes of dark red wine.

In a moment the rancher came in with a woman on his arm. Her beauty drew their attention—all three—and they had trouble keeping their jaws from unhinging.

She could have been his daughter as young as she looked compared to the rancher, but he introduced her as his wife.

"Gentlemen, this is my wife, Lily. Lily, these are business associates—the ones who brought in that herd of fine-looking horses you saw when you returned from your ride," he said and held the chair for her to sit down next to him at the head of the table.

"Oh," she said. "Just the three of you, who brought in all of them?"

"That's right, Miss Lily," Einer said.

Her skin was translucent, the color of skimmed milk, her hair as black as a moonless night and her eyes a vivid violet.

She smiled warmly at them and they shyly smiled back and John Paul couldn't help but think of the story Atticus had told them about the fellow the sheriff had killed for running off with his wife, and thought, boy, you'd best keep your eyes in your head if you know what's good for you.

Food was served on platters by the housekeeper and an elderly man with white moustaches, and obviously Mexican by his coloration. The platters were full to overrunning with steaks and roasts and potatoes and carrots and peas and all manner of food. Conversation was light, mostly talk about horses and land and such diverse things that mattered little to any of them but the buyer. And more wine was poured and drank and tasted like God's own tears Einer thought, and so too did Pinch whose constitution was accustomed to harder, more vile drink.

Einer couldn't help but remember that in the olden days it was like this a lot of the time—in between all the bad times it was.

Dessert was two kinds of pie—huckleberry and apple—and

hand-cranked ice cream flavored with vanilla beans and dark rich coffee and cream and sugar if you wanted it.

John Paul noticed how delicately the woman ate, and how little. He supposed to maintain her hourglass figure. She wore a peach-colored organdy dress with a low black-velvet-trimmed bodice that made it hard for him—or any of them—to divert their eyes from her exposed flesh, the slightest hint of cleavage.

John Paul wasn't the only one thinking about that story of Ballard's wife and her lover; Atticus was thinking about it too.

It'd almost be worth it, he thought, sneaking peeks at her, and became aroused without meaning to. Hell, if she'd let me be caught in bed with her, he could shoot my lights out twice over just for the opportunity. Atticus was not a particular man when it came to fornicating and had once broken both his ankles jumping out of a married woman's bedroom back in his younger days. The irate husband near beat him to death as he tried crawling away from the scene of the indiscretion. Years later he told the story with pride, though there was nothing prideful about it.

When they'd eaten their fill the rancher invited the men to step out on the porch for a smoke and went and got a box of cigars and offered them each one and then they followed him outside to smoke them.

The evening air was cool and pleasant, damn near cold against the harshness of day sun; even though the season was in its change from autumn to winter, the sun could still be intense and unforgiving.

The housekeeper brought out four glasses of cognac for digestion, the glasses as delicate as if sculpted from ice.

"To good Mexican horses," the rancher said, raising his glass in toast, and they did likewise and drank.

They shared the cigars and the cognac and conversation and stood smoking each with a glass in his hand, and stared out into the darkened land that was endless as the sky above.

They felt of good cheer and whiled away another hour or so before the rancher said it was time for him to retire and told them if they wanted another cigar or more cognac just to ask his *jefe* inside.

"Boy, this is the way to live," John Paul said. "You got some beautiful country round here, Mr. Blaine."

"Thank you," the rancher said. "We like it real well."

"Wonder how much a little piece of ground might run somebody," John Paul said.

The rancher looked at him through the cloud of cigar smoke.

"Not that much," he said. "Why, you interested in settling down in New Mexico?"

"Well, it sure is tempting. I've not seen anything to match it. Real peaceful it seems to me."

Einer said, "Maybe you could get you a small plot of ground with your earnings."

John Paul looked from Einer to the rancher.

"Could be you ever get real interested I could put you in touch with a land agent over in White Oaks," he said.

John Paul felt flush with promise.

"I might just take you up on that."

The rancher nodded.

Soon after they went back inside and to their rooms and bed, John Paul thinking about everything, mostly about Mercy and him and her together out in this pretty country, married and raising some kids and maybe doing a little horse business. It was all dreams, he told himself, but wasn't dreams how things got started?

In the morning they saddled their mounts and the rancher gave Pinch the envelope of money for the horses.

"Twenty dollars a head, seem like a fair price?"

They agreed that it did, but then John Paul piped up and

said, "Forty would seem a lot fairer."

The rancher looked at him oddly, questioningly.

"It would, wouldn't it?" he said. "Trouble is, I pay you forty, I lose my shirt trying to resell them. You all think you can do better go on and take them on with you and find another buyer if you'd rather."

He said this without rancor but as a statement of fact.

Einer said, "You'll have to forgive him, Mr. Blaine, he ain't hardly learned as much about horses as you and me have forgotten." Then cut John Paul a hard warning look.

"You must understand something about horses," the rancher said to John Paul directly. "They're only worth so much no matter how you look at it. Horses aren't beeves that can be shipped east and slaughtered for the plates of the rich and from which a good profit can be made. Horses are just horses."

John Paul felt suddenly foolish as he saw Atticus Pinch also giving him the stink eyes, probably thinking he had boogered the deal.

"I know it," John Paul said. "I was just talking. I've got no sense."

"You are young yet and still learning," the rancher said. "A wise man never stops learning, or wanting to; only a fool speaks without thinking."

"Yes, sir," John Paul said.

"Looks like a lovely morning, doesn't it?" the rancher said.

They agreed that it did.

Einer and Pinch and John Paul rode away, Atticus still upset about John Paul's smart mouth for nearly ruining his deal. He wanted to say something, knock some sense into the boy's knot head, but, because of Einer, he let it go and just rode on out in front of them so as to avoid the temptation.

CHAPTER 19

Ballard and the tracker came down through a red-walled canyon, its sides streaked black like a tarry rain had slid down them. The iron shoes of their mounts rang on the rocks and every sound was an echo.

The tracker led single file as the canyon walls closed in; running down through the canyon was a thin stream of water that afforded them respite at some point, and they dismounted and drank from the stream with cupped handfuls of the water, which was tanged with a muddy taste.

They removed their bandannas and soaked them in the water, then tied them wet around their necks.

"You know where we're at?" Ballard said.

"Yes, this is maybe only one of two or three canyons in the whole goddamn part of this state as I know it."

"But where are we at?"

"We're right here," the tracker said.

"That's not what I meant, you damn fool."

"You ain't got no sense of humor, do you?"

"I got what I need when I need it. Right now I don't need it."

"Another two days' ride and we'll be in El Paso."

"You sure or are you just guessing?"

"I'm sure. Well, pretty near sure. It's been a few years since I was this far south."

"Christ," Ballard said, tapping the ends of his reins in gloved hands.

"It makes sense that's where they'd head if they're aiming to abscond into old Mexico."

"Let's get on then."

They remounted and went on up the canyon and eventually out the other end back into bold sunlight that was still hot as a branding iron.

"How you gone find 'em if they are in El Paso?" the tracker asked.

"If they are there they are there for a reason," Ballard said. "Somebody would have to have noticed 'em if they're there—an old man and a boy riding together—especially a boy with a big red mark on his face."

"El Paso's a fair-sized town these days, I hear tell," the tracker said. "Could be they are there and we might not even find 'em."

"Sometimes the easiest ones to find are found in fair-sized towns. Sometimes they ain't," Ballard said.

"But if they're not there, then what?"

"I don't know yet," Ballard said.

"If you catch 'em and find out this boy didn't have a hand in those people's death, then it will have all been a waste of time, won't it?" Elkhart Truth said.

"I reckon," Ballard said. "But at least I'll know I did my job. It's the last job I aim to do. Once this is over that's it for me. I'm hanging my gun up and turning in my badge. I got a new baby child that needs raising and a daddy to raise it."

The tracker had never seen such doggedness in any man, living or dead. He knew *he* wouldn't have gone to the lengths Ballard was going through just to hopefully learn the truth about a thing.

"In the long run it won't make no difference to them dead folks, will it?" he said.

"No, nothing will matter to them who are dead. It is for the living justice is sought; the dead are no longer of this world or subject to its paltry laws."

"I reckon you'll be paying me off when we reach El Paso," the tracker said.

"If that's where you aim to quit," Ballard said.

"You quitting too, one way or the other?"

"I reckon I probably will be," Ballard said.

The sun was a devil on his neck, the wet kerchief already dried and scratchy. Sweat trickled down the sides of his face from up under his hat and his shirt was dark-splotched under his arms and across his back.

They rode on, the tracker seemingly immune to the heat and privation as long as he had something hard to drink and keep him company. They came across a large rattlesnake scurrying across the trail in front of them and their horses shied and the tracker's reared up and nearly unseated him.

"You son of a bitch," he cursed, whether at the horse or the snake, then spurred the horse on around, not bothering to kill the rattler but instead ignoring it, as did Ballard, whose horse wasn't quite as skittish.

They stopped that night at a ranch house whose light they'd spotted from a mile off.

"Let's stop there and see can we stay the night and maybe buy a meal," Ballard said.

"You'll get no argument from me," said Elkhart Truth.

They rode up and called the house and the door cracked open enough to let the inner light seep through.

"Who is it?" a woman's voice called.

"I'm a lawman," Ballard said, "and me and my tracker are in search of a man and a boy. But right now we're tired and our horses need to rest. Wondered if we might lay over the night and buy a meal off you?"

There was no response for a moment as the woman spoke to someone inside the house, their conversation muted.

"Okay," the woman said. "You can put your horses up in the corral yonder. There's water and if'n you want, some cracked corn, but it ain't free."

"Thank you kindly," Ballard said. The woman watched from the door as they put up their animals and watered and fed them, then watched as they came on toward the house. They paused at a jack-handled pump and pumped up water cold and wet from deep in the ground and washed their hands and faces and drank their fill, then came on to the house where she allowed them entrance.

"How do," she said.

"Ma'am."

"That's Tilly," she said, indicating another woman at the stove—a big four-burner Great Majestic with nickel trim and pots on each of the burners, a stove you didn't see every day, especially in such a paltry house. The air was rich with cooking smells, baking aromas of yeast-risen bread. Lanterns hung from the beam overhead, their glow warm and cozy.

Tilly slightly turned to look at them, then turned back to whatever it was she was tending on the stove, stirring one of the pots with a long-handled wood spoon. She had close-cropped brownish gray hair framing her square face. She was clothed in a man's shirt and man's trousers and brogan shoes. She was thick in the middle but the clothing she wore did not reveal much about her figure.

The other one, who'd allowed them in, was slightly built wearing a common gingham dress. Her reddish hair was loose and hung about her shoulders; the bridge of her nose was sprinkled with freckles and the description of "pretty" wouldn't quite describe her.

"Might I see your badge?" she said to Ballard. He produced

it from his pocket and she nodded and set aside the light rifle she'd been holding.

"Can't be none to careful," she said.

"No, ma'am, you can't. Not these days."

"Used to be just wild Indians, Comanche and such, you had to worry about. Now it's just about everything that forks a horse."

"Yes, ma'am," he said.

She looked closely at the tracker, trying to judge him by his overall appearance, the set of his eyes and mouth, the way he looked back at her, and could not determine if he was of viable stuff or not, determined she'd not want to be anywhere alone with him.

"Sit," she said, indicating the table that had a chair on either end. "We done et our supper. Tilly was just making a rabbit stew for tomorrow. It's best to let it simmer all night."

Tilly dished them each a bowl and set it before them along with spoons, then brought forth from the stove's warmer a half pan of biscuits that had dried to a hard crust but were still somewhat soft in the middle.

"Them biscuits is best if you break 'em up and sop 'em in the stew," the thin one said.

The other woman stood watching them eat.

"You ladies live out here all alone?" Elkhart Truth said.

"Yes, and we have for some time," the freckled one said. Tilly had gotten down a cob pipe from a shelf, packed it with tobacco from a tin, lighted the bowl to life, and stood smoking it as she watched them.

"No men?" the tracker said.

"Why you asking all these questions?" Tilly said suddenly, broken from her reverie, her own question sharp as a whetted blade.

"No reason," the tracker said. "I'm just a real curious type fellow."

"Well don't be," the woman said.

"That stew is a dollar each and the grain for your horses another dollar," the slighter one said. "We'd thank you kindly to pay before you go out and bed down in the yard."

Ballard reached into his pocket and dug out the money and set it on the table.

He and the tracker finished by swiping a biscuit into the bowl to sop up all the juices.

"That's some fine stew," Ballard said. " 'Bout the best I've ever et." It wasn't but he said it anyway to be kindly.

The women didn't say anything, but continued to watch them cautious-like. Finished, Ballard stood, followed by the tracker.

"We'll be gone first light," Ballard said. "Not to worry."

"I ain't worried," Tilly said coldly.

"Yes, ma'am," Ballard said. "I didn't expect you would be. Thanks again for the meal and letting us put up our horses and rest the night." He did not wait for a reply that he knew was not likely to be forthcoming.

They stepped out into the night air and it was dark and silent as the grave but for the glow of inner light of the cabin that spilled through the windows and into the yard.

They'd noticed a lean-to and headed there now, passing the corral where they'd hung their saddles; they took up their bedrolls and went and got in under the partial roof and shook out their soogins and laid down on them.

"You think that was strange?" the tracker asked, lying there in the dark.

"What was strange?" Ballard said.

"Them two, the way they was."

"I don't catch your meaning."

"How that one was dressed like a man and the other'n a lady.

166

Hell, she even looked mannish in the face—that one called Tilly, the mean one. You don't think them two is—"

"I don't think nothing but that they was kindly enough to sell us supper and let us camp here overnight," Ballard said curtly.

"Well shit, it's too bad if they are," the tracker said. "That one is a real nice looker for being so plain. A man could really do something for her, I'm betting."

"Get some sleep, we'll leave early," Ballard said. "I want to make El Paso by tomorrow."

They lay in the dark, restive and saddle-sore, each with his own thoughts and imaginations that involved womanhood and what was and was not reality, and such thoughts burrowed into their brains like blood ticks. The moon rose over the distant mountains so far they could never reach it if they traveled hard for two lifetimes and their horses had wings.

The moon looked cold as ice and the land felt empty of all people but the two of them lying on the outside and the two of them lying on the inside.

El Paso seemed like a dream they were trying to have.

The tracker saw the lights go off inside the house and it seemed darker now than the outer dark he lay in. He wondered did they both sleep in the same bed as he reached in his jacket pocket for the liquor bottle that was nearly empty and swallowed the last of it before letting it slide from his weary hand, then closed his eyes and fell into more darkness still.

CHAPTER 20

Einer cut the money three ways and said, "That's it then."

John Paul reckoned he'd never dreamed of so much money, let alone seen it.

"Lord God," he said looking at it in his hand. "How much is it?"

"You can't count?" Einer said.

"Maybe now you can get that thing on your face fixed," Atticus Pinch said.

It sent John Paul into hot anger and he stuffed the money down into his pocket, then balled his fist and swung on the mouth that insulted him. But Atticus was quick and easily ducked the blow and threw a fist of his own that caught John Paul against the temple and made the world go funny, and made the ground suddenly tilt and rush up to slam into his face.

"Do you have some sort of death wish?" Atticus said, almost amused at the fool kid.

"No, he don't have no death wish," Einer said, stepping over to help John Paul to his feet. "Whyn't you go on. You got your pay."

"Seems I should get more than a third since it was me who knew whose horses to steal and who'd buy 'em once they got stole."

John Paul gained his feet but unsteadily so, his bearings still uncertain.

"That's what you think?" Einer said.

"Goddamn right it is," Atticus said. "So how about each of you forking in an extry hunnert dollars or so. Without me in on it, you'd be spitting in the wind and scratching your sorry asses."

"How about you scratch this," Einer said, jerking the revolver free from his belt, cocking and aiming it with one motion, and stopping the barrel inches short of Atticus's forehead.

Atticus raised his palms.

"Now, go easy with that thing, dad, you liable to fire it off accidental and hurt somebody."

"It won't be no accident if I fire it off, Pinch. It'll be on purpose and I generally hit what I aim at. I might be old but this here don't know nothing about how many birthdays I had. Now get on that cayuse of yours and ride on the hell away from me. I'm weary of your company."

"Okay, okay, goddamn it, I can see now what sort of sons of bitches you are. Don't come calling again you ever want to steal more fucken horses, or nothing else. Jesus . . . !"

"You don't have to worry none about it," Einer said, following Atticus's every step with the barrel of his gun.

He waited until the man had mounted and rode off in real haste before he replaced it back in his belt.

"I told you before, boy, you ought not to let your mouth write checks your ass can't cash," he said. "You're lucky that damn fool didn't kill you. Your head okay?"

John Paul shook his head twice and said, "Yeah, least I can stand without falling down. I never thought that old bastard could hit that hard."

"Always expect the worst and pray for the best might be a thing that will serve you well in the future."

"What now?" John Paul said.

"What now what?" Einer said, tightening his saddle cinch.

"I mean what do we do now?"

"Do whatever you like, just remember that money don't grow on trees and once it's spent it's spent."

John Paul pulled his share back out of his pocket and looked at it.

"You didn't say how much it was?"

"I guess schooling never took with you, did it?"

This time John Paul felt embarrassment instead of anger. He started to put the money back again.

"It's a little over fourteen hundred dollars," Einer said, sticking a foot into the stirrup and hoisting himself into the saddle.

John Paul whistled.

"Goddamn that's a ton of money. Shit, I guess we're rich."

Einer laughed.

"Rich? Hell son, it ain't even close to being rich. It's just walking around money."

"Walking around money. Hell it's more'n a bank's got in it."

"Well then, you ought to open a bank," Einer said and started to rein his horse about.

"Wait, where're you going?"

"Find that woman I'm looking for."

"What about me?"

"If'n I find her, I doubt she'd have a sister and she sure as hell won't want two of us."

John Paul swallowed. Einer thought how lost he looked, then shook his head.

"Tell you what," he said. "If'n I don't find her I'll look you up and maybe we'll steal some more goddamn horses, how'll that be?"

John Paul nodded, uncertain as to what to say. He suddenly felt alone again in the world and didn't care much for the feeling like he once thought he would.

"How'd you find me?" he said.

"Well, that's easy, tell me where you're going and I'll find you there."

There was only one place John Paul could think to go.

"El Paso," he said, "is where I'm headed."

"Be careful you go there, those bunko artists will scrape all the hair off your hide and suck the marrow from your bones before they toss you on the trash heap. Don't go flashing your money around, keep it well hid."

"I'm going to find a woman too," he said. "Like you."

"Well shit, then we are men meant to be of constant sorrow," Einer said, "looking for women who may or may not love us when we find 'em, but do it we must, must we not?"

"It is," John Paul said grinning, feeling better knowing that if he could show Mercy he was a man of means now, she would go away with him and if she did, he would not need Einer for companionship.

"Adios then," Einer said, lifting his Stetson and swiping the air with it before he slapped his horse's flank with it and put it into a leaping gallop.

"So long," John Paul said to a distant riding old man he'd stolen horses with. "I hope the laws don't catch you, 'cause you know they do with horse thieves, don't you."

He smiled and mounted his own horse and swung it around toward Texas, El Paso keenly on his mind. El Paso and the whore, Mercy, high-hoped and full of pure joy, for never before had the world seemed so promising.

First thing I'm gone do when I get there, he told himself remembering how he felt after the bath at the rich man's house, the warm wind raking his face, is get a new suit of clothes and get spiffed up real fine, 'cause she ain't gone want no damn rundown kid, but a gentleman of fine means. Yes, sir.

★　★　★　★　★

Einer sold his horse and saddle and bought a ticket on the A.T. & S.F. northward and climbed aboard and settled in to his seat. Already the day was late enough that through his railroad car window he could see a sky more beautiful than any sky he ever recalled seeing before, smeared with the colors of blood and miracles and a westward slanted sun like the eye of a dreamer getting ready to close into long sleep.

A candy butcher came down the aisle and Einer bought a quarter's worth of taffy; he sat enjoying it with his boot heels propped on the seat across from him and watched the landscape slide by under a roiling cloud of black engine smoke traveling in the opposite direction.

He could not but think of Maggie as he relaxed, chewing his taffy candy. His teeth were still good enough to crack walnuts. His people had always had good teeth, if not good sense, he thought with a smile. Every mile, every crosstie that flowed under the engine's steel wheels brought him closer to Maggie.

I'm coming for you, girl. Ol' Einer is on his way.

He told himself now he didn't care if she was married or not, that fate had long ago dictated their outcome and love was a thing that could never be broken, no matter the passage of time or distance. If it was meant that she'd be there waiting for him, then she would be, and if not, well, he'd somehow make it all work out.

You was a damn fool for ever letting her go, he told himself not for the first time. Well, you're coming back just like you said you would.

He never regretted any of the other things he'd ever done— not the robberies nor the men he'd had to kill, not even the prison time—not now that he'd paid his debts. That was all just the hand he'd dealt himself, but her, he'd regretted.

I know I should have taken you with me, and would have but

for the laws having jumped me. If I had it to do over again, I'd have become a damn store clerk selling shoes or parasols just to be able to keep you and have you keep me. But no, I had to be wild and unfettered and now I don't know why I did. It was all such a damn waste. They say there is no fool like an old fool, but they are wrong: a young fool is just as bad and maybe worse than an old one.

He gnawed on the candy and had to pry it from his teeth with a fingernail and thought he ought to just throw the damn stuff away, but he didn't. He just kept gnawing on it until it was all et and by the time it was the land had fallen into darkness and here and there—out there, outside the car's window—he'd see a light glowing in some hacienda or shack, and it would cause him to wonder about them who lived in such places, what the folks were like.

He reckoned most of them were families set down to supper, a man and his wife and maybe children, maybe talking amongst themselves or getting ready for early bed. Maybe the kids were already in bed and the man and his wife were in theirs and touching each other, maybe him on top of her or vice versa and enjoying the pleasures of the marital bed, like he could have been doing if things had gone different. But they hadn't, and now he found himself envious and wanting to be like them folks.

His heart lurched at the thought, those nights so long ago when he and she had ridden under moonlight, the way it mirrored in water of some river or lake they'd ride to. The way the silence of wind brushing the tree leaves over their heads whispered to them as they kissed, her mouth light and delicately placed against his. In a moment of pure clarity he saw once more her perfect features for the briefest moment before they faded away again.

It felt, thinking about her, as if he was drowning in the deepest waters of sorrow, and yet he did not want to save himself, but instead let the water take him and keep him if it meant that was as close to her as he would ever again become.

Wetness gathered at his closed eyes and small tears leaked down his weathered and creased cheeks without him realizing it.

The conductor, dressed in black suit and a black cap, came up the aisle calling for "Tickets, tickets please," and Einer reached up and took from the band of his hat the tickets and handed them forth for the conductor to punch.

"Are you all right, sir?" the conductor said, noting that the old boy seemed to be crying.

"Sure I am," he said defensively. "I'm just on my way to Santa Fe to attend a death."

"Oh, my condolences, sir." The conductor, a stately man near as old as himself, with salt and pepper hair, and moustaches, said, "Is it a relative what's passed?"

"Yes," Einer said with a wry smile, taking back his punched ticket. "Me."

The conductor blinked.

"You?"

"Just been a long day is all," Einer said and closed his eyes once more as a means of shutting out the world of his unknowing, for he cared not for any of it but her.

After a time he felt the need to stretch his legs and went out to the coach's platform and fished out one of the cigars the horse buyer had insisted on giving him for the road's journey. He was glad to be shed of the closeness of the car and feel the cool wind rushing around him as he cupped a match and put the end of his stogie to it and drew till it came to life. It tasted good and he propped a foot on the half-moon railing and took in the night sky overhead and saw that it was near smeared white with the galaxies of stars so close it was like he could reach up and swipe their sugary whiteness with his fingers and taste them.

The *clack-clack* of the steel wheels over rails was to him a soothing sound. It was completely different riding on a train as opposed to trying to catch and rob one.

Sure beats the hell out of sitting a horse, don't it, he told himself. He felt that this was the beginning of an altogether new journey he was traveling, a course that would take him to the most unexpected places, and that after years of dormancy he'd opened a door and let himself out again into a world that had just been waiting his arrival. Yes sir, something had sent that boy to him and kicked off the ashes and he was glad he did.

"Lord forgive me my past sins," he muttered, though he did not count himself as a true believer in ghostly things, but just saying it felt the right thing to do. He could have stood out there forever, all the way to Santa Fe, he thought, but there was a weariness still troubling his legs from all the horse riding and so he tossed away the rest of his smoke and watched it burst into sparks as it hit the rock bed, then he went back inside. He thought now perhaps he could sleep under his hat and maybe when he awoke they'd be there in that high lovely town of old conquistadores, trappers, and tamed Navajo Indians selling their wares in front of the Palace of the Governors. He figured he might stop and buy her a silver ring and watch her surprise as he placed it on her finger.

The thought brought him a joyful peace, just as the night and the rush of cool wind and the good two-bit stogie had brought him joy.

He told himself he could use a drink but there wasn't any to be had and returned to his seat. And sitting across from him now was a young woman with a sunlit-haired child of five or six years old.

He sat down and she watched him carefully and offered a

weak smile and he touched the brim of his Stetson and said, "Miss."

The child looked up at him with large curious eyes.

"Young'n," he said.

The child did not speak.

"He's deaf," she said "He can't hear."

He nodded.

"Would he eat some taffy?"

She looked at the child and made some hand signs and the child nodded.

He stood and went up the aisle and found the candy butcher asleep in a forward seat, his tray of candy beside him. He took a quarter and dropped it on the tray and took up a piece of the paper-wrapped taffy and came back and handed it to the woman.

"He'll probably take it better from you," he said.

She smiled kindly at him and unwrapped the taffy and tore off a piece and handed it to the boy and rewrapped the rest. The child chewed it with obvious delight, still watching Einer with those same curious large eyes. There was something wondrous in those eyes, Einer thought. Something you couldn't buy nor steal nor appoint. It was in every human being at that age, even himself. He felt emotion collect in his throat.

The woman was pretty and he loved her for having such a wondrous child and accepting his small kindness on the child's behalf.

"Well," he said. "I reckon I'll get a little shut-eye," and leaned back and settled his hat over his eyes.

He was so goddamn tired. The hat was to hide his watery eyes as well.

CHAPTER 21

"Well, shit," said the tracker as they rode down El Paso Street with the Franklin Mountains in the background. "It looks like something both grand and terrible, don't it—the way this city has grown along just some old muddy damn river. Just sprung up like weeds."

Ballard rode silent going in search of the jail and when he found it, they dismounted and went in.

"Why, hell," a man behind a desk wearing a city marshal's badge said when he looked up and saw Ballard. "What brings you to our fair and murderous city?"

"Tom," Ballard said. "Not sure if you remember me or if you don't. But I recall you from the last time I was down this way."

City Marshal Tom Moad stared at his newly arrived counterpart.

"Hell, yes, I remember you. What you doing down this neck of the woods?"

"I'm on the scout for a boy with a wine-stained face," and he added to the description by indicating the side of the face the stain was on. "He might be traveling with an old man, too. We pretty much tracked them to here," Ballard said.

Tom Moad stood, a stoutly built man who looked all hat and boots, his trousers stuffed down in them, and offered his hand.

"And who might you be?" he said.

"I work for him, tracking," Elkhart Truth said.

The tracker was uncomfortable around any sort of a peace

officer and especially inside of a jail where he felt caged. He didn't much like it, being assessed by a badge wearer with inquisitive eyes.

"You look familiar," Moad said.

"No, I ain't never hardly ever been to El Paso, but once or twice maybe. Never no trouble though, not even for loitering."

"And your reason for having been here, once or twice before, maybe?"

"Once was a funeral—a cousin of mine, and the other . . . well, hell, I don't rightly recall the other reason I was here. Fact is, maybe I wasn't here at all but one time."

The marshal shifted his gaze to Ballard.

"He's okay, been tracking these fellows I'm looking for."

"What these two do that you're looking for?"

"Maybe something, maybe nothing. I won't know till I find the boy and question him in the deaths of two people."

"Shot, stabbed?"

"Burned up in their place. Real bad fire."

"So if this boy did it, had a hand in their deaths, he might just be a real bad actor is what you're saying," the city marshal said.

"He might could be, or he might could be just a boy riding the earth with an old man. Anyway, wondered if maybe you or one of your officers might have seen them in town."

"If they came, they likely crossed the border if'n he's guilty of a killing. But then again, we got our share of bad actors on this side of the river too, and that's a damn fact. I don't recall personally seeing such as you describe, but I'll sure enough ask my deputies about it."

"How many you got?" Ballard said.

"Six, currently, and the damn newspapers think that's too many for El Paso."

"Big grown-up town like this, looks like six's not enough,"

Ballard said.

"I agree. But tell you what, the six I got are as mean a sons a bitches as any of the rowdies out on them streets at night. Have to be. I'll tell you God's own truth, they ain't nothing more dangerous than an armed drunk Texan cowboy. Then too, we got Mexicans coming across the river, and every swill of humankind you could ask for, all mixed in together. We also got whorehouses galore, dope dens, and gambling parlors about every other door. Days ain't too bad, but come night, fireworks goes off right regular."

"Maybe you wouldn't mind asking your men sooner rather than later. I'm about reached the end of the line here, Tom."

"Sure, not a problem. But was it me looking I'd probably start with the bars and whorehouses. The whorehouses especially. Show me a man on the dodge who don't take time for a piece of ass now and then, and I'll show you a queer sort of hombre."

"Good advice," Ballard said and they shook hands.

"Where you boys staying, case I get a line on the paint face boy and the old man?"

"I reckon the El Paso Hotel for a couple of days if I can get a room there." He looked at Elkhart Truth. "Likely just be me," he added.

"Will do," Tom Moad said. "Now I got to make my rounds, rattle a few doorknobs, and maybe knock in some heads before the lovely dawn comes again."

Tom Moad wore two gunbelts strapped to his middle and also took a Winchester rifle down from a rack on the wall.

"Loaded for bear," he said confident, if cocky as well.

They all went out together.

Ballard turned to Elkhart Truth.

"Well, this is as far as we can go," he said. "If they've crossed the river, they're into Mexico and I sure as hell ain't gone chase them into Mexico if I don't have to."

" 'Cause you ain't allowed," the tracker said.

"You think that would stop me?"

"No, I reckon it wouldn't, not you."

"No," Ballard said. "I'm just ready to go on back home to my wife. You believe in signs?"

"Signs?"

"That if something is meant to be it will come to pass, and if it ain't, it won't. Signs like that?"

"Shit if I know anything about signs unless they have the word ICE BEER written on 'em. I believe in what I can see and touch and taste, like a beefsteak, or a pretty sunset, or a big ass on a whore."

"I believe in 'em," Ballard said. "Let's go find a watering hole and I'll buy you a farewell drink; you earned it."

"Hell, just point the way," the tracker said, and they untied their horses and led them down the street by the reins. They reached a place Ballard remembered, but when they arrived, there stood just a vacant lot but for carpenters and bricklayers putting up a foundation of something or other.

"Damn town's changed," Ballard said. They walked a little farther up the street and found a place called the Rio Grande. A sign in the window featured 6 BILLIARD TABLES. They tied off their mounts and went in and found a table in the cool interior.

A consumptive-looking barkeep came and took their order and Ballard ordered coffee and said, "Whatever he wants."

"I'll have a glass of your best whiskey," the tracker said. "And is that lunch free?"

Up nearer the oak bar itself, on a plank table, was a spread of various luncheon meats and cheeses, and deviled eggs the color of old blood in a large glass jar.

"With drinks the lunch is free."

"I could eat the ears off a donkey," the tracker said and went over and fixed himself a plate.

Ballard sat, weary and more than ever wanting to go home to her and his child. Something seemed to be warning him that he might not make it home at all, though he had nothing concrete on which to feel that way. He was not afraid. It was just a feeling he'd begun having.

He did his best to shake it off.

The tracker returned, his plate stacked high with some of each of everything on the sideboard and began wolfing it down using only his dirt-grimed hands. Halfway through he looked up at Ballard.

"You mind I order a beer to wash all this down?"

Ballard nodded and the tracker raised a hand to summon the barman and ordered a mug of beer.

"You ain't hungry?" Elkhart Truth said.

"I've got other things to think about," Ballard said.

"I don't know how you drink hot coffee on a hot day," the tracker said, chugging down nearly half of the beer and swiping beer foam from his mouth with a finger before going back to work on the lunch.

"I'll front you a room for tonight and pay you off in the morning," Ballard said. "I'll need to have it wired down from up north."

"Suits me," the tracker said.

Ballard was anxious to settle things one way or the other. He felt maybe some of it had to do with failure. He wasn't used to failure; he usually got his man. But this case was baffling to him because all he knew with any certainty was that he didn't know anything about what happened to Foley and his sister other than they had died in a fire.

And battling this sense of himself, he was more and more just plain losing interest in the boy and if he didn't find him

181

here in El Paso and find him in the next couple of days. Well, he wasn't so sure he might not just pack it in and take the loss.

He stood.

"Where you headed?" the tracker said.

"Need to send a wire for the money."

"Oh, well, hell, don't let me stop you."

"I won't."

The tracker still hadn't gotten used to Ballard's no-nonsense style of behavior—couldn't tell whether he was joking half the time or what.

Ballard went out and the sun was settling into the west and in the distance its light transformed the muddy Rio into something close to bucolic and peaceful. He heard guitar music and raised singing voices from the other side of the border. Nights could be raucous on both sides of the river, raucous and deadly. If you didn't like the hell raised on one side you could find a different hell on the other—often better, or worse. He knew that the Mexican people loved their music, found both love and solace in it. It was hard to not be charmed by their world when it was so inclined.

He'd gone over there in the early days. Gone there with some friends and they'd wandered the streets and alleyways and it didn't take much effort to find what they were looking for— prostitutes mostly, pretty young prostitutes who seemed waiting desperately for the gringos, knowing that they would come with the darkness and full pockets and that they could charm them and the musicians would charm them and the joy and the laughter from the cantinas.

These señoritas were as equally skilled in satisfying a man as emptying his pockets, and the rowdy young men in their big Stetson hats didn't seem to mind one bit and hardly ever returned north of the river without smiles on their drunken faces and memories to tell for years to come

He thought about those early times and smiled as he went in search of a telegrapher. It wasn't always thus. There were good people over there too and it left a memory a man didn't soon forget.

Ballard stood staring at the sprinkle of lights that was just then coming on along the hills south of the Rio and fixed himself a cigarette and smoked it, enjoying the night air and the música. And though nothing could stop him of thinking of his wife and child, the distraction allowed him to put them out of his thoughts—at least for a little while. Maybe he would meander over just to hear the music better, to watch couples dance in the plaza.

First things first, however. He rode his horse up to a livery and paid the man there to put it up, water and grain it, then pulled his Winchester from the boot and untied his bedroll with its soap and razor and fresh change of clothes.

He went in search of and found the telegrapher's office but it was closed and so he went on to the El Paso Hotel and rented a room and told the clerk that his assistant would need a room as well and paid for one night's stay for the tracker and two nights for himself. He told the clerk he wasn't sure when the tracker would be along but most likely he would be eventually.

"How will I know him?" the clerk asked.

"Just look for a real nasty fellow," Ballard said. "Can't miss him."

The clerk handed him a key and told him it was for room number seven upstairs and three doors down on his right.

"You want a bottle or a woman sent up?" the clerk said. "I can arrange it easy enough. Cheap too, seven dollars, unless you want a better one."

"Better one?"

"Gal that has all her teeth and pretty," the clerk said. "One like that will cost you ten dollars, though. Most just want the cheaper ones. And if you want her to stay all night, that'll cost you extra, but you'll have to work that out with her."

He knew the clerk had taken the measure of him, had seen what he'd so desperately tried so hard to keep hidden—a man longing for something, if only a kind word or gentle touch.

"No," he said resisting any temptation. "I'm fine the way I am," and went on up the carpeted stairs stained with tobacco spit and mud and burn holes from cigars or cigarettes dropped or ground out underfoot. He'd lodged in better, but he'd lodged in worse too.

He found the room, inserted the key, and went in, closing the door behind him. He set his bedroll on the bed and leaned his rifle against the wall, then stripped out of his clothes all the way to bare skin and lay down.

The room was hot and airless and he rose and opened the window, not without some small effort, and lay down again. He tried sleeping but couldn't, tossed and turned, anxious for something to happen one way or the other—either catch the boy or catch a train for back home. Figured he would sell his horse and saddle and purchase a ticket with it and use the rest to stop off and buy her a pretty dress, some ribbons for her hair, something for the baby. He lay in the dark smoking a newly made cigarette, it's small orange glow a burning shifting eye in the dark, a thing to contemplate as he listened to the street sounds from below, the growing revelry of night crawlers—those souls who sought the darkness and their pleasure in it.

He grew feverish as if he had caught something and his bones ached and he finally sat up and lighted the lamp on a stand beside the bed. There was a black Bible next to it and he opened it at random and read silently from it.

Then went Samson to Gaza, and saw there a harlot, and went in unto her.

His hand trembled, holding the page as thin and fragile as a butterfly's wing, and he closed the cover quietly and turned out the light again and lay back. Lying there the urges in his blood added to his fever, making him more restless still—those Biblical words.

He rose and sat on the side of the bed, his bare feet planted on the worn carpet, which was like the hide of some long dead animal the way it felt against the soles of his feet.

"I wish, I wish . . ." he muttered and the words fell hollow into the room somewhere reminding him of his aloneness. He had cause to wonder what words and conversations and acts, both sinful and otherwise, had taken place in the room, in the very bed he sat upon now. What of all the men and women who'd passed before him here in this room, this bed? Harlots and cowboys, miners and slatterns, husbands and wives? He knew not, and the not knowing left him more unsettled than before he'd asked the questions. He just knew he had to do something. Anything.

He pulled on his trousers and his shirt, went out barefooted down the hall and then down the stairs, and rang the bell at the desk, and the same clerk appeared from behind a door and looked at him through wire-rimmed spectacles. He might as easily have been a schoolteacher as a desk clerk, as a pimp.

"Okay," the clerk said without Ballard's having to ask. "The better one, I guess is what you'll be wanting. I'll have her sent up in fifteen or twenty minutes. You can just pay her direct when you're finished. You've a preference on what sort of liquor you want?"

"No," he said and turned and went back up to his room and lay down and waited, and the night was the same as all nights but he knew it would not stay that way much longer. He cussed himself for his weakness and told himself he would order her to go away and forget the whole filthy business of unfaithfulness.

Loneliness was no excuse he told himself. Loneliness made him like everyone else.

Soon enough a knock at his door. Still wearing pants and shirt he opened it. A young pretty girl with loose curly hair stood there.

"Wilton said you might need some company?"

She was dressed in a loose-fitting silk wrapper and held in one hand a small reticule and in the other a bottle of liquor by the neck.

He did not order her away but instead stepped aside, then closed the door behind her.

Maybe it was the soft lighting in the room, the honeyed glow, but she seemed to him exotic as well as pretty as she came close to the stand and set the bottle of liquor next to the lamp, then straightened and turned to face him again.

She was tall, not at all like his wife who was petite, and he liked that about her as well. His first wife had been a tall woman. Maybe that was it, some of it, anyway.

"What's your name?" she said, unloosing the cloth belt that held her wrapper closed.

He lied, said his name was Ben. It wasn't, but Ben was the first thing that popped into his mind. He didn't know why. It wouldn't have made a difference if he'd told her the truth.

"Mine's Rita," she said and dropped the belt and shook free from the wrapper allowing it to fall at her feet, offering him a full view of her nakedness.

Her breasts were large and full with dark circles around the nipples, her hips wide but her waist narrow. His gaze stopped momentarily at the dark thatch between her legs.

"Are you going to undress for me?" she said. "Or would you prefer I undress you?"

"You," he said and stood as she pulled his shirt over his head and then unbuttoned the front of his trousers and tugged them down; then with him seated on the side of the bed, she tugged the trousers off.

"There you are," she said and leaned and kissed him on the mouth, a long passionate kiss, wet and soft as she held his head in her hands.

He felt himself respond immediately and pulled her down on the bed with him.

"Do you want to leave the light on?" she asked.

"Yes, on," he said.

She was supple and sleek with a feline grace as she maneuvered over and under him and became serpent-like. He allowed her to do whatever she wanted. She wasn't the first whore he'd ever been with. There had been others before his late wife, and two or three after her and before he met Mayra. But none did he recall such as this one and he did not try and control her nor control himself either.

If you've gone this far, he thought in the midst of their passion, you might as well just go on all the way.

"Would you like a drink first?" she asked.

"Yes," he said, and she handed him forth the bottle and he uncorked it and took a long swallow and handed it back to her and she drank too and set it on the nightstand again. For a moment, the time it took for each of them to drink, he thought he should stop now, just pay her whatever her fee and tell her he'd changed his mind. Stop before it was too late. Then he thought maybe if she was willing, they could just sit and talk and drink until he fell asleep. He told himself he didn't need much, just needed not to feel alone. He'd never before felt alone as he did now, did not suffer from loneliness, but was a man unto himself, could keep his own company without the absolute need of others. But something in this journey had transformed him and only just now had he recognized it.

He closed his eyes then as if that act could shut out what he was about to do, what *they* were about to do.

She touched his face and then her fingers traced along his bare chest and she kissed where her fingers traced. "Would you like another drink?"

"Only if you'll have one with me," he said.

"Okay," she said and reached for the bottle and turned it up to her mouth and he watched then as she so delicately drank before holding it out for him. He made no such effort to drink delicately, and when he held it back to her, half of it was gone and she set it aside again.

"I reckon I've changed my mind," he said, for he knew if he didn't stop now, he wouldn't.

"Changed your mind?"

"I'm married, got a wife and child back home. I can't do this to them. I'm sorry I wasted your time. I'll pay you." He reached for his wallet inside his pants pocket.

"Are you okay?" she said.

"Yeah, I guess so."

"Do you want to just sit and talk?"

"That would be nice."

"Do you mind if I put my wrapper back on?"

"No, go ahead."

He looked away from her nakedness now. He'd already seen it and though she was beautiful in a way his wife wasn't, it was his wife he favored.

She came and sat on the bed next to him and he built a cigarette and handed it to her and struck a match and lighted it for her, then reached again for the bottle.

"I think I'm about drunk," he said, the sense of floating just a little above the bed as he sat there.

"Is your wife pretty?" she said.

"Yes."

"I get lots of married men, if that's any consolation to you."

"It's not."

"I wish every customer I had was like you."

"Would you lay with me for a bit?" he said.

She nodded.

"Sure."

He turned down the lamp light and they lay together and he held her and thought of her as Mayra, that he was really holding his wife. He just needed to hold her, that was all.

He didn't know how long he held her but when he awoke, she was gone. He checked his wallet; all the money was still there but for what he owed, and the bottle was empty.

"An honest woman," he said.

He was glad he didn't do anything with her, well, at least almost nothing, he told himself. He didn't know if it was a betrayal to go as far as he had, but he thought he could live with a fairly clean conscience and for that he was glad.

He closed his eyes and went back to sleep.

CHAPTER 22

He was a big bastard.

John Paul sat in the dim corner of the saloon watching her coming down the stairs with the man behind her.

He was big as a damn ox. Hands like rocks at the end of his arms, head the size of a bucket.

John Paul figured him for a teamster. All the teamsters seemed like big rugged bastards. Big and mean and ugly as a gut wagon. What'd she want with something like that, something so big it'd crush her with just the weight of him atop her? Jesus, didn't she care who she did it with?

That's okay, he told himself. He had things planned out. Didn't matter who she was with. They were leaving together. He had the train tickets for the midnight run on the El Paso–Northeastern already in his pocket. The stationmaster said it generally ran on time and it only stopped long enough to change passengers and take on water—"Ten, fifteen minutes at most. It has to be in Tularosa by seven in the morning. It won't wait even on Jesus."

"Jesus?"

"Even if you was him, sonny."

He timed his arrival at the saloon for twenty minutes before the flyer was to arrive at the station.

He ordered a drink and looked around for Mercy. Didn't see her at first. Got worried she might not be there, that maybe she'd quit working there. He swore his frustration under his

190

breath amidst the smoke haze and noise. He had his heart set on taking her with him to that sweet land where they'd sold the stolen horses, go and see Blaine and hold him to his word he'd put him in contact with a land agent.

John Paul didn't worry he might not have enough cash to buy land outright, but he damn sure had enough down payment. Even figured maybe Blaine would take a liking to him and maybe hire him on to help with his horses so he could earn the rest of what he needed.

It's all he'd done ever since they'd sold the horses there—him and Einer and Atticus Pinch—think about Mercy and owning a piece of ground up that way.

He'd sold his horse and saddle and rifle too and used it to pay for the tickets and still have enough left over for the new suit of clothes he wore now, haircut and bath. Even the new beaver bowler he wore cocked on the side of his head—the latest in fashion the haberdasher said. By selling the horse and saddle, he wouldn't have to dip into his horse money.

Damn if you don't shine up like a new penny, he thought. Mercy will be pleased to see you like you are. He was going to buy her some flowers too but couldn't find any place that time of night to buy any. Well, he'd just buy her all the flowers she wanted when they got to where they were going.

He'd sat there about ten long minutes before he saw her—coming down the stairs with that big bastard. His heart sunk like a rock in a barrel of cold water.

"Mercy." He wasn't sure if he'd said it aloud or just thought he had.

The ghostly figures of other patrons moving about in the smoke-filled den seemed to waver like wind-touched candle flames, like spirits searching for their owners in a fog-shrouded graveyard.

Without thought his fingers touched the grips of his revolver there under the flap of his new suit coat, cold steel hardness pressed against his lower ribs.

Before having spotted her he'd prepared how it would go:

"Oh, John Paul, you've come back for me, just like you said you would."

"Yes, Mercy, I'm a man of my word."

"I've missed you so much," she'd say, sitting down next to him, her arm draped around his neck, her mouth close to his ear, the smell of her like sunshine after a rain, her skin damp and warm as he touched her cheek.

"I love you, Mercy. I knew from the first moment we were together that I loved you."

"And I you, as well, John Paul. I knew it too."

"Then you should have gone with me," he would say.

"I would have had no way to sustain myself," she'd reply.

"I'd sustain you."

"With what? You barely had enough for our time together when last you were here. I hated so to take your last five dollars. Were I not in such desperate straits I would not have."

"I know it. But I have plenty of money now—more than enough to last us forever."

They would seal their pact with a kiss and then would leave together and catch the train and every sin they'd ever committed would be forgotten and all their past lives up till then would be forgotten too.

But then he saw her with the big man. His anger flared and he stood away from the table and shouted her name and she turned and saw him and so too did the man with her.

Mercy started to cross the room to him but the man grabbed her arm and said something to her as she tried to break free.

John Paul crossed the room, raising the pistol, cocking it at the same time, not even conscious that he was doing it. And as the man saw him now, what the boy with the marked face was doing, he turned loose of Mercy and shoved her aside and that is when John Paul pulled the trigger.

It was a sound like the crack of thunder, sudden and startling and those all around scattered like startled quail, thus clearing a circle as the big man grunted and grabbed himself and when he did not go down but kept coming, John Paul fired thrice more and this time he did go down, hard and heavy as if dropped from the balcony of the upper floor, the whole of him crashing to the floor, a spout of blood arcing from his neck.

And for the briefest of moments there was just a silence, then chaos, and John Paul took Mercy by the wrist.

"Come on," he said. "We got to go."

She looked stunned, but he pulled her along anyway.

Somebody shouted something and John Paul swung the pistol around and fired into the ceiling just for good measure, just to dissuade any who might threaten their departure. And then they were outside running up the street just as the midnight flyer's whistle shrieked its arrival at the station.

She had trouble keeping up with him but he pulled her along, even as he looked back toward the saloon to see who, if anyone, was after them. He saw some had gathered at the front of the saloon but had not advanced into the street to pursue them. Good, good, he thought.

It was several blocks back to the train station and as they neared they heard the whistle again signifying it was about to depart and he hurried her along, and she nearly tripped but he got her to her feet again and they arrived just as the engine began to move, its wheels digging in for traction on the sleek steel tracks.

He half picked her up and set her on the steps to a passenger car, then hopped on himself, and they moved up the aisle until they found an empty seat and took it and set down, heaving to catch their breath.

He watched through the window, the darkened night, then the slow fading of town lights as the train pulled out and carried them northward.

"You killed that man," she said at last, her lower chin trembling.

"Maybe I did and maybe I didn't," he said.

"But you shot him."

"Damn right I did. I wasn't going to leave there without you."

She swallowed hard, her eyes wet with fear or disappointment or something, he didn't know what exactly.

"I told you I'd come back for you," he said.

The car began a gentle swaying as the train picked up speed. There was nothing more to see out the windows, just darkness and for that he was relieved.

"They'll catch you, John," she said. "They'll catch you and hang you."

"No they won't," he said.

"Do you know who you killed?"

"I don't know I killed anybody," he said stubbornly.

"But do you know who it was you shot?"

"Don't," he said. "And to be honest with you, I don't much care. He should have minded his own business."

She lowered her eyes.

"My God," she sobbed. "Oh, my God."

"What?" he said.

"He was a city policeman," she said. "That's who you shot. His name was Bo Bird. And as if that weren't enough, he has four hard-case brothers and they'll sure as hell not let his death go unavenged."

"Next time maybe he'll learn to mind his own damn business," he said. "I seen you coming down the stairs with him. I just couldn't stand it, Mercy."

"You did it out of jealousy?"

"No," he said. "I did it because he grabbed hold of you and wasn't going to let you come with me."

"God, John. God . . ."

Mercy had her own thoughts about him now, this boy, so young and foolish, she thought, so intense and serious, so dedicated to having what he wanted, and it was her that he wanted most of all. Wanted her so bad he'd kill for her and she felt a strange mixture of fear and pride. No one before had ever cared enough to put themselves at such risk for her, had ever even kept their word when it came to her. She did not know whether to be afraid or relieved that she was free at last from a life she thought would eventually kill her.

She started to say something, had looked at his face as he sat there staring straight ahead, saw the fierce determination in him, and wearing that silly suit. Thank god he'd at least lost the bowler hat in their escape. She inclined her head and laid it on his shoulder and he clasped her hand and held it, comforting. It all seemed too much, like a wonderful dream that had gone momentarily awry.

And when he looked down at her, her eyes closed now, he felt himself fill with happiness.

It might not be perfect, he thought, but it is what you wanted.

CHAPTER 23

Einer knew the places to ask questions and how to ask them and soon enough he got the answers he sought for the price of liquor, though he'd had to do a lot of asking in a lot of places before someone told him what he wanted to know. Liquor was always good oil for the creaky tongues of the reluctant and not so reluctant alike. And eventually he learned of both the existence and location of the woman he sought, Magdalena. Was told she lived at the edge of town in a large hacienda behind a low adobe wall with a front courtyard. The fellow who told him called her the Widow Magdalena Lopez y Lopez.

Widow! Well, that was a piece of startling news, he thought. It wasn't what he'd hoped, that she'd married, but it was reasonable in spite of his disappointment. This news had saddened him a bit. His hope was and always had been that she would have waited for him to return, though he'd never specifically promised her he would—he'd not the time to tell her anything when the laws jumped him. He could but ride away on a fast horse. But still, his hope had been she would have loved him greatly enough to have waited and spurned all suitors in the interim—that she'd loved him enough. He realized that by the time he found the fellow who spoke of her, he'd drank enough to have become maudlin over her.

Just proves what a damn fool you are, he commiserated silently with himself.

His spirits were tempered by the fact that at least she was still alive and at last he'd located her. The thought of being now so close caused his pulse to quicken and the rush of blood to his heart seemed to swell it to the point of bursting in his chest. After all these years it seemed almost impossible that he was so near, but it was also frightening too. His fingers trembled as he held the glass of the saloon's best. What would she think when she opened the door?

He went first to a bathhouse to wash his ancient hide, then touching fingers to his gray stubble he had a barber shave him and trim his moustaches along with his haircut. Finally he went and bought a new suit of clothes of black broadcloth and the whitest shirt in the store and put these on, and lastly a new pair of elk-skin boots that fit his feet like soft gloves.

"How do I look?" he asked the haberdasher.

"Like a gentleman," the clerk said approvingly.

"Not some old bandit?" he asked.

"Oh, no, sir. Far from it."

In the double mirror he inspected himself and agreed.

"Damned if I don't," he said. "Where might I buy a dress?"

The clerk blinked, wondering why a man such as this would want a dress, then realized that he did not want it for himself, and directed him two doors up the street. There were beautiful dresses on dress dummies in the store's windows and he marveled at the fashion, realizing as he did that the old ways were changing and that women wore more than gingham and Mother Hubbards, that new better ways were at hand. He saw a dress in the store window that shimmered, blue silk with black velvet trim and threaded with pearls along the bodice. It was the sort of dress a true lady of quality would wear and then he went inside, his arrival announced by a little bell above the door.

A tall well-dressed woman greeted him.

"Good day, sir. How may I assist you?" she said.

He told her he wanted the blue dress in the window and she went and took it off the mannequin and laid it out on the counter. Its material sounded like women whispering as she handled it.

"It is a very fine dress," she said, lightly running a palm over the material. "For your wife?"

"Oh no, ma'am, I ain't married. Leastways not yet."

She smiled and he wondered if she was thinking he was too old to get married and he wanted to tell her about Maggie and how long he had loved her and traveled all this way to see her again. Hell, he even wanted to tell her about stealing Mexican horses for the walking around money, the money he was going to use to buy this very dress with. But he didn't tell her about any of that.

"Can you put it in a box and put a ribbon on it?" he said. "It's a gift for someone."

She smiled and went into a back room and returned with a box and folded the dress with care and wrapped it in thin paper, then put the lid on and tied it with a matching blue ribbon.

"Say, I don't suppose you'd have some nice shoes to go with it?" he said.

"Do you know what size?" she asked.

Damned if he knew.

"No, I guess I'll just take the dress," he said.

The dress came to eighteen dollars. He dug out his money and counted it off and set it atop the counter.

"She's a lucky woman, your friend," the woman said, "for you to buy her such a nice dress. And, of course, if it needs alterations she can just bring it in and I can fix it for her."

"Thank you," he said.

She wrote him out a receipt and he folded it and put it into his pocket.

"Might be I can bring her by later for those shoes," he said.

She smiled.

"Yes, of course, Mr. . . . ?"

"Einer," he said. "My name is Einer. Just that."

"You look a bit familiar," she said.

"Oh, no, Miss. It's been years since I been anywhere near Santa Fe. I guess all us old men look about alike, don't we?"

"Not really," she said.

He didn't know what else to say and so put the dress box under his arm and thanked her again and went out the door and the little bell rang farewell and he felt pleased he'd stopped and bought the dress. It made him feel like he was courting again. And maybe that is exactly what he was doing, but only he was aware that he was.

He went up the street toward the direction he'd been told that Maggie lived but stopped halfway there to get another drink of whiskey to fortify his nerve. He'd never before felt so nervous, not even walking into a bank in broad daylight to rob it.

He drank one shot and then another and waited till the whiskey found its way into his limbs and settled him.

You're making a damn fool of yourself, ain't you? Maybe. Maybe I am, but then when has that ever stopped you?

"Pour me one more," he said. And he drank that shot too. He didn't know why but instead of making him light of head and thought, the liquor now seemed to have worked just the opposite, had brought everything into a stark reality.

The saloon was small and pleasant with a handful of silent drinking men that hour of the day, men who might be contemplating the life ahead of them, the lives they'd already lived, the joys and regrets, and how none of it mattered what you did before this very moment. Wasn't nothing you could do to change what had gone on before that moment. Time was forever running out and not a damn thing you could do to keep it from running out. And someday that last hour, minute, second, would be upon you, quick or slow, expected or unexpected, painful or painless, and then that was it. No more you, and goodbye world. Adios. His mind was a jumble of unconnected thoughts. What the hell?

He took a deep breath and let it out and said to himself, well, you've come this far you might just as well go on and see it through, and he paid for the drinks and went out, clutching the dress box under his arm.

The sun was a bright blaze settling in the west, but the air cool that high up and he could see the sun's light gleaming against the snowy slopes of the Sangre de Cristo Mountains. He remembered seeing them years ago when the sun set on them like it was now, and how beautiful they were with that unique coloration—*The Blood of Christ* mountains. Whoever named them named them right.

Wind riffled through the dry leaves of the cottonwoods, their trunks like mottled bone.

He went on and found the hacienda—large and round-walled, the color of mud—the hacienda beyond the low wall as described and had a courtyard. Facing outward the large wood door with a wrought-iron knocker seemed to summon his hand. So through the gate of the wall he entered and crossed the courtyard and faced the door.

He stood for a moment knowing she was just feet away, inside and unsuspecting of a ghost from her past. Sweat trickled down his ribs and gathered there under his collar and he inserted a finger and ran it around to swipe the sweat away, then wiped the finger on the leg of his trousers and said, "Ohh, boy" and knocked twice and waited.

Almost too soon the door opened and there stood a woman looking at him. Her gray hair was twined and tied like thin ropes atop her head. She was heavy breasted with wide hips and dressed in a bright skirt and blouse like one of the natives. It was the eyes he remembered most now, this woman's eyes as seen through gold rim spectacles, dark and curious. But for those eyes he might not have recognized it was her. He hated that he felt a staggering sadness at seeing her this way—someone old and not at all like the image he'd forever held of her in his mind.

He removed his hat.

"Yes?" she said. "May I help you?"

"Magdalena," he said, barely able to get her name off his tongue, for it had been stuck inside his mouth for so many years. And when she at first seemed confused and canted her head to one side as she studied him, he said: "It's me, Einer."

Her hand jumped to her mouth, disbelieving what she now recognized in this old man who stood before her.

"Einer?" she said. "No, it cannot be? You are dead."

"It's me," he said. "I ain't dead though I might look it to some." He tried to make light of it, but wasn't sure he had.

Trembling she swung open the door wide.

"Oh my, oh my word."

He took hold of her hand with his and held it comfortingly, noting its fragileness—her tiny hand with the skin so thin and mottled.

"My God!" she blurted and crossed herself. "I can't believe it's you."

Then she was hugging him and weeping at the same time and her tears wetted the side of his face.

"Einer, Einer," she repeated. "I can't believe it. You're here. You're alive still."

She drew him into the house and he willingly followed her in, down a floor of brown Mexican tiles past small rooms of heavy furniture and beyond to a kitchen that was larger than the line shack he'd lived in for years. It was a well-lighted room full of afternoon sun that gleamed off the tiles, and then midpoint she stopped and turned toward him and hugged him to her still crying and it was all he could do to sustain himself and keep the tears from falling from his own eyes.

He set the boxed dress on the large table so that he could hold her better.

She repeated his name over and over again as she wiped the tears from her cheeks with the heels of her hands and touched his face as if trying to read the truth of who he was, as if trying to recall him through her touch.

"I just can't believe you're here," she said again.

"I know it," he said. "I can't hardly believe it myself."

"You've not changed a bit. You're just like I remember you," she said.

"Oh, heck, I've done got old," he said. "Just an old broke-down cowboy, you know."

She took his face in her hands and drew him close and kissed him lightly on the mouth, a motherly or sisterly kiss but not the kiss of old lovers who'd found each other again. He wondered if she was afraid to kiss him, to give herself to him. He was the one who felt suddenly shy. He didn't know quite what to do, whether to kiss her back or if he did, how to kiss her, passionately or just friendly-like. He never felt so flummoxed in all his life.

"This is for you," he said and took the package up again and held it out to her.

"What is this?"

"Open it," he said.

She did, undoing the ribbon and lifting the lid.

She stared down at it, then looked up at him and again her eyes brimming brightly.

"It is beautiful," she said.

He felt relieved and pleased.

"I thought you might like it. You always liked pretty things."

She set it aside and took his hands in hers.

"Einer," she said, then seemed to struggle for the right words. She said his name as if it was the first word in a prayer she'd forgotten the rest of.

He held her close and she allowed it and laid her head on his shoulder and could smell the newness of his clothes and the hair tonic the barber had sprinkled in. But still she knew he was not the same man she'd known and she was not the same woman as he had known, and the sadness squeezed her heart that they'd had to see each other this way, at this stage of their lives, but for all those lost youthful years they might have spent together.

"I missed you," she said. "I've thought of you so often over the years, wondering where you were and how you were. Then I'd read in the newspaper that you had been killed in a robbery somewhere in Texas and I cried for two days."

"It must have been some other fellow with my name," he said.

"Yes, it must have been," she said.

"All I ever thought about was you," he said. "I knew I had to come and see how you were. I'd always wanted to find you again. But every time something come up and I got sidetracked. Then here lately, I just made up my mind I was going to."

It wasn't the speech he'd prepared in his mind—not the one that said, "I've come to take you off with me, and marry you, and live out the rest of our days together if you'll have me." No, it wasn't *that* speech at all.

For long moments they were silent, holding each other that way in the large sunlit kitchen with pots and pans and strings of red chilies and two windows that looked out onto a back courtyard. The silence was great but for the constant knock-knock of a grandfather clock somewhere in another room, a sound like a wooden heart beating slowly.

"Come, let's sit out in the back courtyard," she said, "so that you can tell me all about you. Where you've been and what all have you done."

He followed her out and from the courtyard he could see the risen tips of the Sangre de Cristos and they sat in heavy chairs next to each other.

He told her of the years of wandering, of working all sorts of jobs—the ones he could do from horseback and so forth. He did not tell her of the other women, of the crimes he'd committed, of prison, of his growing fear he'd thrown away the best years of his life and now it was too late to rectify any of it. And he did not tell her of the number of times he'd put a loaded pistol to his head, his finger on the trigger, and nearly shot himself to death from loneliness and the sense that there wasn't any reason he could find to go on living like he was, and that it was only the thought of seeing her again that had made him take his finger from the trigger.

He did not tell her either of his attempts to salvage his soul by going to church two or three times in a row before he quit it because none of it made much sense—that a father would sacrifice his own son in order to save a man like himself, to save the souls of sinners. Too much blood and sacrifice to suit him; he'd had enough of such doings in his own life.

The only thing the preacher ever said that made any sense to him and stayed with him was that loneliness was the greatest disease in the world. He believed it to be true.

And when he had finished telling her about himself the light in the sky had turned to near gunmetal as the sunken sun threw up the last of its light against fingers of clouds that held no portent of rain and she suggested that they go inside again for she was cold and they stood and went inside and she went about the rooms lighting several lamps.

"Are you hungry?" she said.

"I could eat."

He wasn't really hungry, in fact his nervousness had left him without an appetite altogether, but he wanted to stay with her for as long as possible, for as long as she would let him, hoping somehow something would change and revive that spark he'd carried for so long but that had now mysteriously left him full of disappointment and he couldn't say why. The best he could come up with was he hadn't really allowed for the passage of time, for the change it wrought in both of them. The image of her in youth had been there so long he just couldn't shake the reality that was her now.

Why you're probably a bigger damn disappointment to her then she is to you, he thought almost bitterly.

Soon enough another woman, a thin younger woman, entered the house from somewhere outside carrying a tote of groceries she placed on the table with Maggie following her into the kitchen. She introduced the girl as her cook and housekeeper and asked her to prepare them a meal, and then led him into a front parlor where they sat together on a settee of tufted horsehair and leather.

"Juanita is such a help to me," she said. "I don't know how I'd manage without her. My arthritis has gotten so bad it won't allow me to do much. Isn't it a disappointment to realize that you've grown old and feeble?" Her smile was wan, telling, bitter.

He didn't quite know what to say so he merely nodded.

"You've heard about me," he said. "Tell me about you."

"I married two men," she said. "Both were of long tenure and both died. I am twice a widow and will not tempt fate again. I think I am cursed when it comes to love."

Again, a bittersweet smile and he didn't know if she'd included him in that statement about being cursed when it

205

came to love.

"And besides, at my age, what would be the point?"

"You loved them, these men?" he said.

"Yes," she said. "It is why I married them."

"Children?" he said.

She shook her head.

"No," she said. "I tried, but I couldn't have them for some reason. I wish that I could have. Albert, my second husband, had two from his previous marriage and they became like my own. One of them lives in San Francisco and the other in Boston."

He felt the rope of promise of her and him slipping through his hands, the weight too heavy to hold much longer.

"Did you ever marry?" she asked. "You didn't say."

"No," he said. "I never met anyone I wanted to marry but you."

She smiled softly and squeezed his hand.

"What is love?" she said with a shrug. "It's just an idea like all the other ideas we have, both foolish and accomplishable. Love is at first life its very self to the young; we think we can make love and life last forever and that death will never come for us. But we're wrong on both counts, aren't we?"

"I reckon so, you put it that way."

She smiled.

"We are foolish enough to believe we will be the exception, but we're never the exception, we are always the rule. I suppose were the truth too soon revealed, youth would be a terrible thing to have to go through." He wasn't sure if she was talking to him or just speaking aloud.

"I know what it feels like, love," he said. "I know what I felt for you was something special, and if you want to call it love than that is what it was. At least for me, anyway. I know I never again felt for another woman what I felt for you, Maggie."

She kissed his cheek.

"I feel humble to hear you say that," she said.

He didn't ever think it would be possible to be anxious around her. But now he was. He wanted to get said what he'd come here to say, but now he wasn't sure he could say it. He wished he had a drink of something strong.

You can't back out now, he told himself—not after all this time.

"I want you to go away with me," he said. "I want to marry you, Magdalena." And even as the words left his mouth, he wasn't sure if he really meant it, or it was just that he'd committed to saying it.

Her eyes were fixed on him for what seemed forever.

She shook her head softly.

"Marriage? No, I'm too old and you'd not want me as I am, Einer. I'm still this idea you've had of me all these years. You don't see me as I am, but as I used to be so long ago when I was young and beautiful. I'm just an old widow woman now. You don't have to try and convince me otherwise."

She hugged him to her and brushed his ear with her lips.

"It's okay, honey. It's okay."

"You're wrong," he said. "I know what I want."

But his resolve was crumbling like some adobe wall weathered by time and seasons of rain and wind and snow. Still he told himself he didn't want to just walk away without giving it a fair shot. Maybe, given time, he'd feel again about her as he had.

"We don't have to get married then," he said. "We can just live as man and wife if that is what you want?"

"Is that what you want?" she asked pulling back from him now, her gaze never leaving his, never wavering so much as a candle flame in an airless room. "I'm Catholic, you know. For me it would mean living in sin."

It occurred to him that she'd said that last part about being

Catholic as an excuse to let them both off the hook. But now that he'd committed, he couldn't just turn tail and run.

"I . . ."

He wanted to say that he could become Catholic too and learn to believe in ghostly matters as she did, but somehow the words wouldn't come to his throat.

"I have an idea," she said. "If you'll excuse me just a moment." He stood with her, then sat back down again and waited as she left the room. He heard muted voices, the two women talking, and then she returned. She held forth her hand.

"Come with me," she said and he followed her down a hall of framed photographs of people he did not know. She was in some of them standing next to men he did not know—her dead husbands, he supposed, is who they were.

She led him into a large bedroom with a massive oak framed bed and other furniture of the darkest wood, hand-carved and expensive looking. There were two large armoires and a tall, framed mirror.

"I told Juanita to forget the meal and go home," she said, their reflections in the mirror.

"Come to bed with me," she said. "And then we'll know."

He hadn't expected that, but watched as she slipped out of her clothing, the room's only light coming from an oil lamp with hand-painted globe. She got into bed and he shucked out of his new clothes and got into bed with her, feeling like some scrawny chicken of an old man to her larger fleshy frame.

"Do you want me to leave the lamp lighted?" she said. "So we can see the truth of our bodies?"

"No," he said. "Leave us remember how we once were."

"Fine," she said and leaned and turned down the wick, letting the room fill with darkness, with just enough outer light they could still make out the shapes of each other. He reached for her and she kissed him on the mouth, full and long and wet, her tongue entering and his darting to play with hers, his hands reaching for her, feeling when he did, the soft loose skin of her large flanks and then rising up to feel the weighted and sagging breasts, heavy in his hands.

"And what of sin?" he asked, not sure why he asked it but to deter her from allowing this thing to happen.

"God forgives those who are contrite in their sins. Tomorrow I will be contrite, but this evening I will just be me."

She reached for him but he deterred her hand from going to his vitals and she said, "Is something wrong, Einer?"

"It's just I don't want it to be like this, Maggie," is all he could think to say.

She lay in the crook of his arm.

"I'm sorry," she said.

"For what?"

"For how I am, how I've become. What age has done to me. I am not beautiful enough to excite you."

He coughed and wished he had a drink, a cigarette or cigar simply to contemplate the situation.

"Listen," he said. "We can't expect it to just come back like it once was. We've both changed and nothing's to be done for it. Can't stop time or what it does to us, we can only just ride it on out to the end. Besides, it's me. I ain't had relations in years. I reckon I just forgot how is all and I'd not want to embarrass myself further. It ain't you, Maggie."

"I was hoping," she said in a near whisper. Her scent now was cloying, like old funeral flowers and it caused tears to well in his eyes, tears of great sadness for having come here at all.

"What was you hoping, Maggie?" he said.

"I was hoping it would be okay, that we could pick up where we left off that night so long ago by the river—the last time I saw you. Why did you run off and leave me if you loved me so damn much?"

"No point in lying to you now," he said. "The laws were after me."

"Why were they after you?"

"I helped rob a bank."

She fell silent.

"I just wanted money," he said. "Money I could afford to offer you something, maybe offer myself something too. I was young and wild and a damn fool and fell in with the wrong crowd is all it was."

"Oh, honey," she said, her voice breaking and he could feel the wetness of her tears on his shoulder.

"I guess too I always wanted more than what I had. I just . . ."

"Other women," she said. "Did your longing include other women?"

"No," he lied, but he only lied, he told himself, to keep from hurting her more.

"You thought there were women more beautiful, more exotic, who could give you what I didn't. But I would have given you everything of me."

"Maggie, I'd just as soon not talk about anybody else—what I was back then. I was wrong, that's all there was to it."

"And now, you've come back to me and it's not the same—how you thought it would be, and for that we're both the worse off," she said.

He shook his head.

"I don't know . . ." he said.

"I'm tired," she said. "I'm just so tired, Einer."

"Me too, honey. Me too."

"Let's sleep and see how we feel in the morning," Magdalena said.

"Yes," he said and they kissed each other goodnight, then sought sleep, each onto his or her own journey to the land of dreams that had awaited them somewhere in the deepest recesses of their souls—that fragmented world where little made sense—a refuge from reality.

He sighed and listened to her light snores before falling off to sleep himself, thinking: It was a mistake. You should have let it be, Einer, you should have been happy enough with the memory and not despoil the dream—the only goddamn thing you was able to hold onto, and now you've ruined it.

Somewhere in the outer darkness he heard quail cooing as they dusted themselves, a sound like loneliness.

CHAPTER 24

When Ballard awoke the whore's scent still clung to the pillow and his head felt half pounded in. He lay a time staring at the ceiling, the cracked plaster and a water stain in one corner. He felt raw and disjointed and had a headache the size of Texas. The near-empty liquor bottle lay on its belly on the floor.

He sat up and placed his feet on the floor for a moment trying to get his bearings before remembering the hours earlier, how he'd almost been unfaithful to Mayra. Almost, not entirely. Cursed himself for such weakness. He couldn't even remember what the prostitute looked like, just the scent of her, and how it felt more like he'd wanted to take his anguish out on her than to get any degree of gratification.

Lord, he thought. Lord. You're going to blow this yet, ain't you? Lose everything you love, and for what? Chasing down a damn kid who's probably innocent to start with. Lord.

He thought of his wife and the feeling of what he'd done was brutal and unforgiving and he knew it but a weakness, his own failing, as though he couldn't stand to have anything good and worthwhile in his life. He felt sickened at his own mortal weakness.

He bent and reached for the bottle and drained the few lingering drops from it and laid it aside and stood and dressed and went out, pausing only long enough to knock on the tracker's room door. He waited but nobody answered and he went on out of the hotel and down the street to a café, figuring the tracker had got an earlier start of it and might be eating.

He'd yet to pay the tracker off and diverted to the telegrapher's officer and sent a wire for the funds and asked the telegrapher which bank in town he could have them wired to and the telegrapher told him and so the wire was sent.

"How long will this take?" he asked, and the telegrapher said he didn't know, but maybe an hour or two depending on the bank.

Ballard went to the bank and forewarned them of who he was and that he was having funds transferred down and filled out the necessary paperwork and was told to return later.

The man he spoke to at the bank had a soft malleable face, like a bowl of pudding set too long in the sun that had sagged in upon itself. The banker's eyes were not exactly marked true, one to the other with the left one offset to the side while the other looked straight ahead—a face that couldn't easily be forgotten.

He asked about an eatery and was told of a nearby café a couple of blocks up the street and one block north and headed there but did not make it before he passed a large plate-glass window with something in it that stopped him dead in his tracks: two corpses stood upright in coffins side by side in macabre display.

He saw painted in green and gold lettering on the edifice of the building:

MORTON'S FUNERAL PARLOR—EMBALMER

The bodies were in the truest sense an advertisement attesting to the proprietor's skills that he had earned upon the battlefields of the War Between the States.

One of the dead was a large man who looked bloated, his skin bluish gray like fancy marble, but it was the other man who'd stunned Ballard—Elkhart Truth.

213

The tracker looked exactly as if he'd fallen asleep, darker in death than he was in life. It seemed to Ballard that everything about him was not right: his hair was neatly combed and parted down the center; he was dressed in a white shirt and had on black trousers. He was further shoeless and just in stockinged feet. He was better groomed in death than ever in life. And, he looked as peaceful as a saint.

"What the goddamn did you do to get that way?" Ballard said aloud without realizing it. A woman passing by on the sidewalk with a child in tow cast him a horrified look. He muttered an embarrassed apology and touched the brim of his hat, then hurried inside.

There was an acrid smell to the room that looked like an ordinary house with oak plank floors, a large Belgium carpet, wallpaper of some romantic street scenes, and vases on pedestals. It was spare of furniture but for two chairs facing each other from opposite sides of the room, high-backed with curved arms. Off to the right and to the left were arched doorways leading to other rooms and to the rear a heavy grape-colored velvet curtain hid the entrance to whatever lay beyond the curtain. A bell sounded when he entered. Seemed like everyone had a damn bell over their doorway. The smell he knew to be formaldehyde used for the preservation of the dead. He'd witnessed an embalming once and only once. Once was a time too many to suit him.

A man came from behind the curtain. A smallish man with deep-set eyes and high forehead. Wisps of hair lay across his skull like pencil markings.

"Yes?" he said in a soft voice. "Have you come to pay your respects to the deceased?"

"That man in the window," Ballard said. "How'd he get that way?"

The question seemed to momentarily confuse the man; his

black suit of clothes made him seem like a messenger of dire news.

"Well, I embalmed him, sir. Is he a relative?"

"No, I mean how'd you come to embalm him? What'd he do to get dead?"

The man's shoulders slumped a bit and he looked toward the open window, the backs of the standing coffins held propped by stanchions.

"Er, are you referring to the deputy or the other fellow?"

"The other fellow," he said.

"It was an odd circumstance. That poor fellow was killed from a stray bullet that passed through the deputy—er, the other fellow—you see. The deceased you're referring to was doing nothing more than having a drink at the bar when the shooting started."

"So the deputy didn't shoot him?"

"The story is that it was just some simple boy stealing a whore and the deputy tried to stop him. As I understand it."

It was a piece of poor luck, to be sure, Ballard thought. Elkhart Truth's thirst for liquor had finally done him in, but not in a way anyone would have guessed.

"Sir?" the mortician said.

"What?"

"Again, sir, are you a relative? I'll need compensation for my work."

"How much is your work worth?"

The man gave him a price written on a due bill and Ballard said he'd be back later to settle up and went in search of Tom Moad.

He found the city marshal having breakfast at the café, Sunrise, the very breakfast Ballard had expected to have fifteen minutes earlier.

Moad looked up at Ballard's approach but did not seem

surprised as Ballard sat across from him.

"My tracker was killed last night," he said.

"I'm aware of that. So was my deputy, and you want to know the best part?"

"What could be the best part of two men getting gunned down?" Ballard said.

"That kid you was looking for?"

"What about him?"

"I do believe by the description given that he's the one who shot your man and my deputy. They said he had a red mark on his face big as a saucer. Said you couldn't miss it."

"You're kidding me, right?"

Moad shook his head, took a bite of toast and washed it down with coffee.

"Looks like you found your man. Oh, wait, you ain't found him yet, have you?"

"You didn't arrest him?"

Moad shrugged.

"Didn't get the chance. He came in there for a purpose."

"What purpose might that have been?"

"One of the whores who worked there, gal by the name of Mercy Love. Now ain't that something? Killed two men over a whore. Said they took out of there and jumped the midnight flyer. They're long in the wind."

A waiter came over and poured Ballard a cup of coffee and asked him if he wanted anything to eat.

"Toast is all," Ballard said.

"Look at this as your lucky day, Ballard," Moad said, forking some more egg into his mouth.

"How so?"

"My deputy, the one your boy put a bullet in? He's got four brothers who've already decided to hunt him down. And they'll by god do it too. Save us all the expense, them boys will."

Now what, Ballard wondered. Maybe it was a good thing, how it was working out. He could go home knowing he'd done everything he could. Except . . .

"Birds," Moad said, a pleased look on his face.

"Birds?" Ballard said. "That supposed to mean something?"

"That was my deputy's last name, Bird. And his brothers are named Bird." He snorted, drank some more coffee, set the cup down, reached for a cigar sticking out of his shirt pocket, thumbed a match head to life, and lighted it, then snapped it out and dropped it on his plate.

"Those Bird brothers are read bad people. They won't bother bringing that boy in for a trial. They'll kill him where they find him. Most likely kill that little gal with him if they think she was in on it. You know, set my deputy up."

"You think she did?"

Moad studied the ash of his cigar.

"I doubt it, but try and tell them that."

"Let me ask you something," he said.

"Go on and ask it."

"What if he shot the deputy out of self-defense?"

"He didn't."

"You know this for a fact?"

"I know what I've been told by those who were there."

Ballard nodded and stood from the table.

"I'll see you around," he said, and the city marshal watched him walk out.

Standing outside he wondered if it wasn't as Moad said it was. That the boy just killed that deputy. Most certainly Elkhart Truth's death was accidental. He built a smoke.

He couldn't decide if the boy was just a cold killer or a victim of bad circumstances. What if the kid was innocent in the deaths of Foley and his sister? And what if, like the other killings, what happened last night was about them not giving him a chance to

217

do anything but defend himself? What if he had this romantic delusion about being in love and trying to take the girl and the deputy had tried to stop him but those in the saloon didn't see it that way?

It's a lot of what-ifs, he told himself. He cursed his own doubt. Just go on home, he told himself. You done what you could.

He walked back up to the bank and waited for nearly two hours until the money was transferred and then went back to the funeral home.

"I want him shipped back to his people, can you see to it?"

"Yes, I can pack him in ice, but the lead-lined coffin and freight bill will cost extra."

Ballard wrote down the address and name of Charley Redleg, the tracker's cousin, and handed it to the mortician and said he should send the body there with a note as to the circumstances; then he paid for the service in cash money and left out again.

He went to the telegraph office and sent a wire to Charley forewarning him about Elkhart Truth's body arriving by train, and then decided to send another, to his wife, unsure of what he'd say to her and thought hard about it before writing out the message.

Dear Mayra. I am in El Paso City. I think I know where the boy is now. There has been some trouble but not to worry. I hope to be home soon. I promise this is my last time away from you. Give my love to our child. Goodbye for now.

"Send that right away," he told the telegrapher.

"Will you await an answer?"

"No."

He went outside again and straight on up to the train station. A bald-headed stationmaster was wrestling a wood barrel out front on the dock. Ballard showed him his badge.

"Yes, sir?" the man said, glad to be shed of the wrestling for a moment.

"I understand a boy with a stain face bought some tickets last night for the flyer?"

The man mopped at his forehead with a blue kerchief.

"He did."

"Where to?"

"Carrizozo, the only run last night, that's how I know. He just wanted two tickets for the first train out. Tularosa was it."

Ballard nodded.

"If you're aiming to catch him," the stationmaster said, still patting his face, "you're likely too late."

"Oh?"

"The Bird brothers all climbed aboard this morning's run." He shrugged. "It was supposed to go to Santa Fe but those boys stuck a gun in the engineer's face and said, 'No, it ain't gone to Santa Fe, Harvey, it's gone to Carrizozo.' and by gar that is where it went."

"When's the next run?"

"This evening, same as every evening."

"Give me a ticket."

Ballard bought the ticket and cooled his heels the rest of the day, only leaving the station once to go get something to eat, then came back and smoked cigarettes in the leaning shade of the stage office's overhang.

His only thought:

What the hell is wrong with you, Ballard?

CHAPTER 25

Morning brought a light drizzling rain accompanied by a cold warning wind sweeping down off the Sangre de Cristos, and when Einer opened his eyes he discovered himself in a room only vaguely familiar.

He sat up and swung his legs over the side and rested his bare feet on the cool tiles and looked around trying to get his bearings.

She lay still sleeping next to him, her back toward him, her body drawn up like that of a child, and he did his best not to disturb her as he rose achingly to his feet.

He didn't know quite what he should do: stay or leave. His disappointment in how it had turned out—nothing at all like he imagined—left him confused and off balance, a feeling uncommon to him.

He worried that if she awoke and decided to take him up on his offer of the evening before he'd be beholding to see it through. But beholding was not something he wanted now. He felt uncomfortable being as he was now, less certain of everything then he could have ever imagined.

He pulled on his trousers and put on his shirt loosely over his head and went out into the morning-filled courtyard, barefooted, his hair tousled, and his appearance startled a pair of mourning doves that flew off in an explosion of wings.

Why if I had wings I might fly off too, he thought, watching them disappear in distant chaparral.

He took out his makings and built a cigarette just for something to do, to buy some more time, and looked off toward the mountains hoping for an answer, as if God was still living up there, hid away from His believers, so many were they in number—but for himself.

He finished smoking and tore down the remnants of the shuck and scattered the tobacco leavings. He remembered that the Indians held belief that scattering tobacco paid tribute to the earth somehow. Maybe it did. He didn't know.

When he came back inside he found her in the kitchen sitting at the table, a cup of steaming coffee in front of her. Her face was puffy and her hair undone and loose about her shoulders. She appeared to him in the truest light then, he thought: old. It was the only word he could come up with.

"Good morning," she said.

"Good morning," he said. "I was wondering where the jakes are?"

She nodded toward a side door and he went out and relieved himself inside an adobe-walled privy, though it took awhile to get the plumbing working—another goddamn reminder of how old he'd become—and he cussed under his breath as he held himself and waited.

Then he went in and washed his hands at a zinc sink with a cast-iron red pump handle to draw up water with.

She'd poured him a cup of coffee and set it down next to hers. He drew out a chair and sat down.

"I didn't mean to wake you when I got up," he said, his hands encircling the cup.

"Thank you for consideration," she said. "But I too rise early. I don't want to lose more time than necessary at my age—every hour is precious."

He nodded.

"I hear that," he said.

"Are you hungry?" she said.

She wore a collared shift gathered at the wrists, a long muslin affair, and what he saw was simply a woman sitting across from him, one who'd lost all her youth and beauty and had become common, and it rattled his cage to see her thus.

"I can have Juanita fix you some breakfast," she said. "You are so thin, Einer. You should eat more."

"No, I'm good with just the coffee," he said.

He knew, or suspected, that she was also seeing him in the light of the present and not of the long ago and that most likely she was disappointed in what she saw—some old man with spotted hands and loose skin and thinning wisps of cotton hair and that she also thought about her two dead husbands, the children that were not hers but were grown now and living in California and out East and who she had not seen in several years. And what was he offering her that was any better than what she already had?

Then he thought about last night, how everything seemed other than what he'd long dreamed about—how it wasn't nowhere close to all his fantasies and how the realization seemed to crush his very bones. She'd made him feel like just another old fool without even meaning to.

"I'll have some more coffee," he said at last, and she started to rise but he stopped her.

"I can get it," he said and stood and went to the stove and poured himself another cupful and came back and sat down again.

"I . . ." she started to say but then did not finish her thought.

"You don't have to say nothing, Maggie," he said. "We both know it's done too late for us, ain't it?"

She raised her tired eyes to him. They seemed more clouded than before, less light coming from them. He could tell how she felt just by looking at her because he felt the same way. It was a truth there between them that neither wanted to put into words.

She nodded at his quasi-question of it being too late for them.

"Yeah, I know. I shouldn't have never come," he said. "All I did was upset you and I sure didn't mean it to be that way. I'm sorry."

"Einer," she whispered and placed a hand on his wrist. "You didn't know. We remember things as we'd want them to be and not as they are. For me, I see myself as young and pretty—the way I was when I met you. But then I look in the mirror, or see one of those photographs on the wall of me, and I know I am no longer the person I remember, the person I believe that I am. In here," she said tapping her temple, "I still feel the same as I once did. But that's just my imagination."

She'd started to cry.

"Our minds refuse to accept the truth about ourselves, don't they? It seems indecent to have grown old when we were once so young and full of life, such a damn injustice. Why can't we just stay the way we were? Can you tell me that, my love?"

"Damn it," he said. "I wish . . . I wish . . ."

His own tears ran down the rivulets of his creased cheeks but he was not ashamed to cry in front of her, and together they wept holding each other's hands across the table, their tears like a soft unwanted warm rain.

"I'm sorry about last night," she said. Then quickly added: "I mean that I didn't please you. I don't blame you for that. Who wants an old woman?"

Her smile was an effort to be reassuring, to alleviate whatever doubts about himself he might have, even as she heeled the tears from her eyes.

"Oh, I feel so foolish," she said.

"Hell, it wasn't that, Maggie," he said. "I just reckon I ain't up to the task no more—even though in my mind . . ." He let his argument fade into silence. What good would it do him to explain it since they both knew already the truth of themselves.

"Just trust me," he said. "It wasn't you. Please trust me on that."

"I believe you."

She leaned and kissed him on the corner of his mouth; he kissed her back and then he knew it was officially over, settled. He'd come to do what he'd wanted to: he'd found the only woman he'd ever truly loved and not just a woman for a night, a passing diversion, but a real honest to god love. He'd done that, hadn't he?

It's all you can expect, ain't it so, Einer?

He'd found her and in the finding, the truth of them was revealed and the truth was too much to bear, too heavy of a load to carry anymore. She was settled in and he would never be. They'd taken entirely different paths and one could no more change course than could the other.

"I hope you like the dress," he said and drained his coffee and swiped his moustaches to and fro with a forefinger and knuckled the wetness from his eyes. "The lady at the shop said you could bring it in if you needed it altered."

"I will do that," she said. "I want to wear it to church next Sunday."

This pleased him.

"Good, good," he said.

For moments more they sat in silence. Then he said he had best get on, there was something he needed to do—to meet a friend of his so they could go on a horse-buying expedition and she nodded, looking almost relieved.

She stood and walked with him to the door, lightly brushing the back of his coat with her hand.

"It is a nice suit, Einer. Did you buy it just to wear for me?"

"Yes," he said. "I wanted to look nice for you."

"You look very handsome in it," she said.

"And you very pretty," he replied.

They held hands a moment and then he bent and kissed her on the cheek and she hugged him with surprising strength and for a moment, with their eyes closed, it seemed like they were as they once had been that time beneath the moonlight by the river, her body naked and her limbs strong, and something seemed to break inside him, some vital part that would remain forever broken, unfixable.

"Well," he said. "I best get on, that damn kid I'm in business with is hot to trot all the time. Kids these days. Can't be patient for nothing. Maybe I'll write you a letter someday if that'd be alright."

"I would very much like a letter from you, Einer, as many as you want to write." They both knew he never would.

She came to the gate with him, the morning air bright and clean, the air cool but gentle and without the roar of winter winds that would soon enough come roaring down from those mountains.

He went up the street pausing but briefly to turn and wave a final goodbye to her as she stood there at the gate, and then made his way to the train station and purchased a ticket.

"Where to, sir?" the ticket agent asked.

"Hell, anywhere," he said. He didn't know where.

The agent was befuddled.

"Anywhere?"

"Where's the next train going?" he said.

"Well, if you mean of consequence," the agent said, "Albuquerque, and beyond that, El Paso."

"Give me one that will carry me through to El Paso," he said, suddenly recalling where John Paul said he'd be. "Now where can I buy some cigars?"

"Just down the street two blocks is a tobacconist."

"A what?"

225

"A tobacconist, where you can buy cigars."

"Oh," he said. He was lost in his mind thinking about her, them, the terribleness of time's passage, what it revealed to the seeker and how smart men left old times alone.

He found the cigar shop and bought four good ones and a small sack of horehound candy and went back down to the station and sat on the bench outside the ticket agent's window, smoking. His mind seemed an empty place, a landscape without house or church or even a horse. Just a barren plain where nothing grew, nothing lived.

He shook his head without knowing he was doing it.

Boy, you're in the jackpot now, ain't you? You couldn't have screwed things up worse if you tried.

He saw a man riding down the street leading a short string of horses. They were sleek-looking animals with good formation. He watched as the man and his horses passed and he found himself thinking about John Paul, about them Mexican horses they'd stolen, him and Atticus Pinch, and gotten clean away and made some quick walking around money. He felt inside his pocket and took out the silver money clip and counted what he had left, a fair amount but dwindled down some.

This sure as hell ain't gone last you the rest of your life—less you die next week. And hell, you just might.

Shit, this world is full of horses waiting to be stole, ain't it? And that damn kid's just the one to help me steal 'em. Horses? Hell, maybe we'll rob us a nice fat bank. This thought pleased him, filled the void of his disappointment with love and all things love.

For the first time since yesterday standing at her gate, a small flame of hope lighted itself in his darkness.

"Maybe that goddamn boy is realizing that women and love, false or otherwise, ain't enough to carry a fellow to real glory and high adventure," he said, without realizing he was saying anything at all.

"Sir?"

He looked up. It was the ticket agent speaking to him through the open window. "Did you say something?"

"Nah," he said. "I'm just an old man mumbling nonsense to myself. Ignore me if you would."

"Yes, sir."

He looked at the cigar burnt down to gray ash but for the last little bit and lighted himself another from it and smoked it and paced, awaiting the flyer to announce itself with shrill whistles coming out of the mountains like a god descending the heavens of hope.

Son of a bitch, you're talking to yourself again, he thought, and put the bag of candy into his new suit-coat pocket.

"There," he said. "You'll be all right there."

CHAPTER 26

He wasn't sure if they were going the right way or not with the advent of darkness upon the land. Questioning himself about his decision, he thought maybe they should have kept to Old Mexico rather than try and return to near where the horse buyer was—in that rolling sea of grass with its rivers and creeks and juniper-sided hills.

They'd gotten off the train in Tularosa and purchased horses, along with some grub for the trail. John Paul was pretty certain he could find Mr. Blaine's ranch again. They reined into a grove of trees he'd spotted against the night sky, uncertain what time it was but sure it was way past midnight.

"We'll rest up here," he said and dismounted and helped her down. She was leg-weary and butt-sore and slumped to the ground as he unsaddled their horses and tossed the saddle blankets down on the ground to sleep on.

"I'm sorry, it ain't much," he apologized. "We'll likely come across some town or other tomorrow and if they got a hotel we'll stay for a time to get rested up."

"Where are we?" she asked.

"New Mexico," he said.

"Why are we here, John?"

"I know a fella's going to put me in touch with a land agent," he said, building a fire. "He's a good man, rich, and the country is real nice. We'll get us a piece of land and settle down, Mercy. Like regular folks do."

"So you had all this planned out from the start?"

"Once I met you, yes," he said. "Before that, I was just doing what I had to every day to get by. But once I met you I knew what I wanted, and this is it."

He lay down beside her, pulling the small horse blanket up over them, pressed together for the warmth. The blankets smelled like horse sweat.

"What you did back there . . ." She'd been harping on it right along, fearful.

"I did what I had to. It was them who pushed it, not me. They could have just let us go on, but they didn't."

She lay against him shivering.

"I reckon that fellow had reason for not wanting to let you go with me," he said.

"Do we have to talk about it right now?"

"I'd like to know," he said.

"He was just a customer of mine, is all," she said. "He said I was his favorite. I'm sorry to have to tell you that," she said. "But you asked. I guess he just didn't want to let me go away with you."

"He acted like he owned you," John Paul said.

"I reckon in a way he did."

"How the hell does anyone own anybody?" he said. "Slaves was freed a long time ago, and 'sides, you're white."

"John, there is just a lot about life you don't know," she murmured.

"I reckon not," he said, trying not to let his teeth chatter. "I reckon there's things in this world that just make no sense to me. But he don't own you no more, Mercy. Nobody owns you. Not even me."

"You mean it, truly, John?"

"Yes. I mean it. I love you," he said.

"You keep saying that. I wish you wouldn't say that."

"But it's true."

"They'll come after us," she said. "He's got a passel of brothers and every one of them mean as hell."

"Shit, I ain't afraid of no damn body."

"They're all bounty hunters. They know how to track a man," she said. "I've seen them bring in men for the reward money. Dead and slung over saddles like they was some animal they'd hunted and killed."

"I don't see how they'd even find us," he said, though doubt had begun to creep into his bravado.

"I'm afraid," she said.

"Don't be. Now get some sleep."

"I can't."

"Why can't you?"

"I just can't."

He kissed her and held her close and cooed to her like she was an infant.

"There, there, Mercy. Go to sleep now."

It seemed to her in that moment that he'd become a man and she merely a girl who the man was comforting and she allowed herself to be held and comforted because she was tired and afraid and needed reassurance and the night was so black, that darkest hour before dawn. Something moved in the brush but then went on.

He lay there holding her, feeling her slowly relaxing, followed by her steady breathing, the warmth of her open mouth against his neck. His nerves were too raw to relax himself but she was a comfort to him nonetheless. He stared straight up into the starless night and his mind drifted back to Foley and Uda, how what happened to force his hand. How she'd abused him and Foley had beat him with that harness strap like he was a dog or something. How she'd lied to Foley about him, the terrible things she accused him of doing to her so that Foley went mad and beat him down, the strap cutting his flesh every time he swung it. How he'd come close to killing them both right there and then. How much he'd hated them both.

He saw again the hot yellow flames of fire eating away the night, felt its heat, heard the screams of folks being burned alive.

Stop it! Stop it! his mind screamed.

"What is it, John Paul?" Mercy said. For he'd been muttering without realizing that he had. "Are you all right?"

Yes," he said. "Go on and sleep now."

She pressed even closer to him.

"It's me should be sorry," she whispered. "Wasn't for me you wouldn't have had to shoot him."

"It hurt me to see you with him," he said. "With any man."

"It's okay now," she said "Let's both sleep while we can."

"I don't believe I can sleep," he said.

Her sudden yearnings for him came unexpected and the pleasure of it eased him into thinking about only the now and not the before and later they lay holding onto each other in the unspoken afterglow of physical love.

"I love you, Mercy," he whispered again into her hair.

"I know," she said. "I know you love me, John Paul."

They lay like that for what seemed like the longest time, till the first gray light of new dawn that grew along the very edges of the eastern horizon.

They were like sleepy children pressed to each other and trouble seemed like forever away as if they'd made their way from hell back into paradise, as if they were where they were supposed to be all the time.

He never recalled having been so happy nor did she. A happiness so abiding that either was afraid to even mention it one to the other for fear it wasn't real. So instead they closed their eyes at last and fell into a rested sleep, listening to their horses chomp grass.

CHAPTER 27

They were awakened by a light rain that caused them to shiver from wetness. They could not sleep further and so rose and John Paul saw that one of the horses had gone off in the night and he cursed their damnable luck. He saddled the remaining horse and gave Mercy his jacket, even damp he figured it was better than the simple dress she wore. He swung aboard his horse and reached for her and swung her up behind him even as he tried to figure the right direction.

"We're bound to find a town or a village sometime soon," he said as a way of encouragement. "I know Mr. Blaine's place is somewhere not far from here, it's got to be. I should have paid more attention when we come up here last time."

She rested her head against his back.

"I dreamt that they came for us," she said.

"Dreams are just dreams," he said. "I wish you'd not fret, Mercy."

"The dream just seemed so real," she said. "They'd trapped us inside an old house and just kept firing their guns in on us. The noise was so loud . . ."

He did not argue with her about the meaning of dreams but instead heeled the horse into an easy trot, wanting to hurry on and find a place for them to get in out of the rain and get her some dry clothes and the both of them a warm soft bed to sleep in and something to eat.

He kept his gaze fixed straight ahead on the road they soon

found scarred across the land like a healed-over knife wound, a road he didn't know the name of. The Mexicans called their roads *caminos*. He thought it was a prettier name for roads. But they called their horses *caballos* and he thought horses was a better way to call them. He glanced now and then off to the sides in hopes of spotting a town or village set back off the road, maybe a ranchero or just some homestead they could take refuge in. The land all looked familiar and yet none of it looked the same as where the horse buyer's place was, as he remembered it.

"If they come and they find us," she said, "they won't take no pity on either one of us."

"Well, if they come, I don't plan on taking no pity on them either," he said.

By the time they topped a rise and saw in the distance what looked like a village, the rain had quit and the air was again cool and clean as scrubbed glass.

"Look yonder," he said.

"I see it," she said.

"We'll get us something to eat, get you some proper traveling clothes and out of them wet duds. We'll rest up and get you your own horse to ride too, how will that be?"

"You can afford it?" she said.

"Hell, I can afford it that and more," he said.

"How'd you get that kind of money?" she said.

"I helped steal a herd of Mexican horses," he said with a laugh. "You might as well know who you're dealing with here."

She wanted to say that she already knew who she was dealing with, but instead chose to make light of it. She was so awfully tired of living on the dark side of life.

"Damn, you really are a outlaw, ain't you?" she teased.

"I reckon so but now I've got what I want, I'm gone give up and live a straight sort of life."

She hugged him all the tighter.

"You like outlaws?" he said.

"I don't know," she said. "I never met one until now."

He whooped and spurred the horse to a lope.

CHAPTER 28

Ballard scouted the shacks and haciendas of Tularosa, noting the watchful eyes of the habitués, knowing he was a gringo among them, but surely not the only one ever to be among them. He bought some food off a vendor there in the main part of the small town. He asked about the boy. "No, señor," the young man shook his head.

Ballard ate in the shade of a remade. The day was unusually warm for that time of year and in the heat he could smell the junipers and it was not an altogether unpleasant smell. He watched two kids ride by on a donkey, slapping its haunches with a stick and laughing as they went along. He saw Mexican women gathered at the community well chattering in their tongue to one another. A dog came by and sniffed his boots and he said, "What do you want?" and the dog looked at him and he said, "Here," and tore off a piece of the fry bread and fed it to the dog. Then he said, "Now go on and get. I ain't feeding you all day. Go on home or wherever you belong," and the dog continued to look at him for a time longer, then turned and went off.

He went around the town then and asked others about seeing the boy with a girl in tow and finally he found one old man with a thick head of white hair and bushy white eyebrows who said yes, had seen them, that they bought a pair of saddle horses off a man named Domingo, but that Domingo wasn't around to ask more.

"Buscadero?" the old man asked him.

"Sí," he said. The old man frowned.

"You see which way they rode off?" Ballard said.

The old man pointed and Ballard said, "What lies that way, what town?" And the old man said it was Ruidoso lay that way and Ballard thanked him and rode off in that direction.

By evening's glow Ballard rode into the small town of Ruidoso. Riding down the main drag he saw what he thought to be another white man leaning against an adobe wall with a mug of beer in one hand, a smoldering cigarette dangling from the corner of his mustachioed mouth. He reined in.

The man stood away from the wall and stepped forward.

"You looking for something?" he said.

"Somebody," Ballard said. "A white boy with a red mark on his face."

"Step into my office," the man said, indicating the cantina doors.

Ballard dismounted and tied off and followed the gringo inside where it was cool and dim with the familiar smells of every drinking den he'd ever entered. They went straight to the plank bar.

"I do better with something in me."

"Do better what?" Ballard said.

"Talk, fornicate, fight, you name it, I just do better with liquor."

"I didn't come to fight or fornicate," Ballard said.

The gringo eyed him suspiciously, then grinned, getting the joke. He motioned for the fat barkeep to bring them something to drink, but Ballard said, "Just him."

He waited till the barkeep filled the gringo's glass and watched him toss it back, then tap the empty on the plank, and the barkeep poured another.

"Now what is it you want to talk about?" he asked Ballard.

Ballard explained it—about this boy he was after, the facial stain. "He might be in the company of a slattern and/or maybe an old man as well."

"Yeah, sure, I see them come through the other day. Hard not to notice, a boy with a face like that. And yeah, he had a slattern in tow, but no old man did they have in the company."

"You notice if they left town or maybe they're still around?"

"Yeah, I noticed."

"And?"

"You know, sipping this whiskey one glass at a time seems like a slow way of going about it."

Ballard nodded, and motioned the barkeep to leave the bottle. He did.

"Okay, now you can drink it at the pace you are comfortable with," he said but when the gringo went to take hold of the bottle Ballard stayed his hand.

"First you tell me what you know."

"Saw them leave out on the road that takes you up to Refugio," the gringo said.

"Where is this from here?"

"Not far. I can take you there."

"Then let's go."

Within the hour the gringo had feigned something wrong with the shoe of his horse and dismounted as Ballard sat patiently trying to think ahead.

The gringo suddenly had a revolver in his hand and shot Ballard chest high, the blow knocking him out of the saddle. It felt as if somebody had reached inside him and snatched his soul.

"You dumb sumbitch," he heard the gringo saying from what seemed a long way off.

Then blackness, pure blackness, swallowed him whole.

CHAPTER 29

John Paul and the girl came into the village of Capitan, among low juniper-scattered foothills and white oaks. The place looked familiar; he felt they were close to Mr. Blaine's ranch, somewhere around here, he thought.

The red ball of sun stood balanced atop one of the hills, lending a scene of peaceful beauty that gave the boy cause for hope renewed. A community well where women gathered to draw water into wood buckets and clay jars and exchange the day's gossip, commiserating lives lived and unlived, seemed the heart of their every exchange. The old señoras and the young señoritas like magpies chattering about men, who were usually at the heart of their conversations, for what else was worth talking about?

And they traveled back and forth carrying their water, even children helping the older folks and their mothers.

"Look there," John Paul said.

"Look at what?" Mercy said.

"Just how peaceful it all seems. How different it is from El Paso. Look at this country all around. It would be a nice place to have a little spread, don't you think?"

She shrugged and they led their horses to the well and John Paul tried to communicate that they were in need of food and possibly a place to rest for the night. But no one spoke English.

Mercy spoke to them in Spanish instead and a couple of the women nodded saying, "Sí, sí" and pointed to one of the haciendas and Mercy said, "Over there, John. They said there is a woman over there who will sell us food and maybe a place to rent for the night."

"Where'd you learn to talk Mexican?" he said.

"John, are you forgetting where I worked, and it's right across the border? Don't you think I had Mexican men who visited me?"

"Jesus, Mercy, but I wish you wouldn't keep reminding me of what you used to do."

"Well, you asked."

He shrugged and the two of them led their horses over to a small hovel of a place. There was a woman there in the yard hanging up a string of chilis to dry and Mercy spoke to her explaining what they were in need of. She looked at them with curious eyes but smiled knowingly.

"Yes, come and sit and I will get you something to eat," she said in Spanish and pointed to a small alameda stripped with shade and they went and sat under it and waited for her to bring them something to eat.

"This around here looks real nice. Don't you think so, Mercy?" he said.

She looked about, not sure if she could adjust to such a slow way of life, though she thought maybe she could if everything else was right. But she had a dark, dark feeling that everything else would not be right. Though she hadn't told John Paul, she'd been visited at one time or another by every one of the Bird brothers and knew them to be rough and dangerous men and she feared for her and John Paul if they ever caught up to them.

The woman brought them a platter of warm tortillas, frijoles, and shredded chicken breast and glasses of water.

"Agua and pollo," Mercy said.

"What is it?" John Paul said.

"Water and chicken and they call beans *frijoles*. Eat up."

They ate and fed their starved appetites and John reckoned he'd never tasted anything so good and it all just went together with his vision of the place and he kept thinking how nice it would be to live around here, him and Mercy and have a brood of kids and trade in horses, even if he had to go and steal them himself. He could do it now that he knew how. Hell, yes, he thought.

"I wonder why there are so few men?" Mercy said looking about.

"Men?" he said. "Why do you care where men are or where they're not?"

"I'm scared is all," she said.

"Of what?"

"Of the men I cannot see."

"Better than the ones you can see," he replied, trying to keep his jealousy out of it.

He looked about. It was true. There were very few men lingering about, mostly old ones and boys. He figured they probably were off working somewhere, maybe drinking in a cantina.

The dusky evening settled over them like a cloak and beyond the hills where the sun was setting, the land held the redness of a fresh wound the way the light played.

"Don't worry about the men," he said.

The woman returned bringing them more food and they were grateful to get it and Mercy asked her if there was a place they could rent for the night.

"Sí, sí," the woman said and John heard the word *pesos* amid their conversing.

"She said that a friend of hers will rent us a room if we have money to pay."

"How much does she want?"

"Cuanto cuesta?" Mercy said.

"Eyiee," and she said something else, raising her hands in supplication. "She will have to ask her friend," Mercy said. "But leave her something for the food, John."

John Paul took out a dollar and laid it on the table.

When they finished eating the woman led them to another hacienda at the far end of the village, out away from the rest of the buildings. The woman she led them to was blind, the first woman explained, and added that this woman sometimes let a small room off the back of her house—a very nice room. And when they arrived the woman knocked and the blind señora answered and stood listening as the other woman explained it. Mercy and John Paul looked on as the blind woman listened and saw her smile and nod her head.

"Yes, she will rent you the room for however long you need it," the woman said, herself seeming happy to have accommodated the two young gringos. She said she would rent the room for one dollar a day and that included meals. John paid for five days in advance and told Mercy to tell her in Spanish, they might stay longer if things worked out.

Mercy relayed the message and the blind woman and the unblind woman led them around to the rear of the house to an off room separated from the main house by a breezeway.

"Her son used to live here," the woman explained, "but then he left for California and she never heard from him again."

There was a sadness in her voice for the blind woman's situation.

They're arrival also had drawn a gaggle of curious children, one of them a boy of ten or twelve.

"Ask that boy if he'll care for the caballos," he said to Mercy. Mercy spoke to him and he quickly stepped forward and took the reins, smiling with teeth white as new snow.

"Give him something for his troubles," Mercy said.

John Paul dug a quarter from his pocket and handed it to the boy, who looked like he'd just been handed a fortune.

"You make sure you don't run off with that *caballo*," John Paul said in a stern but friendly way before jerking free the Winchester rifle from the saddle boot.

"No, no, señor. I take good care."

The women stood aside and John let Mercy enter the room first and followed her in, Mercy thanking the women and closing the door.

John Paul leaned the Winchester against a wall by the bed. They stood for a moment looking around. The room was cozy and nicely decorated with a good bed.

"Damn, this is pretty decent, ain't it?" he said testing the bed by sitting on it. "Feels like we're almost there, don't it?"

"Almost where?" Mercy said.

"Wherever it is we're meant to be," he said, tugging off his boots.

"How do you know where we're meant to be?" she said.

"I believe we'll know it when we get there."

"Maybe this is it?" she said undoing her shoes. They lay clothed on the bed as the room began to fall into evening darkness.

"I'm so tired," she said.

"I feel as whipped as a borrowed mule myself," he said.

"A borrowed mule?"

"Just an expression I remember hearing somebody always saying." It was Foley who said it and John Paul felt bitter even about recalling that much of the man.

"What do you suppose will come of us?" Mercy asked.

"I reckon we'll be all right," he said.

"But you can't be certain of that," she said.

"I reckon I can be as certain of that as anything else."

She rolled toward him and he put his arm around her.

"Hesh, now. Why do you worry so?"

"I just always have, my whole life," she said. "I don't know why. Maybe it's how I grew up and what all I've done to survive."

"Well, you can rest easy," he said, "because from here on I'll take care of you."

He sounded so sure of himself, she thought, and it brought her some small comfort, even though she knew he wasn't yet a full-grown man and surely there was no way he could stand up to the Bird brothers if they came and found them. I guess if they do and they . . . Oh, she didn't want to think about what she'd do, but she knew there was no turning back.

"Hold me tighter," she said.

"Of course," he said.

"Just hold me till I fall asleep, John."

"I'll hold you," he said.

The blind woman could hear them talking as she sat outside smoking a small thin cheroot, her head and shoulders covered by an orange rebozo with long tassels that her own mother had given her as a wedding gift, so many years before.

Listening to them transported her back to a time when she was young and full of life and being courted by various young men. Her father anguished over the purity of his only daughter, but her mother did not.

"Don't let our conventions keep you from finding your joy," her mother had said out of earshot of the father. "You only are young once."

Oh, so very long ago, she thought, against the ice-bright stars now fully in bloom in the sky above her, stars she could only imagine. She missed so much now that she was old. Her books she missed especially, for they carried her to other worlds and let her peer in at the lives of others and she missed her books even as much as she missed her lovers. She felt trapped in a world not of her choosing and longed to be touched just once more by a young man with soft lips and read the sonnets of Señor Shakespeare.

She sighed and smoked and rocked in her chair and far off, beyond the lovers' conversation, there was the call of coyotes on the move in search of something—or perhaps calling out their own loneliness.

Aren't we all in search of something? she whispered and wept.

CHAPTER 30

Ballard sat in the sun, the heat soaking down into his muscle and bone. She said the sun was healing and daily helped him outside soon as he was able to get out of bed. Three long weeks she'd nursed him as he hovered between this world and the other one.

An old man in a burro-drawn cart had found him near dead there along the road to, as it turned out, the mythical El Refugio, for there was no such place. The old man had gone and gotten his son and together lifted Ballard into the cart and taken him to the healing woman.

"What have you got there?" she'd said when they brought Ballard to her.

"A near dead gringo," the old man said as he and the boy lifted him out of the cart and carried him inside to a small room with a narrow bed, the only bed, her bed.

Her name was Carmelita Areas and the locals knew she had a natural gift for healing the sick and injured. But when she first looked at him, touched his fevered skin, saw the bullet wound crusted black, she said to the old man, "I cannot raise the dead, Pablo."

"No, but you can try," he said.

"Only if God has a hand in it," she said.

"God has a hand in everything," he said, then he and the son left the gringo in her care, to live or to die. Whatever would be God's will.

By the third day he was still alive and by day five the fever had broken its grip. She spoke little while ministering to him and he felt too weak to ask many questions. It felt like someone had scrambled his brains for he had trouble stringing thoughts together as he drifted along.

But two weeks later he was able to get around on his own and sit out in the sun and the sun felt good, seemed to help sweat out the bad blood and heal the new nicely enough.

"You are very lucky," were the first words she'd spoken to him that he could remember.

She'd bandaged and re-bandaged his wound, cleaning it with great care and bandaging it daily, sometimes twice a day, and all the while he watched her closely but she in turn diverted her gaze, bashful-like, and he felt foolish for feeling so weak, so incapable.

"Do you remember who shot you?" she said.

"No," he said, not because he didn't remember but because he had no need to remember. It was enough to be alive, to know that he could soon go home again and be with Mayra and his child.

He believed that the shooting—a simple robbery he believed—was a sign that it was time to quit the search. Nothing good could come of it, he told himself, there in those private hours under the sun as she brought him drinks and soups and later regular food.

Quit while you still can. She'll never forgive you if she gets word you've been killed.

It was foolish, he knew to think of it that way, but that is the only way he could think about it. He'd been lucky.

Toward the end of the third week he was able to get around pretty fair, though stiff and sore still. He didn't know much about doctoring—but a bone was broke that joined his shoulder to his breastbone and it made it painful to lift that arm. And

247

when he'd looked down the first time she'd changed his bandage and saw where the bullet had gone in, he realized that a few inches lower and it would have exploded in his heart. The thought that it had just missed killing him caused his hands to tremble. Death and near death weren't the same things.

Old women came every few days and prayed over him and when they did, he feigned sleep. He had no wish to tolerate their kindness, misplaced on him he believed as it was.

She slept on a pallet on the floor by his bed and would alert at the least little stirrings, then fall back asleep. He felt embarrassed when she washed his body with a cloth rinsed in a pan, the water turning pink.

He came to wonder what she thought of him in his nakedness but she seemed not to notice but was efficient in her nursing and for that he appreciated her discretion.

In another week, week and a half—he tended to lose track of time—he was feeling near normal but for the soreness that didn't seem as if it would ever go away. The sun bearing down on him felt as if it was knitting his bones and muscle and sinew together in the right order again. She'd taken to preparing him stews of goat meat she said she bought from the same old man who'd found him and brought him to her place. She even gave him cool goat's milk to drink and it was surprisingly rich and good.

Then it dawned on him, without rhyme or reason, that he'd come to love the young woman. Sometimes at night there in the darkness as she lay sleeping on the pallet by the bed, tears formed in his eyes and spilled down the sides of his face for thinking about her kindness.

It wasn't just the way she cared for him, it was also the conversations they'd begun sharing, how easily she was to talk to, how she sometimes looked into his eyes so intently he was sure that she knew him better than anyone ever had, even his wife.

He denied his feelings for her until he could not and when he realized that he had to confess them to her, he worried and fretted that she would see it as some sort of betrayal for her kindness, that she was far too young for him. He didn't want her to feel badly toward him.

Then, too, what of his wife? Was it possible to love two women at the same time? If it was, it wasn't anything he'd ever been taught before. And, after all this time of not hearing anything from him would Mayra think him dead? Might she be vulnerable to the proposals of other men if she thought he was dead?

"What's wrong?" Carmelita said that one afternoon.

"Nothing," he lied. "Why do you think there is something wrong?"

"You look worried, as if something is troubling you. You will finish healing just fine. Soon you'll probably be able to ride a horse again."

He tried making light of it.

"If I even had a horse," he said.

"We'll find you a horse and anything else that you need," she assured him.

We, she'd said.

When she wasn't busy healing others, carrying for their wounds and broken bones and preparing homemade concoctions, she would sit there in the yard with him and talk about everything and anything.

She asked if he had a sweetheart back home waiting for him.

He told her he had a wife and child and watched closely how that would affect her. She simply smiled and said she bet that his wife and child were pretty and he replied yes, that they were.

Then without even meaning to say it, he blurted: "You're

pretty too, Carmelita."

Her gaze lifted to meet his and her eyes were wet and troubled and she'd excused herself that time and went into the house and he waited, then followed her inside and found her sitting on the side of the bed, head in hands, her shoulders trembling.

"You know, don't you?" he said.

"Yes, I think so," she said.

"I didn't mean for it to be this way," he said.

"Nor did I."

He sat next to her on the side of the bed.

"How'd this happen?" he said.

She shook her head.

"It just did."

"I know it."

He kissed her then and she leaned into him, face lifted and he kissed her again.

"I can't help how I feel," he said.

"I know."

That night she crawled into bed with him and drew the blanket over them.

"I don't want you to think I'm a whore," she said.

"I don't think that and I never would."

It was the turning point, one that comes into the lives of men and women often unexpected and unplanned—like a discarded match that touches a patch of grass aflame and before anyone realizes it, an entire prairie is a wall of raging inferno no one or nothing can stop.

With the passage of time he found himself in no hurry to do anything but be with her. Sometimes he dreamt of his wife and child and other times he did not. He was torn between guilt and longing, the source of both sprung from somewhere deep in his core.

Half the time he felt dazed by the confusion and when he was there with her, intimate and loving, she was all he could think about, but when she was off helping others and not with him, all he could think about was his wife. It sometimes got to the point where he almost wished he hadn't survived the assassin's bullet. It would have been easier just to be dead.

They rarely spoke of Mayra or his child and he knew why they didn't and for that too, he was ashamed. He did not want to use his family as an excuse for his confusion, for his unfaithfulness.

He had no answers for the questions he asked himself, nor did he even ask them when he was with her.

And then too, he'd already been somewhat unfaithful with the whore back at the hotel and for that he was truly contrite, but he was not contrite for his feelings for Carmelita, which only made him feel worse about it.

He was not a religious man but he found himself praying for an answer to his dilemma. But no voice answered his prayers and he understood why, for what sort of God would answer a faithless man?

This is all on you, he told himself. You made your bed and now you have to figure out what to do. He told himself a hundred times he ought to just go on home and forget everything. But that would mean if he did, he'd be hurting Carmelita, and if he stayed it would be hurting his wife.

And though he was a nonbeliever he did remember that at times in those first days of his fighting for his life that he seemed to be in the presence of a warm light that he had not wanted to leave and he wondered if the light was God or if it was just death waiting for him to come to it.

He often dozed in the sun thinking of such things, the wind ruffling his hair, and only awakened when she touched his hand or leaned and kissed his cheek.

"You are very beautiful," he found himself saying each time. "But even more is how you have shown your love in the way you care for me."

His words caused her lips to tremble, caused her shyness around him.

And thus they would talk of other things but the one thing they needed and inwardly wanted most to talk about—what, if any, future they had together.

"How old are you?" he said among these days after realizing he loved her.

"I am twenty," she said.

"I am nearly forty," he said. "Probably about your father's age."

"Does it matter so much to you?" she said.

"That I'm old or that you're so young?"

"Either one?"

He shrugged.

"I guess not. You?"

"No," she said.

And that put an end to that potential obstacle.

He knew it couldn't go on much longer—he was far too attached to her, and he must make a decision. The strange thing was, however, that as he healed and felt physically better, the desire to still find the boy, to complete the mission, had returned as well. A job yet unfinished and he knew that if he did not finish it, he would have that burden to bear on top of all the rest of what he'd begun to think of himself as.

She heard him muttering in his sleep and woke him and asked if he was okay, if he was having bad dreams.

He sat up and fumbled for a match to light the lamp with and waited until the room filled with the glow of wick burning.

He took hold of her and drew her close to him.

He'd come to a decision.

CHAPTER 31

It was the ugly little trollop who sidled up to him who intervened on Einer's behalf as sure as if he'd written it out.

He hadn't been in El Paso more than an hour, hour and half, and had begun to search the bars and bagnios for John Paul, drinking and asking questions. It was the third bar he had been in, the one him and John Paul had been in before, with the rooms up top, when she came out of the smoke like some misbegotten angel.

"Say, dad, I don't suppose you'd like to buy a girl a drink?"

He appraised her as he might a horse he was considering buying. Tiny little thing with pocked cheeks and a missing incisor, lank brown hair.

"I'd consider buying you a drink," he said. "But I'm in search of a friend of mine, a boy with a red stain on his face. I don't suppose you might have seen him around here? As I rightly recall, he'd fallen in with some Cyprian or other, and I'm thinking maybe this might be the place?"

"Well," she said coyly, "I never screwed nobody looked like it, if that's what you're asking."

"No, I'm not asking if you have, I'm just asking if you've seen such a boy about?"

"You don't mean that boy that killed the deputy and took Mercy out of here do you? Such a boy came in not but a week or so ago and shot the hell out of the place. Fact is, he killed two men that night. One of 'em was standing right there at the bar having a drink by his lonesome—all the other gals was taken and I reckon he was waiting for one to be free. Fact is I had my eye on him when he come in. Sort of looked half Indian. First that kid dropped Deputy Bird, then he dropped the other one, bang, bang, just like that," she said snapping her fingers. "I was upstairs with a teamster when it happened. Wouldn't even take off his boots. Boy, you don't know how bad us girls got it with some of these galoots."

Einer looked at her with startlement.

"I never heard a woman talk so much in her life," he said. "I just want to know about this boy."

"Well, to hell with you, Mister Charmer," she said in a huff and turned to leave but Einer stopped her and said, "I'll buy you a drink, I'll buy you a whole damn bottle if you'll tell me what happened to him."

She allowed the perceived offense to ease off her face.

"Whyn't you just give me the cost of that bottle instead?" she said.

He took out five dollars and handed it to her and watched her stuff it down the top of her dress.

"He ran off. Took Mercy with him," she said.

"They didn't arrest him, the city marshal didn't?"

"No, he fled like the devil was after him, and the devil surely is by now," she said. "A whole bunch of devils."

Again, he'd never talked to anyone who talked so much and said so little that could be made sense of.

"How so, woman?"

"Deputy Bird has himself a pack of brothers, bounty hunters, and they done took off after that boy and Mercy and they might have even cotched them by now if I know those Birds."

Einer didn't stick around a moment longer but headed out and went in search of the jail office.

Tom Moad was eating himself a liverwurst sandwich with a

slice of onion when Einer came in.

"Help you, old timer?"

"Maybe you can, and maybe you can't," Einer said. "I'm wondering about the boy I heard shot up the place not long back—over in the saloon."

"You a bounty hunter, then, are you?"

"I might could be."

"You might could be?"

"Well what difference does it make if I am or I ain't?"

"None, I reckon. What you want to know for?"

"I just want to know is all. Can't a man want to know things?"

"Well, I reckon he might can."

Einer was anxious to get the hell out away from any laws.

"Let's just say that if you *are* a bounty hunter, you're probably way too late because there are already a bunch gone after him."

"How'd they know which way he went? Across the river, I reckon?"

Moad shook his head and swiped a piece of sandwich from the corner of his mouth.

"No, sir, you'd be wrong there. You was to go down to Mexico looking for that boy you'd die of old age before you found him down there, and judging by the looks of you, that wouldn't take more'n a week or three." Moad grinned at his own humor. Einer failed to appreciate it and finished off rolling himself a shuck and lighting it, exhaling twin streams of smoke through his nostril to form a small cloud in the air.

Moad was anxious to get this old goat out of his office.

"Far as is known, that boy and harlot jumped the cannonball that very night."

"Which cannonball was that?"

"Only one runs out of here that hour."

Jeez Christ, Einer thought, everybody in El Paso was a gum flapper.

"You care to elaborate?" he said.

"North, up on up through New Mexico."

New Mexico, huh. I know where that boy is bound to head. He's gone head back up to Blaine's, see about getting him a piece of land like the two of them had talked about. Yeah, that sure as hell was where that boy was headed. Thing was, could he get there and be safe before these bounty hunters caught up to him?

"Thanks," he said and turned and walked out without bothering to close the door. Moad narrowed his gaze after the exited man, the door standing open allowing flies and any other stray creature, including humans, to come in and disrupt his meal.

"That damn old fool's got no manners," he said to the empty room. "Next thing I know a circus lady will show up carrying a midget and asking where she can buy some short pants for him."

Just then another deputy came in.

He stood looking around.

"Who you talking to, marshal?" he said.

Moad looked at him.

"Nobody," he said.

"Oh," the deputy said. "Thought I heard you talking to somebody."

Moad flicked a hand to hasten him away and said, "Can't a man eat his lunch in peace no more?"

The deputy turned and left.

CHAPTER 32

A thunderclap louder than any pistol shot awoke him from a troubling dream he was having—his wife had discovered his unfaithfulness, had caught him with the woman who now lay beside him.

The very earth trembled with the storm. It seemed directly atop them.

He rose from bed and went naked across the cool tile floor to the door and looked out. A merciless sky dark but for the wires of hot lightning crashing across it and all around seemed like death and hell had descended on them. A black wind moaned in between the thunderclaps.

"Bad storm," he said when she came up behind him, her arms encircling him, and looked over his shoulder. She pressed her naked body to his and again it felt as if he was joined to her flesh and blood and bone and had become one with her. Being thus aroused him and with the arousal came a sense too of shame, for each time, in spite of himself, he could not help but think of his wife.

"I think it is the devil singing," she whispered of the moaning wind.

Rain washed down the streets in torrents that turned into gullies that terminated into puddles.

"Come back to bed," she murmured. "There won't be anyone coming today for healing, at least not until the rain lets up."

"I've been thinking," he said.

"About what?"

"That I should go."

She stiffened and drew back and wrapped her arms around herself and stood shameless and naked before him, her mouth tensing with expectation of bad news.

"I need to finish what I started, and when I do, I need to go home and see can I work things out."

She went over and lighted a lamp, then sat heavily on the side of the bed and pulled a blanket over her shoulders. Tears formed in her eyes but not yet spilled down her cheeks. He knew she was doing her best to accept what he was saying but that she didn't like it.

"But you're not fully healed from your wounds," she said. "Some still bleed even."

"I know," he said. "But if I don't go now, I'll never go."

"What does that mean? I don't understand."

"It means I've fallen in love with you and the easiest thing in the world would be for me just to stay here with you and forget everything else."

"So why don't you, if you love me?"

"I can't. It wouldn't be fair to you and I'd come to regret not doing things the right way and that includes my wife and child."

Now, the tears spilled from her eyes and down her face and she made no effort to wipe them away. She wanted him to see what his words had caused. She wanted him to hurt the way she was hurting. If only she could explain to him how she felt and how she'd never felt about another man the way she did about him.

In their time together she'd come to see how much he'd needed her and in that seeing had come to realize that there was something powerfully moving in giving to another who needed you and you could save them.

"Why now?" she said.

"I don't know why now. I just been thinking about it for a few days is all. It feels right, the time, I mean. I've gotten used to depending on you, you've made my life too good, too easy, and I admit it scares me a little to have to depend on anyone, even you."

"You never felt that way with your wife?"

"Not like I have with you. She's a good woman and gives me everything I ask for, but she needs me more than I do her . . ."

"But there is something she does not give you," she said.

"I've thought about that too. I guess I realize that nobody can give you everything you need—that each one gives you something, but not everything."

"Including me?"

"I reckon it must be so," he said. "But you're as close as it comes. I'm sorry if this hurts you."

He reached for a shirt hanging on the back of the chair, one she'd purchased for him when she'd determined his other was too bloody to wash and mend. She watched as he put it on with some difficulty. He was still so very sore and the shooting had aged him in more than just his movements.

"What is that thing she doesn't give you? I'd like to know," she said, her cheeks wet, the tears having rained down to her breasts and in between her breasts and he could hardly look at her, for to look at her would only weaken his resolve and he forced himself not to want what he wanted more than anything.

"I don't know what it is," he said. "But it has to be something."

She stood and came to him and pressed herself against him, her arms locked around his waist, her head nestled against his neck, and he laid a hand upon her head, the silken hair that covered the smooth roundness of her skull.

"Please stay with me," she said. "Don't go out there. You see what can happen to you out there."

He drew gently away and sat on the side of the bed to pull on his trousers and she sat next to him, one arm around his neck, pleading with him not to go but her pleading became overly needy and it made it easier for him to keep his resolve to go and find John Paul. He did not want to make her weak, needy of him—she was too good a person for that.

With great and painful effort he donned socks and tugged on his boots and stood and stomped his feet down in them.

She followed him out of the room and into the kitchen. He was tall and bareheaded and without weapons or money or horse and relayed this dilemma to her with a downcast look as he stood there.

She went to a cupboard and took down a can marked AR-BUCKLE COFFEE and opened the lid and reached in and took out a fold of money and gave it to him.

"I will pay you back," he said.

"There is no need," she said. "Go and do what you need so that you can find this important boy and then you can return to the north to your wife."

He did not need to say it, what he knew she was feeling, the depth of her pain and sorrow and disappointment in him, for he felt as much about himself.

"I can't promise you anything," he said as he reached for the latch. "But once it is finished, I'll go home again, and if . . ."

"No one is asking you to promise me anything," she said.

"Can I kiss you once more?"

She shook her head.

"It would be best if you didn't," she said.

"I know it," he said. "But I'd like to anyway."

She turned her back to him and went to the stove even as the rain hammered down and the cold winds blew in from the west and the world seemed shattered and wet all around them and he dreaded going out into it, to leave the safety and comfort of her bed, of her love. But he had always believed that the world would turn as it must and people would act as they believed they should regardless of surrounding circumstances.

"Goodbye," he said.

"Vaya con dios, hombre," she whispered and listened for the door to open and close again and with the closing, the finality of it struck her like a fist and she sat down heavily and wept without reserve for he or no one else was there to witness her shame and heartbreak at giving herself to a man who in the end did not want her enough to stay.

CHAPTER 33

Over the ensuing days John Paul grew restless to get on, him and Mercy. He had her ask around to the few men in the village about if they had heard of a big horse ranch anywhere near. Surprisingly they had not hesitated to say that they did. Yes, not but a day's ride on north, up around a place called Capitan.

"Yes, yes," John Paul said when he heard the name. "That's it, that's near where Mr. Blaine is. Ask them how we get there."

So she asked and the men told her the direction to take and said that when they got close to Señor Blaine's they'd recognize it by the horses and fences.

"We got to go right away," John Paul said.

"I hate to leave here," Mercy said. "Everybody has been so nice to us."

"I know it," he said. "But we got to get on. I ain't giving up on my dream. You'll see when we get up there what I'm talking about. It's like a paradise."

Still she was unenthusiastic about going. The village was the first place she'd been in memory where people were so friendly and wanted nothing from her, demanded nothing, but instead were willing to do whatever they could for her and John Paul. And especially the old blind woman whom Mercy had become accustomed to talking to while John Paul was out riding his horse, just to scout around he told her, not knowing that his real reason was to check their back trail for men who might be coming for them.

The old woman had shared her thoughts on men and love with Mercy and Mercy had asked her a lot of questions.

"I rightly don't know what love fully is," Mercy had told her.

"It is what you believe it to be," the woman answered.

"That's it?"

"Well, it gives you a feeling of happiness like nothing else can, and the truth of when you've found it comes unexpectedly and it is all you can seem to think about, this man, whoever he is, who brings you such love."

The blind woman was like a mama to her and Mercy felt that she could learn an awful lot about life from her if only she could stay around.

"I'm not sure I love him," she told the woman.

"Then you probably do not," the woman advised. "For if you did, you'd know it and have no doubts. There are many types of love," she said. "But real love is unquestionable and rare and so when you find it, you don't give it up short of death of one or the other."

"What should I do?"

The woman shrugged.

"I can't tell you this. It is something you must decide. Either go with him or stay, or go somewhere else."

"I'd like to stay here."

"Then do so."

"I'm afraid of what he'll do if I say I want to stay."

"Love has no room in it for fear," she said.

"I guess I'll go with him," Mercy said at last.

The old woman simply nodded.

"I don't know what else to do."

"The answer will come when the time is right," the woman said.

And the morning of their leaving the woman gave Mercy a rosary, put it around her neck, her sighted friend saying, "She wants you to wear it for safekeeping."

The rosary was black-beaded with a small silver crucifix.

"I'm not Catholic," she said.

"You don't have to be," the sighted woman said. "God watches out for us all."

She kissed the two women on their cheeks and then she and John Paul rode away to the northeast, toward Capitan, and Mercy remained silent in her longing even though she didn't know what it was she longed for, but for something. It felt as if somewhere deep inside of her was a dark corner she was afraid to look into, a place where she feared they were going, she and John Paul, and her love for him was in doubt if it existed at all. She thought maybe she *did* love him, but it was impossible to know since she'd never loved anyone. She found it strange considering her line of work as a prostitute. So many men who took their pleasure from her, and admittedly, some who afforded her physical pleasure in return without meaning to. But it had been a dismal life at best and she felt so very old at such a young age yet.

"We'll be happy once we get there," John Paul assured her their first night camped out after leaving the village. "I just know it."

CHAPTER 34

Finding Mr. Blaine's place was easier than John Paul imagined once they got close and the country around looked familiar.

"That's it yonder," he said excitedly, pointing at the large house. Mercy privately was impressed that John Paul would know such a man no matter what the circumstances.

John Paul rode right up and helped her down from her horse and led her to the porch and boldly knocked on the door, and it was answered by the housekeeper. She didn't seem to recognize him at first, what with his new clothes, even though they were dusty from the ride. She looked toward Mercy and Mercy saw the disapproval in her eyes but she had them wait just inside the door while she went to get Mr. Blaine.

"Sure is something, ain't it?" John Paul said looking about.

"Yes, it's something," Mercy said.

Soon enough Mr. Blaine came down the hall and smiled when he saw John Paul and offered his hand as he looked toward Mercy.

"I'm back, sir," John Paul said. "This here is my girlfriend, Mercy. Mercy, this is Mr. Blaine, the fellow I've been telling you about."

"Won't you come into the front room?" Mr. Blaine said, and they followed him up a hall. He called to his housekeeper to have her bring them something to drink, but Mercy swore off anything until Mr. Blaine said, "Oh, it's only tea, this hour of the day," and Mercy relented and said, yes, she'd have some tea to drink.

They'd barely got seated before John Paul stated his reason for coming, to be put in touch with the land agent Mr. Blaine had mentioned. Mr. Blaine listened intently, but all the while seemed to pay Mercy more attention than John Paul.

"Yes, yes, I understand," he kept saying at everything John Paul was explaining. "And yes, I can put you in touch with my man."

And it went like that for a brief time before Mr. Blaine said he had to be somewhere but invited them to stay the night and John Paul quickly accepted and they were shown to a room by the housekeeper. Mr. Blaine said his wife was away for a few days and it really wasn't any bother.

And so they'd stayed overnight and had a nice supper of it, Mr. Blaine listening to John Paul shed himself of the long-held dreams to have his own place and Mr. Blaine seeming to understand well enough.

And in the morning, Mr. Blaine said at the breakfast table that his man would be out shortly to take them to see a piece of land adjoining his own property that even had a small stone house on it as it stood.

"Not much of a house, but something to live in while you get another built," Mr. Blaine said.

John Paul felt like he was about to dance right out of his skin, and when the land agent arrived in a couple of hours he said he'd take the young couple out to look at the property. But Mercy said she had a headache and would prefer to remain behind, and even though John Paul begged her to come along, she said she simply wasn't up to riding just then. The land agent said he could come back another time but it might be several weeks before he could do so and that there was someone else already interested in the property; then he shrugged, waiting for John Paul's decision.

"Let's go then," John Paul said, and he and the land agent rode off leaving Mercy behind with Mr. Blaine.

He asked Mercy if she'd like to join him outside to sit in the warmth of the sun and she said she would and together they went out and sat in finely constructed chairs of antlers of all things, antlers with leather seats and the housekeeper brought them out coffee. He engaged Mercy in conversation, innocent-seeming conversation, asking about her past, where she'd come from and how she'd met the boy. Called John Paul *the boy* instead of by his name. And she did her best to answer his questions but found herself having to lie about her past in order to present a good front to Mr. Blaine, who she could tell was a man of substance.

And then after an hour or so he looked at her and said, "You probably don't remember me, do you, Mercy?"

She studied him and shook her head.

"No, sir."

"I reckon you wouldn't, considering the number of men you must entertain. I was in your place almost a year ago. They said you were the new girl. You certainly looked very sweet and innocent," he said.

She felt herself growing crimson, flushed with embarrassment. "Please don't say nothing to John Paul," she said.

"Oh, not to worry. He seems rather an impetuous boy and probably has a hell of a temper I imagine, when it comes to you, I guess."

She didn't know what to say so kept quiet.

"He know what you did for a living?"

She nodded.

He arched one brow and half-smiled.

"Doesn't care then?"

"No, I suppose he doesn't," she said, her embarrassment

267

quickly replaced with anger.

"Well," he said lighting himself a cigar he took from his shirt pocket, inhaling it and exhaling a plume of smoke above his head, one leg crossed over the other, "I reckon he probably sees the benefit in it."

"How do you mean?" she said.

He leaned toward her and patted her knee.

"He won't have to pay for it anymore."

She stood to leave.

"Oh, hell," he said. "Don't act so damn'd high and mighty. I was just making small talk."

"It sounded like more than small talk to me," she said.

"Sit."

She didn't sit.

"Sit down!"

She sat.

"Now, here is how this is going to go," he began. And he explained it, how in exchange for him helping John Paul obtain that piece of adjoining property, there'd have to be some benefit in it for himself.

"Such as?" she said.

"Oh, I think you know, such as," he said.

"No," she said. "I won't do it."

"Why not?" he said. "You've certainly done it for a lot less."

She felt the bitter hot tears there just behind her eyes, welling, wanting to come forth but she fought them back.

And for a time there was only the sweeping wind.

"Well?" he said. "Do we have a deal?"

She nodded.

"Good. My man won't have him back before two hours. Let's go inside."

She rose and followed him inside.

★ ★ ★ ★ ★

Later John Paul returned, very excited, and found her lying in their offered room, and she pretended she'd been sleeping.

"You ain't gonna believe, Mercy, but I've got the land, house, and all for just what I have in my pockets as a down payment. Mr. Blaine said he'll give me work enough to make the mortgage until we have it paid off!"

He was like a kid on Christmas morning, she thought, and did her best to not let on the bargain she'd struck with Mr. Blaine in order that John Paul have his dream.

Maybe, she thought most bitterly that night in bed beside him, listening to his breathing, that is what love is, doing whatever you need to so that another person can be their happiest. She sure hoped so.

CHAPTER 35

Their existence had been just as John Paul imagined it to be. They moved into the small stone house and every day he would arise early and go and sit out front waiting for the sunrise. He would smoke a cigarette, fashioning just as the old man had taught him, and he would drink a cup of coffee as he did so, squatting on his boot heels and watching with wondrous eyes at the dawning of a new day.

He often thought about the old man, wondered if he'd ever found the woman he'd gone looking for, and if he had, what had become of them?

He heard the cluck of prairie chickens out in the shrub and liked the sound and they were good eating, too, although Mercy proved not to be much of a cook, so John Paul took over, cooking the fowl with sage and wild onions.

I wish I knew where that old goat was, he often thought. I'd invite him and his lady to come and visit and see how good Mercy and me are making out, see what I've come to. Banditry is a fun life but it's no kind of life you can live for long. He was surprised that Einer was still in the game, or rather, had gotten back into the game after so many years of lying fallow. Einer had shared his tale of going to prison and all the rest. And he in turn had shared his stories about how Foley and Uda was. He had also told him about the fire. How it was him lying out in the barn where he slept, even on the coldest of nights and had heard gunshots—two of them—from within the house, had gone out to look and saw the flames in the windows. He'd run to try and get them out but by the time he got there the heat was too much and drove him back, even though he could hear her in there screaming. He didn't know why she just didn't come out, but figured maybe she couldn't. Maybe Foley had shot her and she couldn't get to the door. And then the timbers of the roof collapsed inward and she was still screaming and so he took Foley's horse and one of the guns he'd stolen earlier and what food he'd hoarded because he had always been hungry, always fearful that someday they'd run him off and he'd need something to eat. And he got aboard that horse and ran away from that insanity, even as the flames ate away the night and finally he'd heard no more screams.

Einer had looked at him and said, "Damn, son, it's just as well you're shed of all that filthiness. It wasn't right what they did to you, John Paul. And it sure as hell wasn't your fault what they did to each other. Folks die, often in terrible ways. Don't blame yourself."

It hadn't made him feel much better, but at least that old goat had acted fatherly about it and for that John Paul was grateful. Of course he would have felt much better had everything he told the old man been the complete truth, but it wasn't. That part about always sleeping in the barn—well, that wasn't the case, not by a long shot. Only sometimes did he sleep out there just to get away from the two of them. And maybe some of the rest of what he told about that night wasn't true either. He wasn't sure what was true anymore and what was not because he didn't want to believe the terrible things about himself. Hell, he thought, sitting there one morning watching the first piece of red sun edge up over the horizon, that old man wasn't so bad. I sort of miss him, damn'd if I don't.

Then, one morning, unknowingly, rode two men looking for John Paul and Mercy: Einer and Ballard, each on different

271

tracts. They were closing in on the object they'd been in search of.

But before either of those two men could arrive, John Paul and Mercy were awakened by the shouting of the voices of men outside the stone house. The one morning he had not risen early to go and sit and watch the dawn with a cigarette and cup of coffee. He and Mercy had instead made love, then fell back into slumber.

"You inside, come out empty-handed!" a loud voice shouted.

She shook him, for he was yet in a half drowse and dreaming of a child that had her eyes and his hair coloration. A small shambling child running toward his open arms: "Da-da, da-da."

"John," she said shaking him, "someone's out there yelling at us."

Groggily he awakened and sat up.

"What? What is it, Mercy?"

"There are men outside calling us to come out. They have guns, John."

She'd left the bed and had gone and stood peeking out the window and saw four riders each holding the butt of a rifle rested on his thigh, the barrel pointed skyward. She'd seen clearly enough their faces and knew who they were and the knowing caused her to tremble.

He was still trying to unwind himself from the dream.

"It's them," she said. "It's the Birds."

"Birds?"

"His brothers, John. They've come to kill us."

He rushed out of bed reaching for his pistol but then tripped with his feet tangled in the legs of the chair and he came crashing down but scrambled quickly up again and pushed her away and looked out.

Yes, there they sat, loaded for bear. How the hell had they found them? He did not consider the possibility that they may have gone to Blaine's and Blaine told them where they were. No, Mr. Blaine would never do a thing like that, he was too decent a man.

"You can send the woman out," the rider called. "We'll not hurt her. We just want you, boy."

John Paul looked at her.

"You best go," he said. "Otherwise they'll kill you if you stay with me. I intend on taking out as many as I can, but . . ."

She shook her head and he didn't know if she intended not to go or was agreeing with him.

Instead she crawled on hands and knees and went to the other side of the room and got his Winchester and it was very heavy in her hands and brought it to him and he took it and levered a shell into the chamber.

"I ought to have known it couldn't last," he said. "You were the best thing to ever happen to me, Mercy."

She saw he had tears in his eyes and wiped them away with her fingers.

"Let me go out and talk to them, John. Maybe they'll listen to me. I'll tell them how it happened, that he drew first on you and you had no choice, that you didn't mean to kill him . . ."

He shook his head.

"It won't do no good, Mercy." The tears were now running down his cheeks.

"Please just go on. Let me at least know I did all I could for you before . . ."

She threw her arms around him.

"I love you, John," she whispered in his ear, her own tears mixing with his.

He kissed her and their tears tasted of salt.

"I will stay with you," she pleaded.

"No, you won't!"

He called out the window.

"She's coming out!" Then he told her to put on some clothes and he did the same, pulling on his trousers, but not a shirt.

"No, John . . ."

He picked her up by the waist and carried her to the door and kicked it open and pushed her forth.

"Go on, Mercy, go on."

Then he closed and latched the heavy oak door and stood for a moment breathing hard.

He could hardly stand the thought of being without her.

He heard one of them say, "Don't shoot her, it's Mercy. She's a good screw, ain't she boys!"

Laughter.

Then one rider said loudly enough for John Paul to hear: "We're going to have to whip you, gal, teach you your place. Whip you right after we take our pleasure."

He was at the window, rose up and fired, and saw the man who had threatened Mercy pitch from his horse. And then the peaceful morning was peaceful no longer but shattered by the racket of gunfire, a hellish sound that caused the least of God's creatures to take flight and the world to stand momentarily still in the breath of murder all around.

And when it was finished, two of the riders lay dead, and two others terribly wounded, so much so they could not so much as mount a horse.

Mercy removed her hands from her ears and opened her eyes when the shooting stopped and saw the carnage, saw the two groaning survivors twisting on the ground and the other two lying still, one face down, the other face up. She ran to the house calling, "John, John!"

And she found him there, sitting back to the wall as though he'd become tired of some chore and had sat down to rest awhile, but for the blood soaking the front of his shirt, and the blood that dripped off his outstretched fingers.

His face was peaceful, unharmed, eyes closed.

"John," she said softly as though afraid to awaken him, "John." And then she came and sat beside him and cradled him in her embrace and stroked his hair.

"Oh, John . . ." How long she'd sat with him she didn't know, but the sun had risen to its zenith when she finally released him unto his final journey and kissed him goodbye, then took up his revolver and walked outside to the still groaning Bird brothers, who seemed mortally wounded but not yet dead.

She didn't know if she shot them out of compassion—to put them out of their misery, or out of revenge—but shot them both she did, once each in the head, then dropped the gun and went and saddled the horse, for those of the riders had fled off. Her intention was simple: as long as she was killing men anyway, there was one more who deserved it.

Blaine.

She hefted herself aboard and was about to turn out toward Blaine's when an old man came riding up.

"Missy," he said. "Is they a boy here by the name of John Paul?"

"You're too late if you've come to kill him," she said.

He looked at her.

"Kill him? No, I ain't come to kill him. Me and him is pards. I came to fetch him." She could see the old boy's face crumble into something most sorrowful.

"You're Einer, then?"

"Yes ma'am, that is me all over."

"John is inside," she said.

She waited as he dismounted and went in and in a few minutes came out again, saw that his ravaged old face was wet with tears and he was shaking his head as in disbelief. It was only then did he seem to see the other bodies.

"Looks like there's been a heap of killing here today," he

275

said. "Did he do it?"

"Some of it," she said. "I finished those two yonder for what they did to him."

He looked at her and she at him.

"Might I ask where you're aiming to go, Mercy, child?"

"There is one more needs killing," she said.

"Lord God, ain't they been enough killing here today?"

Something broke inside of her and she near collapsed because of it, something hard and cold that washed over her like a bitter sea that was set to drown her.

The next she knew the old man was holding her up after she fell earthward from the saddle.

"There, there, now gal. It's okay. It'll be okay," he kept telling her.

"No, no, it never will. He was a good and loving soul and they took it . . ."

"They might have took his life," Einer said. "But they never got his soul. It done fled from this place here."

Still she trembled, afraid and alone in a world that just seemed endless with disappointment and misery.

"What of you now?" Einer said. "Where will you go?"

She shook her head.

"I don't know," she said.

They were standing thus still when Ballard rode up. He looked about at the slain, then at the old man and the girl.

"You're him," he said to Einer.

"I'm who?"

"The one traveling with the boy. And you are his . . ."

"Mercy," she said. "I was his . . ." She didn't know exactly what she was so she simply said, "Wife. I was his wife."

"Was?"

"He's inside if you want to pay a look," Einer said.

Ballard dismounted and went inside and saw the boy he'd

been trying to find and knelt and looked into the slack face, those closed eyelids already growing dark, and reached forth and touched John Paul's shoulder.

"Rest in peace boy," he said and stood and went back out again.

"What'd you want with him?" Einer said.

Ballard started to say but then changed his mind.

"I just wanted to ask him something is all," he said. "But I guess it'll have to wait until we're all in eternity together."

Then Ballard mounted up and rode away.

"Well, that just about does it, don't it?"

Mercy didn't say anything.

"Was you two happy?" he asked.

"Yes, mostly, we was."

"I'm sorry for your loss," he said.

"I got to get on."

"No, not for what you're aiming," he said. "More murder ain't gone solve nothing and it ain't gone to bring you no peace. Take it from a man who knows."

"I still got to get on."

"Get on to where?"

"I don't know."

"Listen," he said. "I got me some walking around money still and I got no place to go, either. Now I don't want you to take this wrong or nothing, but what would you think of coming on with me and maybe us getting some small little place together. No, I don't mean nothing like husband and wife, but just companions helping each other out till we can get our bearings. I got no family and when I'm gone, whatever I have could be yours, give you a fresh start. Or, if after a while you decide to find your own way, I'll help you out with that too."

"I don't know," she said.

"Would you think on it before you say yes or no?"

"I will," she said.

"Then that's all can be asked," he said.

"What about John?" she said.

He went and found a spade and began digging a grave.

"Damn it, boy. I told you I wasn't up to digging no graves," he muttered, some of the words snagging in his throat.

It took him several hours and Mercy helped relieve him as much as she could while he sat and smoked a shuck and at last they'd dug the grave deep enough and got a blanket from inside the house and wrapped him in it and laid him down in the hole and shoveled the dirt back in.

"I don't know much about praying, do you?" he said as they stood there, the wind drying their sweat.

Mercy shrugged.

"Not very much," she said. "Maybe a little of the Lord's Prayer."

"Well go on and say what you know of it, then."

When she finished she said, "Einer, do you believe there is a heaven and John will be in it?"

"I don't know," he said. "I reckon there could be and if there is, he'd be in it, for God I believe is merciful and forgiving more so than man."

And so she did and the wind blew as it always had and always would.

CHAPTER 36

She was there when he returned. Standing out in the yard, what yard there was, mostly just scrub and hardpan, and hanging a fresh wash on the clothesline, wood clothespins pressed between her lips, one of his shirts in her hand, damp and heavy. The baby played on a blanket nearby.

She didn't know why she had, but something had told her within a week of his going that he wasn't coming back. A fear like a curled rabid fox asleep inside her chest waiting to be awakened by truth, by the word of his death, and the fox now awakened would bite into her heart and make her rabid too and she would die of the pain.

She dropped the shirt and spat the pins from her mouth and ran to meet him, her skirts flying, her arms raised out as if to catch him falling from heaven. He hauled up short and threw himself out of the saddle and she leaped into his arms and he held her, lifted her off her feet, and she squeezed his neck and kissed wetly his unshaven face and bawled his name over and over.

"I love you, I love you, I love you!"

He thought sadly of the other one, the one who'd nursed him and yet could not even allow himself to speak her name, not even in silence, for fear of what it might do to him.

"My wife," he said lovingly. "My darling wife."

They stood for the longest time under a clean bright Texas sun and everything else from that moment was simply history.

ABOUT THE AUTHOR

Bill Brooks is the author of 30 novels of historical fiction including *The Stone Garden: The Epic Life of Billy the Kid*, selected by *Booklist* as one of the 10 best Westerns of the past decade. Bill began writing full-time with the ideal of becoming published after he ran out of other things to do when he left the healthcare field at the ripe old age of 45. He had always read that for writers, "Write what you know about." Bill loved the West and anything historical, including the "gangster era" of the 1930s—a period in which he wrote two novels: *Bonnie & Clyde: A Love Story*, and *Pretty Boy: The Epic Life of Pretty Boy Floyd*. Bill's Westerns have been praised by *Booklist*, *Kirkus Reviews*, and *Publishers Weekly*. His John Henry Cole series has been well-received and he continues to write from his home in Indiana.